Last Resort

**Center Point
Large Print**

**This Large Print Book carries the
Seal of Approval of N.A.V.H.**

Last Resort

Hannah Alexander

Center Point Publishing
Thorndike, Maine

In loving memory of Ray Overall,
February 2, 1913 to August 9, 2004,
stepdad extraordinaire, whose kindness and gentle support
gave hope and renewed life to his wife and stepsons.

This Center Point Large Print edition
is published in the year 2005 by arrangement with
Harlequin Books S.A.

The text of this Large Print edition is unabridged. In other
aspects, this book may vary from the original edition. Printed in
Thailand. Set in 16-point Times New Roman type.

ISBN 1-58547-670-6

Cataloging-in-Publication data is available from the Library of Congress.

Therefore, there is now no condemnation
for those who are in Christ Jesus.
—*Romans* 8:1

ACKNOWLEDGMENTS

As with every book we write, we depend heavily upon others to help us reach our deadline with integrity. We very much appreciate our editor, Joan Marlow Golan, for enthusiastic support, patience and kindness. She and her excellent staff make our job so much easier.

Our agent, Karen Solem, guides us with expertise and wisdom when we stumble through the often-confusing world of publishing.

Cheryl's mom, Lorene Cook, keeps us going when deadlines loom and the world threatens to fly apart around us. What would we do without you, Mom?

Thanks to Vera Overall, Mel's mom, who never stops spreading the word about the books she loves to read.

Thanks to Marty Frost, who has always believed in us, always served as a sounding board and inspiration.

Thanks to Barbara Warren, who rubs her hands in glee, red pen in hand, eager to attack and critique our latest work until it shines.

Thanks also to Jackie Bolton, for serving as an expert into the mysterious mind of the teenager.

Thanks to brainstorm buddies Nancy Moser, Steph Whitson Higgins, Deborah Raney, Colleen and Dave Coble and Doris Elaine Fell, for helping us plot late into the night.

We owe a debt of gratitude to some wise individuals who helped us mold this book with insight into the spiritual gift of discernment. Sylvia Bambola, Till Fell, Brandilyn Collins, Janet Benrey, Carol Cox, Brenda Minton, Sharon Gillenwater, Barbara Warren, Colleen Coble and Kris Billerbeck, thank you for your patience as we pestered you with questions. Dr. Bill Cox and Jerry Ragsdale, thank you for additional input as you took time out of your church duties to give us direction.

We are always blessed by an online group of writers called ChiLibris, and by the combined wisdom, Christian love, support and troubleshooting that is always available just a keyboard away.

Another group of prayer warriors, WritingChambers, constantly blesses us with their writing—the thing they do the best.

Praise and thanks go most of all to our Lord, without whom we would have no reason to write.

Chapter One

Not again. I can't let it all start over again. I've got to stop this madness, even if it costs me everything. I can't live if I take another life . . . and now Carissa.

She's the light that fills Cedar Hollow. She brings sunshine from the gloom that seems to haunt Cooper land. I'll take my own life before I lay a hand on—

But she knows too much about me. She's been searching for secrets that have to stay hidden, telling everybody she's gathering information for her school report. What if she's lying? Maybe the report is a cover-up. . . .

Now that I think about it, she's been looking at me differently.

The kid is too smart for a twelve-year-old. She has other ways of knowing about me. I can't trust her. I trusted before and look what happened. I can't ever let my guard down or I'll lose everything.

I can't let Carissa tell what she knows.

Carissa Cooper stepped carefully along the muddy lane that led from the sawmill to the house, hugging the old business ledger that Dad had asked her to fetch. Aiming her flashlight at the tire tracks in front of her, she glanced into the darkness. Fear crept up and down her spine like spiders on patrol.

She wasn't usually scared of the dark anymore, but something about the movement of shadows bugged her.

They shifted, changing shapes, skittering along the forested roadside with the movement of her flashlight, like the monsters that had waited for her in her closet and under the bed when she was six. She'd been scared of everything then, right after Mom left.

Now she knew better. Still, tonight she couldn't help imagining that eyes were watching her from those waiting clumps of brush and weeds.

If only her big brother Justin had come with her. If only he weren't still so mad at her.

"Should've kept my mouth shut," she muttered under her breath.

The sound of a quiet thud reached her from somewhere deep in the forest to her right. Horse's hooves? She stopped and listened, but all she heard was the whisper of leaves brushing against each other in a puff of wind. The branches made shadows leap across the trunk of the old walnut tree in the glow of her flashlight . . . like bony arms reaching out for her. . . .

The breeze died and the movement stopped.

Carissa swallowed hard, sweeping the light around her. She had less than an eighth of a mile to go, and here she was acting like a 'fraidy cat. She brought the small circle of light back to the muddy track as she stepped forward again.

What was all the fuss about with Justin anyway? So he was weird. Nothing new. He wasn't the only weird person in their family; he was just acting a little weirder lately. His habits were always making them late to church, late to school. It was embarrassing. This morning she'd counted the number of times he'd checked the front door to make sure it was locked before they left for school. Seven. Same as yesterday. Monday it had been fourteen. Probably to make up for missing his counting process Sunday morning, since they hadn't gone to church.

And she was getting sick of him turning out all the lights in the house at night before everyone went to bed. Last night she was in the bathroom brushing her teeth when he turned out the light on her, and when Carissa shouted at him, Dad got onto *her*. It wasn't fair.

She shifted the business ledger under her arm. If she dropped it in this mud, Dad would freak. He didn't like his stuff dirty. He and her cousin Jill were probably already wondering what was taking her so long, even though the whole family knew she was doing research on the history of the Cooper sawmill and the deaths ten years ago that nobody would talk about. She could get a good grade on this report if she could dig up enough information, but did they care? No. What she wanted never mattered.

This morning had been the worst thing yet, when Mom had called and Dad wouldn't let her talk to Carissa or Justin. Then Dad had freaked when Carissa picked up the extension. How could he pretend Mom never existed? Sure, Mom had been a jerk, but she was their mother. How could kids be kept from seeing their own mother?

That sound again—that thump of something heavy hitting wet earth in a slow rhythm. Horsewalk.

"Gypsy, is that you?" Her mare wasn't supposed to be in the front pasture, but sometimes she jumped the fence.

Carissa shuffled the ledger beneath her arm to keep it from sliding out of her sweaty hand. It continued to slide. She grabbed for it and dropped the flashlight straight into a gooey puddle. The splatter of mud startled her. The darkness seemed to attack her with glee.

"Stop it, stupid," she muttered to herself, reaching into the puddle.

She came up with a handful of mud, and heard the splash of water mingled with a rustle of brush somewhere behind her. Heart banging in her chest, Carissa tried again, feeling through the slick goo for the flashlight. She searched with both hands, forgetting the book until it slipped from under her arm and fell, splashing her with more mud.

Oh no! Dad would freak. He'd warned her not to—

More rustling, closer.

Carissa froze, still stooped over, grasping the mud-slicked book. Had she really heard something? Was her mind playing tricks on her? She waited, holding her breath, listening.

Nothing.

"Justin? That you? You'd better stop it or I'll tell Melva." Reporting him to their stepmother was a threat that sometimes worked.

Still no answer.

"Justin, I mean it. Stop it right now."

It had to be Justin playing a trick on her. She listened for his soft snicker. Nothing.

"Never mind Melva, I'm telling *Dad.*"

She continued to search for the flashlight, but her movements grew slower and slower. She frowned.

Usually Justin would be making weird noises by now, just to scare her. . . .

Was that breathing she heard?

"Justin Cooper! Dad'll skin you alive when he finds out you made me drop the ledger."

No answer. This wasn't like her brother.

But then, Justin hadn't been acting all that brotherly lately.

There was another rustle of brush, followed by another thud that sounded like a horse hoof.

Noelle Cooper's fingers stiffened in the process of making change for a customer. She caught her breath at the sudden unreasoning concern that gripped her.

"You okay?" the bearded man asked as he stared at the coins Noelle held poised over his outstretched hand.

She breathed again. Forcing a smile to her lips, she relinquished his change. "Sorry, Jack." She closed the cash drawer. "Guess it's past my bedtime. Hope you like that yogurt. If you want to cut your fat intake, you can skim the cream off the top, but for better taste stir it all together."

She waved him out the door, casting a glance around Noelle's Naturals, her health-food and supplement store. No other customers had slipped in while she was waiting on Jack, so she reached for the keys to lock up.

It was eight o'clock, straight up. Everyone else had gone home. Mariah, Noelle's silent business partner, kept encouraging her to keep the doors open a few minutes past closing on Thursday nights for a customer who had to drive clear across Springfield after work, but that man hadn't been here in three weeks, and there were hardly any cars parked in the shopping center lot.

Besides, Noelle felt strange . . . enervated . . . weak. Understandable enough, since she'd slept only a total of ten hours or so the past three nights. The insomnia was probably brought on by Joel's return. It had been too much to hope that her ex-husband would disappear from Springfield, Missouri, forever.

On top of everything, Mariah was away on a buying trip to Kansas City, and Noelle had been at the store since seven o'clock this morning. Why was it every time her partner left town all the grouches and complainers descended? For the past three hours, Noelle's face had ached from forcing a smile. If one more crank walked through that door . . .

She locked it and returned to the cash register to balance her money with receipts, but then she paused and leaned against the counter. "Okay, Lord, what's happening here?" she whispered.

A ripple of unease brushed her nerve ends, as it had several times the past few days. But why? Usually, when she felt this kind of spontaneous sensation, she could take a few minutes to focus and she would calm down. This time it felt stronger. Different. She closed her eyes and breathed deeply, picturing her favorite hiking trail, down by Hideaway. She would go hiking again soon. Very soon, she promised herself.

The constant bustle of Springfield tended to get on her nerves, and she tried to escape from the city at least two or three times a month. Although the nearby nature center offered a good occasional respite, she also needed a quieter trail now and then, with lots of trees and without anyone race-walking past her, chattering on a cell phone. Noelle loved people, but the public could overwhelm her. When she was hypersensitive, as she was now, she craved solitude.

She stretched her arms over her head to ease the tightness in her shoulder muscles. Everything in the store looked in place. She straightened a package of pumpkin seeds on the sale rack and returned to the counter, still unable to shake her anxiety.

There was something different about the way she felt tonight. Noelle knew it wasn't simply stress. Not this time.

The last time she had felt this way a loved one had died.

Carissa didn't move. Her heart was pounding so fast she could hardly breathe, and her throat felt so stiff she could barely swallow. She prayed silently, the way her favorite cousin, Noelle, had taught her to do when she was afraid. *Keep me safe, Jesus. Keep me safe.*

Something rustled the bushes at the side of the lane, and Carissa felt a low whimper sliding up her throat.

13

What if it wasn't Justin? Maybe it really wasn't anybody she knew. But who else would be down here in Cedar Hollow at night?

More rustling . . .

Carissa stopped breathing.

A footstep. Between her and the house.

Forgetting about the flashlight in the puddle, Carissa swung around and raced back through the darkness toward the sawmill. She clutched the muddy ledger to her chest like a shield as she stumbled over weeds along the lane.

She heard more rustling behind her, a splash of mud, the sound of labored breathing . . . and a soft whisper that blended so closely to the rustle of brush, Carissa couldn't be sure it was human. . . . It sounded like the wind in the trees, except the whisper kept time with the rhythm of footsteps, and she thought she heard her name . . . *Carissssssaa* . . .

She let the ledger fall to the ground as she raced through the darkness toward the sawmill, stumbling into branches that seemed to reach out from the black line of trees on both sides of the lane. As she emerged into the lumberyard, the moon peered out from the clouds. She pivoted to her right and sprinted toward the side door of the huge building that housed the sawmill.

The footsteps behind her grew fainter, and when she reached the door, she risked a glance over her shoulder. A shadow broke loose from the hovering trees, but she couldn't tell who it was.

She yanked open the door and ran inside. She cracked

her shins on something solid and tripped, falling hard on her left side. Her temple smacked the floor, stunning her. She'd left out a box when she'd been searching the sawmill earlier. Stupid!

The footsteps came closer, slowed and stopped. She sensed her pursuer was poised in the doorway, listening to her harsh, shallow breathing.

She scrambled to her feet, stumbled again, dizzy and confused.

A hand touched her shoulder. She screamed and skittered backward. Something caught her at the ankles. She fell back, slamming against the cement floor. Total darkness engulfed her.

Noelle dropped the bills back into their slot and shoved the cash drawer shut. Time to go home and go to bed.

She looked up to see a customer reaching for the handle of the front door—the door she'd locked a few moments ago. Groaning inwardly, she motioned for the man to wait, then retrieved the keys from the drawer.

She could feel her neck muscles tightening as she walked toward the front of the store. She glanced outside at the dark sky, then at the pale impatient face of the waiting customer. She wasn't up to this, really she wasn't. She needed to get away sometime soon, away from the demanding customers, the complaints and traffic. She couldn't take—

Again, that feeling of focused concern struck her,

more powerfully intense this time. And even more focused.

She caught her breath. It had been so long since she'd experienced this . . . this response. She closed her eyes, ignoring the man at the door.

"Oh dear Jesus." It was a prayer not a curse. "Is this—" She opened her eyes, startled. "Carissa!"

Chapter Two

Nathan Trask gritted his teeth and braked his black Chevrolet pickup to avoid hitting a flop-eared hound darting out in front of him, the dog's black nose following a scent.

"Sorry, fella, but that raccoon's probably long gone," Nathan muttered as the dog plunged into the brush on the other side of the road. "Could be we're both following a false trail."

A car honked behind him, and he increased his speed. Traffic in Springfield could rival the congestion of St. Louis or Kansas City during rush hours, but at 6:30 a.m. on Friday, Highway 160, south of Missouri's third largest metropolis, held some of the attractions of a country lane. Touches of yellow and burnt orange decorated the trees along the road this autumn morning, hinting at more color to come.

But today, the beauty didn't ease Nathan's tension. He knew, from a lifetime of experience, that Noelle Cooper had a formidable understanding of logic, and the idea that Nathan had been considering these past few hours was *not* logical. His best friend from childhood might think he'd gone nuts.

He forced his hands to relax on the steering wheel and unclenched his jaw. Maybe his desperation to find Carissa, along with a night without sleep, had addled his brain. But his memories of Noelle's particular gift were vivid, more so in the past few months, as the friendship that he and Noelle had shared long ago reestablished itself after years of life's intrusions.

He wasn't romanticizing the past, was he? Jumping to wild conclusions about Noelle's ability to find Carissa when the rest of them had failed?

Noelle adored Carissa, and she needed to know what was happening. He was doing the right thing, if for no other reason than to inform Noelle about something she deserved to know, since she and the girl were family.

He turned right before he reached the city-limits sign, then drove six blocks and turned right again, admiring the picture-postcard attractiveness of this increasingly familiar neighborhood. Since running into Noelle in downtown Hideaway earlier this summer, Nathan had started finding more and more excuses to visit Springfield, despite the three-hour round trip.

As he pulled into her driveway—second house on the left, the gray brick with black trim—he spotted her red Ford Escort through the tiny square panes of the garage window, which meant Noelle hadn't gone to work yet. Good. Maybe her partner could carry the load today, so Noelle could be free to come back to Hideaway with him immediately. After a cup of coffee; he really needed a strong dose of caffeine first.

Less than three seconds after Nathan rang the doorbell, Noelle opened the door. She focused on him slowly, pushing back a wave of tousled brown hair. Her brow cleared, and that familiar, affectionate smile lit the sleepy lines of her face.

"Nathan?"

"Morning," he said, casting a glance at her long, teddy-bear nightshirt and terry-cloth robe. "Just get up?"

"Mmm-hmm." She rubbed her eyes. "Thought I'd see if I had a paper yet." She peered out at the empty sidewalk and front yard and shrugged. "Optimistic, I know. Come on in. Did you just get into Springfield? How about a cup of coffee? What are you doing here so early? Another meeting with those rural pharmacy suppliers?" She turned, leading the way back inside.

For a moment, instead of following her, he hesitated. Crazy. Definitely, he was crazy. What in the world made him think he could face this sane woman and blurt out what he'd been thinking? They were both adults now. Was he romanticizing memories? As a child, Noelle had possessed an extra special knowledge of certain events. Could she have that knowledge now?

She stopped and turned back, the tiny lines around her blue eyes deepening. "Nathan?"

"Coming." He followed her into the foyer. "No meeting today. I came to see you. And coffee would be wonderful. Oh, and yes, I just got into Springfield."

Classical music played in the background, and he caught a whiff of pumpkin spice mingled with freshly brewed coffee.

She pulled a mug from a cupboard near the sink. "You came to Springfield at six-thirty in the morning—which would mean you left Hideaway at five? Ick! All this just to see me?" Her movements slowed and she turned, frowning at him. "So what's up?"

"Your sister hasn't called, has she?"

A heightened alertness stiffened her shoulders, and her eyes narrowed with sudden apprehension. "Why would Jill call me this early in the morning? What's happened?"

"Carissa's missing."

Noelle stared at him for a moment, slow to comprehend what he was saying.

"She disappeared last night, somewhere between the house and the sawmill," he continued gently. "We haven't found her."

Nathan's words seemed to strike her one by one, in a timed delay. Then her eyes widened, and she drew in a deep breath.

Nathan reached for her as she paled.

She caught his arm. "Oh, no," she breathed. "What . . . what time last night?"

"It was after dark, maybe around eight. She went down the hill to the sawmill to do some research for a school paper, and she was supposed to bring back a ledger for Cecil and Jill when she returned. She never returned."

Noelle's grip on Nathan's arm tightened. "I can't believe . . . they must be out of their minds with worry!"

"Cecil is blaming himself. Melva's inconsolable." Noelle had grown up in Cedar Hollow, down the lane from her cousin Cecil, and the two of them had been like brother and sister.

"And my sister?" she asked.

"Jill's trying to reassure all of them, but it isn't doing much good. Jill's just as upset as the rest. I thought you'd want to help search."

Years ago, when Noelle was in the process of a painful divorce from her abusive husband, she had returned to Hideaway to stay with her sister, Jill. During those months, she'd spent a lot of time with Cecil's daughter, Carissa, forming a bond that had kept them close ever since. Though Jill lived in town, and Cecil's family in sparsely populated countryside outside Hideaway—a hollow in the hills strewn with cedars, Carissa had used every excuse to visit Hideaway and spend the night.

Noelle released her grip on Nathan's arm. "I'll get dressed, and then I'll follow you back. Put our coffee in a thermos, will you? There's one in the cabinet above the stove." She swung toward the hall, chatter gear kicking into high, as it always did when she attempted to tone down an emotional rush. "I'll take my cell phone and arrange for extra help—"

"I'd hoped you would ride with me," Nathan said before she could disappear into her bedroom.

She stopped and turned back, frowning. "Why? Then

you'll just have to drive me back home as soon as we find her."

As soon as we find her. He'd always loved her positive attitude. "We need to talk on the way down," he said. "I thought you might know some places we haven't looked. You seem to have a special empathy with Carissa."

"Can't we do all that when we get there?"

He hesitated. Why did she have to be so contrary?

"Okay, fine, I'll ride with you," she said, changing her mind before he could speak, then pivoting again toward her bedroom. "Let's just get there, okay?" She shut the door behind her.

Carissa awoke to the throb of pain in her head, and the sound of her own voice—a soft whimper that she had intended, in her dream, to be a loud cry for help. Staring into the thick blackness, she couldn't remember the dream, or even why she'd been afraid—until she reached out and felt the hard, damp slab of stone beneath her, and heard the *drip-drip* of water somewhere nearby.

She barely suppressed another cry. Where was she?

She squeezed her eyes shut tight against the pain in her head and tried to think. Somebody had chased her. She remembered running back to the sawmill, someone grabbing her. She remembered falling. Then nothing. Whoever was chasing her had brought her here. But where was *here?* If only it weren't so dark . . . if only she'd found her flashlight in the mud puddle.

Her eyes strained against the blackness. She blinked. Nothing. It was as if she were encircled by air as thick as tar. But if she could see nothing, then that meant nothing could see her. That thought brought some comfort. The darkness was her friend.

Unfortunately, it seemed she had an enemy more scary than the darkness had ever been when she was a little kid.

The drip of water caught her attention again. She turned toward the sound and gasped at the sudden burst of pain in the back of her head. Had her attacker knocked her out? Or had it been the fall?

And where was he now? Or *was* it a he?

Fear mingled with the pain. Carissa strained to see anything at all through the darkness, but there was no light. Her heartbeat pounded like a hammer on her skull. Her shallow breaths echoed against . . . what?

She raised her hand and tentatively pressed it deeper and deeper into the thick blackness. About a foot away from her face she touched something hard, and jerked back. She rubbed her fingers together and felt wetness. Forced herself to reach out again, she felt damp, gritty rock, forming a wall beside her.

A wall where?

Would her attacker come back? Maybe he thought she was dead. Maybe she *would* be dead if she stayed here.

She tried to sit up. Shafts of pain shot from her head all the way down her back, and she slumped sideways against the wall.

The smell of fresh, damp earth was familiar, but the sound of dripping was different from the sounds of the woods where she'd been walking earlier. She touched the wall beside her once more, and again rubbed her fingers together. Gritty wetness. She heard the water dripping in the distance, with a hollow echo, as though the sound was contained.

An underground cavern of some kind? She'd been in enough caves with Justin to recognize the feel and smell of one. How long had she been here? A few minutes? Hours? She had to get out.

She leaned forward and braced herself against the wet wall, trying to breathe past the pain, the way Melva had told her to do when she'd broken her arm last year. She couldn't let the pain stop her, or she might die here.

Slowly, she stood up. Keeping her hand on the cave wall, she inched her way forward, stumbling in the dark over rocks and pebbles. Was this the right thing to do? What if she was going in the wrong direction?

Pain spread from her head down her neck. She took shallow, quick breaths and thought about sunshine and safety.

She shuffled forward along the uneven rock for a few more minutes, keeping her right hand extended in front of her while staying in contact with the cave wall. A wrong step could plunge her to her death if there was a drop-off. Justin had warned her never to get lost in a cave. Too late now.

She felt along the surface of the mud-slick cavern floor with her toes until the pounding pain in her skull grew too harsh, then she paused to breathe away some of the throbbing.

A moment later, she continued inching forward.

But was she going the right way? Should she wait a little longer, in case someone was coming for her? Dad and Melva and Jill would be looking for her soon. People got lost in these Ozark caves. Some died. Maybe she should wait a little longer. . . .

How had her attacker been able to carry her this way? Maybe she should—

Stone clattered against stone somewhere behind her, and she froze, listening. She almost called out, then she realized that Dad or Melva or Justin or Jill would be shouting for her. There was a shuffle of footsteps, another clatter of rock. Carissa dropped to her knees, pressing her lips together to keep from crying out at the sudden pain.

She waited.

Silence.

She crawled forward, keeping her left hand on the wall to guide her as the soles of her shoes slid across the muddy earth. She could hear her own loud breathing.

A flash of light shot over the dripping rocks, then disappeared. She froze to watch and listen.

Was that a whisper? Or just a change in rhythm of the dripping water?

The light flashed again, and Carissa caught sight of a stalagmite just ahead, with a shelf of white rock beyond it. A hiding place. If she could reach that spot and—

Another whisper, then the sound of footsteps.

Someone was coming, but any other sounds of an approach disappeared in the thumping roar inside Carissa's skull, pain growing worse as her fear mounted.

She scrambled past the fat stalagmite. Digging her fingers into tiny crevices, she pulled herself up the stone wall. A narrow space behind a slab of limestone looked like a perfect fit for her as the light flashed through the cave again. She crawled into the space, then collapsed, gritting her teeth against the sharp stabbing in her skull.

She heard the sound of rocks scattering, then footsteps below her. Light flickered across the white limestone. She cringed. Could she be seen?

There was a loud gasp. "No!" The voice was a whisper. The searcher paused, as if looking around. Then: "Carissa? Carissa . . ." Like the hiss of a snake.

More footsteps, as if the searcher roamed through the cave. More whispers echoed from the walls of rock, like the sound of dry leaves blowing in the wind, but Carissa couldn't make out the words. She held her breath, trembling with terror.

That whisper . . . something about it was familiar. But what? Or maybe it wasn't the voice. Maybe it was something else. She sniffed the air. A scent?

Whoever was holding that light and filling the cavern with whispers knew her name.

The footsteps shuffled past her hiding place, and the light faded in the distance. Darkness and silence floated down over her again like a shield. At last, all was dark, and all was silent once more.

Chapter Three

Noelle fastened her seatbelt and settled the thermos beside her as Nathan pulled out of her driveway. She fished her cell phone out from her purse then punched in Cecil's home number. When a stranger answered, she asked about the status of the search and was told Carissa had not yet been found.

"Thanks." She disconnected. "Nothing yet."

"We can try again in a little while."

She closed her eyes and leaned her head back. Oh, Carissa, where are you?

Nathan's warm hand touched her arm. "You okay?"

She nodded as tears stung behind her closed lids. "I'm fine. Carissa will be, too."

His hand tightened. "You know that for sure?"

She opened her eyes and looked at him, hearing the odd note in his voice. "I'm praying it's true." She hadn't stopped praying since Nathan had broken the news to her. Actually, she'd been praying before that.

He nodded and returned his attention to the road.

She knew this drive well, all the rolling hills, stark cliffs and misty valleys that stretched from Springfield to Branson on Highway 65, and then west on 76 to the Hideaway turnoff. These wooded Ozark hills kept their secrets well.

She closed her eyes, once again picturing her young cousin's smiling face, her mischievous blue eyes and shoulder-length ringlets of soft brown hair. Oh, Carissa.

Tears smarted Noelle's eyes again, and she straightened in her seat. "Tell me about the search. Where have they looked? How many are helping?"

"No one has rested," Nathan said. "Not even Aunt Pearl. They've combed Cedar Hollow from end to end. The police, the forest rangers, even some local guardsmen were called to help."

"So you're saying they called out the guards before they called me?" That stung, and yet she knew this wasn't the time to allow her personal feelings to become involved. She'd called the Coopers last night from the store, and left a message on their machine.

"Sorry."

"How's Aunt Pearl holding up?" Noelle asked. Her sixty-seven-year-old great-aunt Pearl lived on the original family homestead, about a quarter mile from Cecil's home. Cecil and his family lived in the same sprawling two-story house in which he had grown up, halfway between Pearl's house and the sawmill. Ordinarily, a sawmill would need to be situated closer to civilization, but Cooper's had been in operation for over fifty years, with an excellent reputation. It never lacked for business.

"I've hardly seen anything of her," Nathan said. "She's obviously upset."

"How's her heart?"

"She's strong as an ox, you know that. I wouldn't be surprised to discover she's covered the whole property on foot herself."

"Surely there have been places the searchers have

missed," Noelle said. "Nobody could possibly cover all two thousand acres in one night. Who, besides the guards and police, is searching?"

"Thirty people from regional search-and-rescue squads, plus the Cooper sawmill employees. Dane Gideon came over with his ranch hands before I left this morning, and as the word's spread, the churches got involved. Everyone has combed the woods as thoroughly as possible, then started over again. When I left this morning, it looked as if there were more people than trees in that forest."

Noelle felt a rush of gratitude for the strong community that had always been a part of Hideaway, and the surrounding countryside, and once again tears filled her eyes. "And family?"

"Cecil stays out there all the time. He won't eat, won't even sit down for a short rest."

Noelle could easily believe that. The paternal instinct ran strong in her cousin. "What about Melva?" she asked. Cecil's second wife had always adored Carissa and Justin. Indeed, the family joked that Melva had married Cecil because she'd wanted to mother his children.

"She's not holding up well at all," Nathan said.

Noelle closed her eyes and willed herself not to let the tears fall. Why hadn't they returned her call last night? She stayed up late waiting and praying, until she'd finally received assurance that everything would be okay. But now? Where was all that holy assurance now?

"Your sister's been keeping a close eye on Melva," Nathan said. "Typical Jill."

Noelle sighed and turned her head to stare out the passenger window, across a rare open valley. "Jill didn't call me."

Nathan didn't reply.

Noelle gave him a sharp glance. "What aren't you telling me?"

"Maybe you should have a talk with Jill when we get there."

"Why?" She studied his expression. His attention remained on the road, hands at the ten and two position on the steering wheel, back straight, a sure sign he was covering. "Let me guess. She told everyone not to call me."

He grimaced.

"She did!"

"She said you had a lot going on right now, and this would be too much for you."

Noelle scowled and crossed her arms over her chest. She should have known better than to tell her sister about Joel's return. Now Jill was all distressed, begging Noelle to scamper back home to Hideaway with her tail between her legs, like a whipped cur. Again. Jill to the rescue. Again. But Noelle didn't need rescuing this time.

"She's only concerned for your welfare," he said.

"Don't even start with that, Nathan. I'm thirty-six. She still sees me as a seven-year-old child who's lost her mother. For Pete's sake, that was twenty-nine years ago." And Jill never seemed to remember that she'd lost *her* mother, too.

"She mentioned that you had a difficult time after the sawmill accident."

"Sure I did. So did everyone else. It was shocking and horrible, and Jill didn't even take time to grieve. She was too busy taking care of everyone else. Come on, Nathan, she's pulling the big-sister act again. It isn't healthy for her or anyone else. And besides, that accident was ten years ago. I wasn't exactly in the best mental state at the time."

Ten years ago, Noelle and Jill had lost their father and grandparents in an accident at the sawmill when a load of cedar logs had fallen off a flatbed truck, crushing them. Four years later, Cecil's wife—Justin and Carissa's mother—had suddenly left home, abandoning her family. Two years ago, a tornado had ripped through Cedar Hollow, barely sparing the homes and sawmill. Some people said Cedar Hollow was cursed. Sometimes, Noelle agreed.

From her peripheral vision, Noelle saw Nathan give her a brief glance. "You've lost weight," he said.

"Thank you for noticing."

"Haven't been eating?"

She shook her head. "I needed to lose the weight anyway, but I guess I've been a little on edge the past couple of weeks, what with Joel back in town."

There was an expressive silence, and she could have bitten her tongue. Apparently, Jill hadn't shared that tidbit with Nathan.

30

"You didn't tell me." There was a note of accusation in his voice.

She felt an uncomfortable nudge of guilt. She reminded herself firmly that there was no reason to feel guilty. "Now you're beginning to sound like Jill."

"Okay, let me make sure I'm clear on this." His voice bit with a hint of sarcasm. "Your ex-husband—who has proven in the past to be violent—has suddenly reappeared in Springfield. You're nervous enough about it that you've lost your appetite, yet you don't think it's reasonable for anyone to become concerned?"

"I'm simply saying I don't need more than one person overreacting to the crises in my life. I'm capable of taking care of them myself." Okay, maybe *she* was overreacting. Yes, she and Nathan had renewed their friendship, and she valued that friendship highly, but she was answerable to no one but herself. These past few years of independence had given Noelle a sweet taste of freedom. She intended to guard that freedom with everything she had.

She glanced at Nathan's profile, the even features, the high forehead, and resisted a pang of chagrin at the concern in his expression. "I'm telling you now, okay? And yes, I've lost some sleep over it. I just don't think anyone else should have to worry." Especially since she had landed herself in this mess to begin with. She didn't intend to drag friends and family into the ugly aftermath of her past mistakes.

"Has he tried to contact you?"

She hesitated. "Let's just say he's made sure I know he's back."

"Please don't tell me he knows where you're living now."

"He could easily find out if he wanted to, but he's been coming into the store the past couple of weeks."

Nathan's grip tightened on the steering wheel. "He's been *coming* in? As in, more than once?"

"Twice when I was working, but he always purchased things, so it isn't as if he's harassing me."

"Has he said anything to you?"

"He barely looked at me." Okay, so it wasn't completely objectionable to have Nathan concerned about her welfare.

"Do you think he's up to something?"

"I can't tell. Six years ago I was able to read him and know when to expect an outburst, but he's been gone a long time. Now we're strangers, and I don't know what to expect."

They rode in silence for a moment. During the divorce proceedings, which had been drawn out for eighteen excruciating months, Noelle had received several threats from Joel, along with a broken windshield. There had also been numerous anonymous telephone calls to her place of employment, where she'd worked as a nurse for a pediatric group, calls that ultimately had resulted in the loss of her job when the harassment had become too intense—Missouri's status as a "right to fire" state hadn't helped. Three of the five physicians in the group had requested her termination, with no reason needed.

Because of her past work record, she'd found it impossible to find another nursing position, which was her own fault. Testing positive for methamphetamines had cast an indelible smudge on her reputation, though she hadn't touched drugs again. She only wished she'd never taken those pills the first time, had never fallen for Joel's promise that they would "keep her alert."

The situation with Joel had become so frightening that she'd requested a restraining order. She hadn't received one, because she couldn't prove her estranged husband was the culprit. During the final six months before the divorce hearing, she'd gone home to Hideaway and stayed with Jill. And her concerned older sister had stepped back into her "mommy" role, to the point of insisting that Noelle eat three healthy meals a day and attend church twice a week. It was then that Noelle had begun to seek God's direction in earnest, for the first time in many years.

"You don't think Joel's sudden reappearance could have anything to do with Carissa's disappearance, do you?" Nathan asked.

Noelle looked at him, startled. "Like what?"

"Would kidnapping be out of the question?"

"Kidnapping!"

"At this point I don't know, but having met Joel a few times, and knowing what he's done to you in the past, I wouldn't dismiss the possibility. From all accounts, he's a vindictive scoundrel who should be rotting behind bars."

She blinked at him, startled by his adamancy. "But Carissa? After six years? I don't think that's likely." And yet, what if . . . ?

She glanced at Nathan's profile again. Nathan Trask had a kind nature, which was obvious in his expression, in the laugh lines around his eyes. He was also an attractive man, with a high, broad forehead, dark-green eyes, dark-brown hair that he kept short and combed back. Right now, his usual five o'clock shadow had nearly become a beard, and his facial lines were ones of weariness. He had good reason to be cranky.

"Maybe I should be driving," she said.

"I'm okay. The coffee helped."

Sitting back, she tried to relax, and again thought about last night. She shivered.

"Cold?" Nathan reached toward the console for the heat dial.

"I'm . . . fine." She folded her arms over her chest and tried to let the passing roadside beauty calm her—the bright yellow splashes of goldenrod against the deep red of autumn sumac, highlighted by sprays of purple asters.

It was no use. Her mind wouldn't stop whirling with questions.

"Noelle?" Nathan said at last.

"Hmm?"

"What else is going on with you?"

"What do you mean?"

"There's something else you're not telling me."

She gave him a look of aggravation. Nathan Trask

had always possessed an irritating ability to read her mind. "Why would you say—"

"Just tell me, okay? I'm not in the mood to dig it out of you."

"Okay, fine." He really was a grump today. And she shouldn't be saying this. It would only invite more questions and cause more worry. Could she trust him not to share too much with Jill? "It's nothing, really. I had a little episode last night, probably from low blood sugar, since I haven't been eating a lot, and didn't—"

"What kind of episode?"

She had his complete attention now. "Watch the road, would you?"

"I'm watching the road. Tell me what happened."

Rats. She knew he'd get upset. For a few more seconds she stared out at the colorful roadside. Like Jill, Nathan had the "older sibling" complex. He tended to be bossy, and from the time the first of his two younger sisters was born, he had also tried to boss Noelle even though she was his age, and a neighbor rather than a sibling. She'd established her boundaries with him when she was about five. She didn't intend to have to do so again.

Still, it wasn't totally disagreeable to have Nathan so concerned about her.

"Okay," he conceded. "I'm sorry. I didn't mean to snap at you. What happened? How did you feel?"

"I felt very concerned for no reason," she said, then glanced at him to make sure he was watching the road again. "You know how it is when something occurs to you, that seems so real, as though God has spoken?"

He glanced at her again. "That's a lot more than just nerves or blood sugar."

"Joel's arrival is definitely a stressor," she said.

There was a pause, then Nathan asked, "What time, exactly, did it happen?"

She frowned at him.

He met her gaze briefly, then looked away. "This may have everything to do with Carissa."

She thought so, too, but why would *he?*

He took a deep breath and exhaled, then combed his fingers through his hair. The morning sun shining in through the window showed the lines around his eyes and the evidence of his lack of sleep and his worry. "What time did you have the attack? You said it was last night—was it after dark?"

"It was just after closing time."

"You close at eight—which means this happened about the same time Carissa disappeared."

"Yes." She didn't want to go there. Not yet. It was too soon and she wasn't ready.

"You know what I'm talking about." He braked when a car cut in front of him. "It's as if you somehow knew something had happened to Carissa."

"You can't be serious." Hypocrisy will get you nowhere, Noelle Cooper.

He nodded. The tightness around his mouth revealed his determination. He was going to discuss the subject no matter what she said.

"Nathan, I'm not psychic. I'm surprised a former pastor like you would suggest such a thing."

"No, not psychic. But you've always been able to perceive things others don't," he said. "I remember you had dreams several days before your mother died."

"You remember that? We were seven."

"You told me about it, and it stuck with me. It scared me, because every time you had a dream after that, I was afraid someone would die."

She closed her eyes and leaned back against the headrest. Growing up as country neighbors, she and Nathan had ridden horses and bikes, hiked, explored caves, and wandered over the extensive acreage of the combined Cooper and Trask properties. They'd done homework together when they were old enough for homework. She'd shared her thoughts and dreams with him, and he'd remembered, after all this time.

"So you do know what I'm talking about," he said.

"Just because I had dreams before Mom died doesn't mean anything."

"Remember that orange-and-white kitten of mine that got lost when we were ten? I told you about it, and you went right to it. I'd looked for at least two hours, and you found it in five minutes."

She shifted uncomfortably in her seat. This was just great. She was stuck in a moving vehicle halfway to Hideaway with Nathan Trask, who seemed to be very much in the mood for an argument.

She pointed to a sign. "There's your turn. Focus on your driving for a few minutes, will you?"

He shot her a quick glance that said, "This subject is only tabled, not closed," but made the turn in silence.

Chapter Four

I have to think . . . have to get control! Where did she go? What if she knows it's me? She could beat me to the house, she could tell the others that I tried to kill her!

But I didn't kill her. I stopped myself. I can stop this if I try hard enough. I can keep the fear from controlling me.

She's just lost in the cave somewhere, scared and alone. I need to go back and find her and take her home. Maybe if I stay with the others when this thing hits . . . when this slow, shifting spiral into terror strikes me . . . their presence might force me to control my actions.

Yes. I'll have to find her. Everything will be okay.

Carissa won't be able to find her way back without my help. I'm in control.

I can stay in control.

Nathan took a bypass around Branson's busiest highway, increasingly aware that Noelle's silent observation of the passing roadside was a sign that he'd struck a nerve. This new road had very little traffic, but he waited to speak, respecting her wish for silence, until they were on the far side of Branson.

"I wish you'd at least talk to me about it," he said at last.

She cleared her throat but didn't answer. A few moments later, she sighed, but still didn't speak.

"It's okay," he said at last. "I understand. It's difficult. The kind of gift that you've been given can't be an easy thing to live with."

She gave a soft snort. "Gift? You've got to be kidding."

"That's what I'd call it."

"Do you remember where I found the kitten?"

"At my grandmother's, up the road, in the milk barn."

"Big surprise," she said dryly. "Cats love milk."

"I'd just finished looking everywhere in that barn before you led me to her."

"So I got lucky."

"I can't count the number of times you've practically told me what I was feeling without my having to say a word."

"That happens with friends," she said.

Nathan drove in silence for a few more moments while Noelle returned to her study of the passing hills and hayfields. She wasn't fooling him. He knew her too well. She couldn't deny something they had grown up knowing—she had been blessed with an unusual amount of empathy.

No, not just empathy. Intuition, too, and more . . .

They'd never talked about it, when they were children, because then it hadn't seemed like such an unusual thing to them. He suspected that for the past ten or twenty years she had even tried to deny the gift completely. Or maybe she hadn't experienced it. Noelle's lifestyle in her late teens and twenties had not given her much of an opening for guidance by the Holy Spirit.

He couldn't remember when she'd first shown signs of this special sense about other people. She was right, she did have a logical thought process and a natural gift for reading body language. She also had a genuine affection for people.

But there was something extra, besides all that, and the best definition he could find was to call it "a discernment." Some might say it was unnatural, but if anything it was supernatural, a spiritual gift from God, because, somehow Nathan was sure, Noelle had never attempted to "conjure" this gift.

He couldn't help wondering about last night, but for now he wouldn't push it.

"Be gentle with Jill when you see her," he said, knowing Noelle would appreciate the change of subject, even if it did mean talking about another uncomfortable issue.

"Fine. I'll just tenderly punch her in the nose."

He grinned as he negotiated a sharp curve past Reeds Spring. "I think she feels partly responsible for Carissa's disappearance. Carissa was bringing back a ledger from the office for Jill to look at. You knew Jill and Cecil formed a business partnership for Cooper's Sawmill?"

"Yes, she told me. Sounds like Aunt Pearl's not crazy about the idea."

"Pearl doesn't like losing authority, but Cecil and Jill finally managed to convince her that they need to modernize if they're going to retain their edge in the market."

"Meaning computers," Noelle said. "Jill told me two weeks ago that they'd already purchased two. Also that Melva's tackling the job of entering data for the whole year, and Jill's learning the system with her. Aunt Pearl must be fit to be tied."

Nathan chuckled. "She hates anything she can't understand."

Noelle glanced at him. "But Jill has her nursing job at the clinic. How does she have time for both?"

"Maybe you should talk to her about that."

"I did, but Jill wouldn't listen. Remember, I'm the baby sister without a brain in my head."

Nathan heard the frustration in her voice. Noelle and Jill loved each other very much, but they never quite overcame the clash of wills that should have been settled between them long ago—Jill's fierce need to nurture versus Noelle's equally fierce need for independence. Jill nurtured not only her sister, but her extended family, the patients she worked with at the clinic and the clinic staff, as well. Consequently, she had little time to nurture herself. She was often irritable and stressed.

Nathan braked for a slow moving car in front of him. "Jill's working a lot these days, and the clinic is still desperately searching for medical personnel willing to relocate to Hideaway."

"I know. She's asked me at least ten times in the past month if I'd consider a position."

"And your reply?" Nathan resisted the urge to check out Noelle's expression.

41

"I told her it shouldn't be hard to find someone," she said. "The town caters to tourists, including medical personnel, and surely some of them could be enticed to stay permanently."

"It hasn't happened yet. Jill isn't the only one who would like to see you back home in Hideaway."

From the corner of his eye, he saw her glance at him. "Really?" she asked softly.

"Bertie Meyer talks about you all the time. So does Carissa."

"Oh."

Was that disappointment in her voice? And if so, who else had she hoped would want her back in Hideaway?

He suppressed a smile. "They'll need several new staff members if Dr. Cheyenne Gideon manages to convince the city board of directors to support a hospital designation for the clinic." He glanced at Noelle. "You're still a nurse. Why ignore the skills you worked so hard to learn?"

"Don't start with me. I've had enough of that from Jill."

"Have you ever considered the possibility that she's right once in a while?"

"Have you ever considered the possibility that you're a nag?" Noelle teased. "Besides, you're the one who can't settle on a career. From preacher to pharmacist in four years. You never told me why you made that giant leap."

He gave up. She wouldn't be pinned down, and if he tried, she'd just change the subject again. "Not much of a leap. After Natalie died, I felt overwhelmed by the pastorate, so I gave the church my resignation and went back to school to follow in my mom's footsteps." It was an oversimplification of a very complicated and painful time in his life, and her prolonged silence told him she knew it.

"I'm sorry," she said. "Your wife was so young to be taken like that. It must have been awful for both of you."

"I tried to be there for her as much as I could, while still trying to shoulder all the responsibilities of the church myself." And Hideaway Community Church had become his undoing, especially after the aggressive ovarian cancer took Natalie in such a short time. "It became too much for me during her illness. I couldn't cope with the needs of so many, and even though the church was supportive, I guess I felt like a failure." As always, he had an uncomfortable tendency to spill his guts to Noelle.

"I was so caught up in my own problems at the time, I wasn't there for you," she said.

"I brought it on myself, with my inability to delegate responsibility in the church. I had the erroneous attitude, thinking of myself as God's anointed, who should be able to do it all. I was wrong."

"I'm sorry," she said softly.

"I knew what a rough time you were having then, with Joel," Nathan said. "I've heard the comment that a divorce is more painful than a death. In a way, not only is divorce the announcement of the death of a relationship, but it's also, in the eyes of many, a sign of rejection."

"For me it was a sign of failure," she said quietly. "By the time the judge pronounced us no longer husband and wife, I felt as though I'd been released from prison."

He gave her a quick glance.

She shrugged. "The drugs, the abuse." She pressed a forefinger against the small scar beside her left eye. "This is just the most visible scar he gave me. I kept thinking I could hold out and see him through all of it, that I was the one person who could rescue him from himself." She gave a bitter snort. "I discovered I wasn't so special, after all."

"Then I'm sorry I wasn't there for you, either." Nathan risked another glance at her; she was staring out the window again. "And so you changed professions because of the experience, just as I did."

"I didn't have a choice. I couldn't find a job after I was dismissed from the clinic. No one wanted to take a chance on a proven drug abuser."

Nathan's foot involuntarily eased from the accelerator and the truck slowed. He couldn't keep the shock from his expression.

"I did offer to drive if you need me to," she said dryly.

"That's okay." He regained his composure. "I guess there are some things I still don't know about you."

"There are some things you won't want to know. Let's just say I made a mess of things once too often, and I've been paying for it ever since."

"But you shouldn't have to keep paying for it for the rest of your life."

"Maybe I should. Get over it, Nathan. I have."

"But you always wanted to be a nurse."

She returned to her brooding.

Time for yet another subject change. Amazing how they'd once been able to discuss anything together, and now they had to tiptoe around so many areas of their lives.

She pointed to the first outlying buildings of the town of Hideaway, the breathtaking view of the lake to their right and the picturesque town square to their left—a square on which the brick storefronts faced the street that encircled it on all four sides.

Nathan drove past the clinic, general store, feed store, bakery and bank, then followed the curve in the road through a charming residential district, lush with trees and shrubbery and lined with a variety of homes, from colorfully painted Victorian houses to neat brick Colonials and ranches and small lake cabins. This early in the morning, all was quiet. Nathan and Noelle passed Jill's two-story Victorian on their way out of town.

"Nothing stirring in town yet," Noelle said.

"Which means everyone's probably still out at Cedar Hollow."

"Which means they haven't found Carissa yet."

Nathan returned his attention to the road as he picked up speed.

The first sight to greet Noelle as Nathan sped along

the paved country lane toward Cooper land was the trees—lush, green and tall, except for a narrow swath of twisted and stunted growth to the right of the lane for about a quarter of a mile that followed the curve downhill into Cedar Hollow. It was the only remaining evidence of the tornado that had torn through the hollow two years earlier. This was the Coopers' very own tornado alley—with the tops of the trees ripped off and scattered for miles, along with the roof of the old barn behind Cecil Cooper's house.

Turning in her seat, away from the window, Noelle watched Nathan drive. His muscles rippled in his bare forearms as he steered to miss a pothole. Due to the number of logging trucks that came this way, the county road crew had to struggle to keep this road repaired.

Nathan's face seemed to brood in the flickering shades of light and shadow as he drove under an arching tunnel of trees.

Noelle's gaze returned to the road. A few hundred feet ahead, she saw the sturdy cedar stand that supported four mailboxes, belonging to Cecil and Melva, Great-Aunt Pearl, the Cooper Sawmill and the last in the line to Nathan. Forever a country boy at heart, he had returned to his roots when he moved back to the farm where he'd grown up, in the house that was hidden from view to their right, behind a thick stand of lodge-pole pine.

Nathan turned left into the paved driveway on Cooper land. The sawmill was a quarter of a mile along this wooded lane.

"Did you hear Harvey Sand died?" Nathan asked.

"Jill told me." Harvey had done the monthly and annual accounting for Cooper Sawmill for the past fifteen years. His secretary had found him unconscious at the bottom of his staircase at home last Friday morning. "Did he ever regain consciousness?"

"Not that I heard."

"So they still don't know what happened for sure. Is the sheriff continuing to investigate?"

"Probably. You know Greg, always suspicious."

Noelle peered around at the growing gloom as the clouds seemed to congregate over Cooper land. How appropriate today, with Carissa missing. Obviously, some rain had already fallen, judging by the dripping leaves on the trees and the damp pavement. "Nathan, Jill said you were still doing some counseling for the family."

"She did?"

He sounded hesitant, and Noelle glanced at him. Once more, his posture was perfectly correct, his grip on the steering wheel precise, his gaze straight ahead at the road. Interesting.

"Are you trying to get to the bottom of the Cooper family psyche?" She was only half joking.

He looked away. "You know I'm not a counselor."

"I know you're not a *psychologist,* but once a pastor always a pastor."

"Just because someone's a pastor doesn't mean he's a good counselor."

"You have a knack. Don't be so modest." She'd heard

enough local gossip to know that his solid common sense had helped to heal more than one fragile marriage in Hideaway.

"Okay," she said. "I understand all about confidentiality."

"Right. I'm liable."

"Even if it *is* family."

"Exactly."

"Okay." She was dying of curiosity, but that had landed her in trouble before. She studied Nathan's closed expression. Okay. For now, she'd drop the subject and focus on finding Carissa.

Nathan glanced sideways to see Noelle's dark brows drawn together, her blue eyes narrowed in concentration. What was she thinking? He knew she wasn't sulking over his refusal to disclose confidential information to her.

Again, he glanced at the scar beside her left eye. He'd noticed her rubbing her finger over the indentation several times, an automatic gesture that revealed more about her than she probably wanted anyone to know. What did that man do to her? When Nathan and Noelle were younger, she'd had an impulsive sense of fun, an almost constant light of humor in her eyes. She'd often poked fun at herself, but not at others. Her face had always been in motion, expressing her thoughts and feelings without words. In repose, her facial features gave the appearance of exquisite elegance—her nose almost too delicate and straight, her cheekbones almost too high, her dimpled chin too perfect. When they were growing up, it was that beauty that people had seen in her, often missing the sharp intelligence behind the radiance of her eyes, framed by long, dark lashes.

Nathan blamed Noelle's beauty for the end of their friendship. When they entered high school, she'd become a focus of attention for the guys, and Nathan, a nerd, had faded into the background of her life to watch her flit from one relationship to the next in rapid succession. It was then that he'd painfully realized he no longer had a best friend. It was then, with the sense of sadness, that he'd discovered Whom his real best friend had always been.

From that time, the focus of his life had changed. His final interaction with Noelle—the one that had broken their friendship for several years—happened the day he'd overheard some guys in gym class comparing notes about her, shocking notes that had sickened him.

When he'd confronted her, right there in the busy main corridor at Hideaway High, there had been an ugly shouting match between them that had been talked about for weeks afterward.

Funny, until her divorce, Nathan hadn't realized—hadn't allowed himself to realize—how deeply Noelle had been a part of his life during their formative years. Lately, the more he saw her, the more he wanted to see her, aside from any question of romance. In fact, he'd reminded himself over and over again that a romance could put their friendship at risk, and he wanted to keep her friendship.

Nathan's truck topped a wooded knoll and the gray-brown angles of the sawmill came into view. Several cars and pickup trucks were parked in the lot—more than usual. All the employees were beating the brush in search of Carissa.

Nathan's truck bounced down the steep lane into the valley and over the low-water bridge that was already under at least five inches of water from the recent rains.

Noelle gave a sudden, soft gasp, and Nathan glanced at her.

"What's wrong?"

She took a deep breath and blinked.

"Is it happening again?" he demanded.

She nodded and closed her eyes.

Chapter Five

Carissa's eyes opened to complete blackness. All she could hear was the drip of water, and all she could feel was the hard stone floor beneath her. She sniffed the earthy, moist air, and remembered where she was. Tears filled her eyes and trickled down her cheeks. She tasted the saltiness on her lips.

"Jesus, please help me," she prayed in a whisper. *"I'm scared. Where am I? Why hasn't anybody found me yet?"*

Her soft words bounced off the rock that surrounded her . . . but when she stopped praying, the whispers continued, sliding past the rock wall, slithering through the blackness.

Her attacker was back! She clamped both hands over her mouth to keep from crying out.

There was a scuff of shoes on a hard surface, a flicker of light that turned the blackness to dark gray. The footsteps drew closer, the whispering voice became louder.

Carissa cringed against the wall, afraid to breathe. Could she be seen? Her head pounded once more with sudden pain, and she gasped aloud without thinking.

The footsteps stopped, and so did the whispering. Carissa squeezed her eyes shut. *Make whoever it is go away, Jesus. Hide me! Please, Jesus, keep me safe!*

The whispering started again, the footsteps drew closer. Then the words grew more pronounced.

"Control," she heard, on an eerie breath of sound. "I'm in control. I can take care of this. She's here and I can find her."

There was a clatter of pebbles above Carissa's head. The searcher was above her now!

She held her breath. *Please Jesus please Jesus please.*

Then the whispering faded, becoming less distinct. The sound of footsteps moved away. Carissa opened her eyes and peered out at the reflection of a flashlight beam against a white column several yards away. She stuck her head out of her tiny hiding place, but the light had disappeared.

She settled back into her hiding place and waited. Jesus was watching over her.

"Noelle, listen to me, please tell me what's happening," Nathan said quietly.

She blinked at the gloomy daylight outside the windshield, then realized Nathan was watching her intently.

"It's okay," he said. "You're all right." His voice was gentle, reassuring, as though he were speaking to a child. He caught her hands in his.

She tried to withdraw them.

He didn't release her. "What's this all about? Was this the same as last night?" he asked.

She nodded.

"How does that feel? What happens? What goes through your mind?"

"It isn't anything dramatic or overflowing," she whispered, as if speaking aloud might make this sudden knowledge disappear. "I'm sorry, I can't explain, really. It's too . . . new to me."

"Once upon a time, you understood what it was."

"Yeah, well, once upon a time I was an innocent child, but too many things happened to change that. It's been many years since I've felt His blessing." There. She'd admitted it to him. The faith of her childhood had failed her. Or maybe it hadn't failed, but *she* had failed it . . . failed God . . . failed herself.

"What's that supposed to mean?" he asked.

She straightened and withdrew her hands; this time he let them go. She sat back and stared out the windshield. "If this is a gift from God, as you say, then He must have made a mistake."

"You know better."

She raised a hand to stop his protest. "Would you just listen for a minute? You saw the way I was in high

52

school—desperately in need of attention and love and willing to go to any lengths to find it."

"I came to grips with that years ago," Nathan said gently. "You'd lost your mother, and your father wasn't home with you much. Your sister tried to make it up to you, but that was impossible. Why don't you give yourself a break?"

"And why won't you at least let me complete a thought without interrupting?" She kept her voice gentle, but she needed him to hear her out.

"Sorry."

"During nursing school I dated a drug addict, and after graduation I married him. How stupid is that? I'm talking illegal street drugs, Nathan. And I used them myself. You think God wants to give a gift to someone like that?"

"I think you're making judgments you should leave to God. Sure, you got carried away and blew it badly a few times. But you aren't the same person you were then, so stop with the guilt complex and tell me what you were experiencing a moment ago," he said.

"Oh, come on, Nathan, you sound like an overeager newspaper reporter. What do you think I was feeling?"

"I don't have your gift, but you looked very concerned about something."

"You got it." Her voice caught. She cleared her throat. "Very concerned."

"But about what?"

"Carissa. It's urgent that we find her quickly. But we all know that." She focused on the familiar features of

53

his face, at the unusual cedar-green of his eyes. "You really think this is a message from God?"

"Yes I do. Your gift has returned."

She watched for some break in his gaze, some hint of doubt. There was none. "I'm not some holy saint, Nathan. If this *is* a gift, there are many far more worthy recipients who—"

"Worthy?" he interrupted, impatiently. "A saint is simply someone who has put faith in Him. You've been a believer since you were six."

"But you know I haven't—"

"He can use anyone He pleases for whatever work He wants done, with or without that person's help," he interrupted again. "With you, I think He gives you special knowledge that you need to know, not something you conjure for yourself, because He's the one in control, not you. When you dreamed about your mother before she died, I think He was preparing you."

Noelle nodded. "Okay. So what's He giving me now?"

"You're here, aren't you? Obviously you need to search for Carissa."

She nodded, watching the tension in his expression. "You don't look too chipper," she noted. "I thought you dealt with this kind of thing before in your pastoral duties."

"*This* kind of thing? You're kidding, right? This is not your normal, everyday counseling session or grief process." He slid back behind the steering wheel, shifted into Drive and eased forward along the lane.

"Okay, then if these episodes I'm having are connected to Carissa, why can't I see where she is? Why didn't I receive some brilliant flash of understanding, some mental map about where to go to find her?"

"Because you aren't writing the script. God is. He'll guide you when it's time." He glanced at her briefly. "So were there any other impressions a moment ago?"

Noelle gazed at the ceiling of the truck, reluctant to accept that this was even happening. But still . . . "I felt she was alone in the dark and frightened of some unknown threat."

"Something? Or some*one?* Or just the dark itself?"

"Someone." That much Noelle knew, though it was still a mystery to her how she'd reached that certainty. "But that doesn't make sense. I can't believe anyone would kidnap Carissa."

"Could be revenge. You know Cecil. He has a way of—"

"Making people angry," she finished for him. "I know. He's always been quicker to engage his mouth than his brain. But still, only a nutcase would try to take that out on Carissa."

"Excuse me, but a 'nutcase' is exactly who we're talking about here."

"Okay. Fine." Noelle gazed out the window at the bright-red sumac bushes along the edges of the lane, at the red Virginia creeper vines outlining tree limbs, threaded among the canopy of green leaves. "Come to think of it, we sound like a couple of nutcases ourselves. If anyone were to overhear us talking—"

"They won't. We'll be careful."

"Good. So that means you're not going to go blabbing this to anyone?"

He raised a brow of affected disdain. "You can't possibly believe I would do something so audacious as to sully my own good name among the locals. My livelihood depends on my reputation."

She grinned, flooded with relief at this glimpse of her old friend. "Okay, fine. You don't tell them I'm psychic—"

"You're not psychic, you're gifted. They're two totally different—"

"—and I won't tell them about the stray marbles you've apparently been losing because you believe me. Has Cecil fired someone at the mill or the ranch recently?"

"Not in over six months, and the last man wanted to get fired so he could draw unemployment insurance."

"No motive for a kidnapping, then. Could Carissa have gotten lost?"

"That's very possible. Cecil found her flashlight in the mud last night. He's thinking that she might have gotten turned around and panicked."

"But Carissa doesn't panic easily," Noelle said.

"And besides, you have a definite impression that some*one* is a threat . . ."

"I'm not willing to put my faith in some stupid impression," Noelle said.

"Not stupid," he insisted. "Let's not dismiss any possibility."

Nathan pulled up to the sawmill. The paved parking lot surrounding the huge, barnlike building was crammed with cars, trucks, SUVs and trailers, which had apparently carried all-terrain vehicles.

Ordinarily, Cecil wouldn't thank anyone for tearing up his pastureland and traumatizing more than a thousand head of cattle and horses, but if the volunteer searchers found his little girl, he would most likely be willing to give them permanent rights to the land—if those rights were his to give. Though he managed all of the Cooper enterprises, he hadn't yet inherited.

Nathan parked between a van and another truck, then turned to Noelle again. "Are you sure you're okay?"

"I told you, I'm fine. A little rattled, but what would you expect? I want to focus on finding Carissa."

"We'll do that."

Noelle stared at the corrugated aluminum siding on the huge building. Even after ten years, the sawmill brought back the memories of the accident that had killed Dad and Grandma and Grandpa. Carissa's disappearance only resurrected those memories more distinctly.

"We might as well walk from here," she said. "We've got to start looking somewhere."

They climbed from the truck to be greeted by the music of the crickets and the scent of moist earth. Noelle took a deep breath, her gaze traveling over the mossy green of the cedar trees, the splashes of orange and apricot on the tips of maple trees and the rippling green of the hay field, punctuated by huge, silver-gold bales stacked side by side in the field to the right of the lane.

This lane led around the side of the building to the Cooper settlement about a quarter of a mile away. Noelle's ancestors had lived and farmed here for generations, expanding this property into a valuable asset that, combined with the successful sawmill, generously supported family members and dozens of employees. As a Cooper family member, Noelle received a sizable check every six months, even though she didn't work on the property.

Noelle avoided looking at the sawmill, allowing her memories to carry her back to a safer time. She loved country life, especially the privacy and peace of this hollow in the hills. Though she also loved living in Springfield, every time she came home to Hideaway she felt a distinct tug of the heart. She loved the town of Hideaway. Even though she wouldn't admit it to Nathan, the idea of working at the clinic appealed to something inside her that she thought had dried up and died when she'd lost her last nursing position.

Still, too many memories attacked her here on Cooper land.

"Did anyone search the mill for signs of a possible problem?" she asked. "Maybe a struggle of some kind?"

"They checked, but all they found was the ledger alongside the lane, covered in mud. Carissa obviously had been to the mill and gone, and if there'd been a problem at the mill, she certainly wouldn't have bothered with the ledger."

"Could Cecil and Melva have heard a car engine from the house?"

"Not necessarily, but the dogs are usually pretty quick to pick up on the scent or sounds of a stranger, and they never sounded an alarm."

Noelle reached into the back of Nathan's truck, where she'd placed water flasks and a backpack with supplies, including a first-aid kit. "Want to hike from here?"

"I'd love to," he said. "But let me carry the backpack. It looks heavy."

She strapped herself into her pack. "Think I can't carry my own load?"

"No," he said dryly. "I just thought, after all these years, that competitive streak of yours might have mellowed a little."

"I'm not competitive." She shifted the shoulder straps. "You should know that by now."

She gazed along the lane. She wasn't in the mood to talk to anyone in her family right now, especially since no one had called her about Carissa. Still, the lane was the quickest and safest route into the rest of the hollow, with connecting lanes and cattle trails beyond Cecil's place. "Maybe we'll get lucky and make it past the houses without anyone noticing us," she said as they set off.

Nathan sniffed the tealike scent of early autumn leaves and listened to the crickets chirping from the forest on either side of the lane. Cedar Hollow—two thousand acres of fertile farm valley settled deep in the tree-lined hills—had changed little since he'd grown up here. His family's dairy cows had grazed just across the road from the Cooper beef cattle. He and Noelle had played along Willow Creek, which followed the curve of the land until it reached Table Rock Lake, a little over two miles away.

Noelle turned and glanced over her shoulder at the field to the south as the sound of an all-terrain vehicle reached them. "That's Carissa's favorite place to ride Gypsy," she said.

"It's where we loved to ride, too," he reminded her. "The field is level with amazingly few rocks to trip the horses." He and Noelle had often played in the field and along the creek when they were growing up.

"Why do some things stay the same, when other things change so drastically?" Noelle murmured.

"I've asked that enough times myself," Nathan said. "Remember how many times we walked down this lane when we were kids?"

"Or rode our bikes."

"And tried to hide from my little sisters."

"And my big sister." Noelle chuckled. "I felt so secure, so protected then. I mean, I had family all around me, and my best friend lived right down the road." She glanced sideways at Nathan.

He nodded. How many times in the past few years he had thought about those days, wondering if he would have done things differently, given the chance.

"Two thousand acres of Cooper property, joined by Trask property," Noelle said. "The searchers couldn't have covered everything yet, could they?"

"Not every inch, of course, but—"

"But Carissa knows this hollow so well. All she has to do is find Willow Creek and follow it down."

Nathan glanced at Noelle. "Maybe Carissa's done just that. She might be home by the time we get to the house."

"You don't sound convinced." Noelle pulled the cell phone from her pocket, punched numbers again, asked whoever answered about the status of the search without identifying herself, and then expressed thanks. "Not yet," she reported to Nathan, kicking a rock to the side of the track. "Carissa knows this land as well as we did at her age."

"That's true, but everything looks different in the dark. My friend Taylor Jackson thinks it's possible she got lost, and he's working on that premise while others are searching farther afield."

"Taylor's the ranger who's dating Karah Lee Fletcher at the clinic?"

"Yes. He's been helping coordinate the search. The sheriff suggested Carissa might have run away for some reason."

"Ridiculous. Greg should know better."

"That's what Cecil and Melva keep insisting," Nathan said. "But you know Carissa can be headstrong, and she and her parents did have a little confrontation yesterday."

"What about?"

"Gladys."

Noelle's steps slowed. "What about her?" she asked quietly.

"She wants to see Justin and Carissa again." Gladys had given up any right to see her children when she had abandoned them and their father. Her lack of concern for their suffering had outraged the whole community. "Carissa wants to see her, and Melva's pitching a major fit."

Noelle stepped around a mud puddle and ducked beneath a tree limb. "Does Gladys think she can just suddenly walk back into their lives and stir everything up again? When she left, Carissa was devastated. For at least a year, I think she continued to hope her mother would come back to them."

"As you said, Carissa's strong-willed," Nathan said. "So it could be possible that she's in hiding somewhere, maybe protesting."

"No."

"But if she *were* hiding, where do you think she'd hide?" He gestured around him, indicating the expanse of ground they would have to cover. "Where would *you* hide?"

"Not around here, and no, I'm not feeling any kind of leading."

"But just for the sake of a place to look, where would you hide?"

"Does that old dirt track still wind through the woods to the national forest a couple of miles back?" she asked.

"I think so. I heard Pearl complaining about people

trespassing on Cooper land from the logging trail in national forest land. Why? Do you—"

She turned and looked up at him, and he glimpsed an interested quickening in those intelligent eyes. "Where did we go when we were kids? You know, when we got in trouble."

"The caves?" he asked. There were at least four in the vicinity that ranged from mere indentations in the rock to caverns that cut deeply into the hillside.

She gave him a look of approval. "Exactly. Is Bobcat Cave still sealed?"

"I think it is. At least, I hope it is."

She bent over and tucked the cuffs of her jeans into her socks. "We may be beating some brush. Still ticks and chiggers here, I suppose."

"Not in this section, there ain't." A deep, strong female voice suddenly spoke from the trees a few yards ahead.

Chapter Six

Pearl Cooper's tall, rawboned figure emerged from the woods along one of the wildlife trails that intersected the lane. Her hand patted her chest in a long-familiar gesture—Aunt Pearl had claimed heart palpitations for as long as Noelle could remember. The family affectionately accused her of using sympathy to get what she wanted. She never denied it. Aunt Pearl could always charm people into giving in to her, and when she couldn't charm them, she pulled rank—though Cecil and Jill had incorporated the business to save on taxes, Pearl owned the property and everything on it. It had passed to her through the Cooper family trust.

Pearl's iron-gray hair stuck out in haphazard tufts, straggling over her forehead to frame deep-blue eyes— Cooper eyes that saw more, sometimes, than one wanted them to see. She seldom wore anything other than jeans and old plaid flannel shirts, even in summer, and now she had the legs of her jeans tucked into a pair of well-used hiking shoes—she'd been the one to teach Noelle this practical trick for warding off tiny, biting varmints.

"Can't swear to it," she said as she neared them, "but I think the geese running free and the pennyroyal I planted did the trick. No ticks in the yard or this part of the woods all summer. Of course, you've gotta watch close or you'll be ankle-deep in goose poop, but it's better than ticks, to my notion. The backwoods are another problem, though. That where you're headed?" Without pausing, she grabbed Noelle in a fierce hug, wrapping her in the pungent aroma of rosemary that always clung to Pearl from her herb garden.

Noelle's great-aunt Pearl lived in the same house she'd been born in, a sturdy, sprawling rock dwelling that had changed little since it had been built in the early nineteen-hundreds. For as long as anyone in the area could remember, Pearl Cooper had gathered herbs and made her old-time medicines, distributing them to anyone who needed them. She'd protested loudly when the general store in Hideaway had opened a pharmacy, and she'd been only slightly mollified when she discovered Nathan would be the pharmacist.

"Good to see you, girl," she said to Noelle now. "I've been expecting you. Come to search for Carissa?"

"Yes, but I don't know what I'll find that others haven't." Noelle gave Nathan a look of caution over Pearl's shoulder, and was reassured by his small nod of understanding.

"I thought since Carissa and Noelle are such good friends," Nathan said, "that Noelle might have some fresh insight."

Pearl was frowning when she stepped back from Noelle's embrace. "All those searchers probably turned up the same rocks and looked behind the same trees two or three times. Seems this holler's been scoured from top to bottom and end to end. If she's anywhere near here, a feller'd think we'd've found *something*."

"It seems that way, Aunt Pearl," Noelle said. "You haven't seen any strangers hanging around out on the property lately, have you?"

Pearl shook her head. "There's strangers and tourists swelling the town to three or four times its normal size, but nobody ever wanders this far from the fun."

Noelle nodded. It was unlikely that any stranger would have ventured this far into the wilderness on the off chance of happening across a twelve-year-old girl to abduct in the dead of night—if Carissa had been abducted. Noelle prayed it wasn't so, but she couldn't dismiss the conviction—Nathan might call it a message from God—that someone with sinister motives was involved in Carissa's disappearance.

Pearl gestured with a loose-jointed shrug. "Seems like the loggers, mill workers and farmhands are here all the time." She hesitated, her eyes narrowing at Noelle. "Did you hear about poor Harvey Sand? Died from that fall he took last week. I heard tell Greg's investigating foul play there."

Noelle shifted impatiently. Pearl could be a talker when she was in the mood, and this wasn't the time to stand around making idle conversation.

"I don't know what's come of Hideaway lately," Pearl continued, "what with all the new folks moving in and taking over. Mind you, there was no love lost between Harvey and me—heaven knows we went round and round about the price he charged for a couple hours of work every month—but the guy was just a kid, still in his forties. Such a tragic loss." She shook her head. "That new secretary of his had all our files delivered to the shop at the sawmill on Monday. Can you believe it? Fifteen years' worth of tax records she just dumped on us, without even offering to help us find another accountant."

Noelle rubbed her tightening neck muscles and rolled her shoulders.

Pearl noticed at last. She patted Noelle on the shoulder and nodded at Nathan. "You two can look as far and as long as you want. I'm going back out myself after I rest up a bit and give my heart some time to catch up with the rest of me. Melva should be back to the house by now after her latest foray into the woods." She grunted. "Surprised me to see her scrambling through brush so much. She's not exactly the outdoorsy type, if you know what I mean."

"Aunt Pearl, give Melva a break." Noelle kept her chiding voice gentle. Sparks had flown between Pearl and Melva in the past—Melva had taken over the bookkeeping for Cooper Enterprises from Pearl several years ago, and Pearl was not an easy person to please when it came to the family business. "She loves Carissa. I hope you've been nice to her."

"I've been nice as I had to be," Pearl replied grumpily. "Guess you know Jill's here, too. She's been searchin' all night. We all have. I told her to take a break."

"Thanks, Pearl." Nathan took Noelle's arm and stepped along the road. "We're headed in that direction, so we might see them."

"When all this craziness settles down," Pearl called after them, once more tapping her fingers against her chest, as if the rhythm of her heart would regulate better that way, "you come by my house for some iced sassafras tea. Been too long since we visited last, Noelle."

"I know, Aunt Pearl. I will." Noelle fell into step beside Nathan. Pearl returned to the trail through the trees, taking the shortcut to her own house nestled at the foot of the hills that formed Cedar Hollow.

"I should get down here more often," Noelle said. "Last time I saw Aunt Pearl was at Jill's a few months ago. I haven't been to the hollow for a couple of years."

"Why is that?" Nathan asked.

"Too busy, I guess." She broke off a twig from a nearby branch and rubbed it between her fingers, deep in thought.

"Or still avoiding it for some reason?"

"Could be. Pearl implied she thought I was still stuck in the past."

"I disagree," Nathan said. "You wallow in guilt over the past, but I don't think you're stuck there."

Noelle gave him a look of aggravation.

"So what did she say?" he asked.

"She said, 'Noelle, you've got a lot goin' for you now, kiddo. Just keep on lookin' forward, and don't look back so much. The past can't hurt us if we stay away from it.'"

Nathan walked beside her in silence. The crunch of their boots against gravel matched, as if they were marching in cadence toward the house where Cecil and Melva lived with Cecil's children, seventeen-year-old Justin and twelve-year-old Carissa.

Whenever Noelle returned to this hollow, she felt as if she were stepping back in time. She also felt as if she were returning to old, dysfunctional family dynamics. Maybe, deep down, she feared she would once again become the rebellious teenager who'd made so many wrong choices. She knew better, of course. She had a tendency to be oversensitive.

Pearl was right. The past couldn't hurt her if she stayed away from it.

She navigated around a puddle the circumference of

a small car, in which the mud had been churned up into a slick mess with tire tracks. Obviously, there had been dozens of cars in and out of this place since last night, and Noelle glimpsed several vehicles still parked out in the cleared hayfield behind the house.

In addition to the number of automobiles that she and Nathan had seen parked at the sawmill, she judged there might be as many as sixty or eighty people currently searching the place. In the field she counted three pale-green Jeeps with ranger insignias, and seven white police cruisers, all splattered with mud.

"I don't suppose there was a chance to check for strange footprints before the searchers arrived?" she asked, gesturing toward the mud puddle.

"The police looked, but they found nothing out of the ordinary." Nathan skirted the puddle on the other side. "Cecil needs to get some gravel in here before someone loses a car."

Noelle's steps slowed as they drew near the white picket fence that encircled the house and yard. There was a rumble of growls, and two black and white Australian sheepdogs came running from the backyard, barking as if a herd of cattle had suddenly descended on them.

Noelle groaned. "Just great. I'd hoped to slip past the house without stopping."

"Not with Butch and Sundance on high alert. You haven't been around often enough for them to be familiar with your scent or the sound of your voice. They only bark at strangers."

"We can visit later, *after* we've found Carissa."

Nathan tapped her on the shoulder and she looked up at him. "Relax, grumpy. It'll only take a few minutes. Your family needs you."

"Sorry," she muttered.

The racket of the dogs set off the geese at the pond below the house, and the honking commenced.

Noelle gave Nathan a look of exasperation. "And I thought we'd sneak in? What could I have been thinking?"

He grinned at her.

"Speaking of dogs, is the search-and-rescue unit bringing any search dogs in?" she asked.

"They've got three already out in the field, more on the way, but the ones they've got are new, not very experienced."

They reached the white fence that circled the yard around a big, two-story white house. The dogs finally recognized her, and their barking turned to excited whines of welcome. Noelle reached through the slats of fence to pet the animals and quiet them.

The front screen door opened, and Jill, eight years older than Noelle, stepped out onto the broad concrete porch. Jill was a couple of inches taller than Noelle, with stronger features and a more voluptuous figure—and a familiar, piercing blue gaze.

"Noelle Cooper, what on earth?"

"Hi, sis."

Jill glanced at Nathan, disapproval—annoyance? irritation?—sharpening her gaze.

70

"I came to help search." Noelle followed Nathan through the front gate and braced herself for the rambunctious dogs as they leapt forward in welcome. "Any more word about Carissa?"

Jill shook her head, shading her eyes from the warm October sun. Her thick brown brows almost met in the middle as she squinted, and Noelle noticed the shadows of fatigue around Jill's eyes as she stepped into her sister's tight embrace.

Jill held her for a long moment. "This is like a nightmare, sis. I didn't want to drag you down here. You've already got so much on your plate right now."

"I didn't come down here to cause you worry, I came to help with the search."

Unfamiliar voices spilled from the house as Jill released Noelle. The aroma of frying bacon drifted through the screen door. Apparently some of the weary searchers were taking a much-needed break.

"So tell me," Noelle said, "what have they found?"

"One of the sheriff's deputies found fresh horseshoe prints in the mud at the edge of the lane," Jill said.

"Maybe one of the horses jumped the fence," Nathan said.

"None of the horses are even on the front forty right now," Jill said. "They're pastured half a mile in the other direction. That means someone may have come onto the property last night, because we had a lot of rain yesterday, and the print would've been washed away if they'd come earlier."

"Surely they can't think someone carried Carissa

away by *horse*," Nathan exclaimed.

"Can you think of a better way to carry someone through miles of wilderness trails without making a lot of noise?" Jill asked. "The fact that the dogs haven't found Carissa yet probably means she was taken elsewhere, and it's unlikely she walked there herself. They could have followed her scent."

"What else did the searchers find?" Noelle asked.

Jill closed her eyes for half a second, then opened them and held Noelle's gaze. Sorrowful. Suddenly gentle. "Taylor Jackson, one of the rangers, he found blood on the sawmill floor. Looks like someone was injured."

"Maybe one of the employees was injured yesterday," Noelle said.

"Taylor asked all of them, and no one was."

"Okay, but that doesn't automatically mean it was Carissa," Noelle said.

"We'll find out before long." Jill lifted her hair from her neck and stretched her muscles. "I know we can't go jumping to conclusions." She said the words quickly, as if she'd been repeating them over and over to the others. "We can't let ourselves get discouraged and stop searching."

"Speaking of which," Noelle said, "that's what I came here to do. I'd better get to it."

"Okay, but first will you let Melva know you're here?" Jill asked. "She's been wanting to call you since last night—as if one more person searching would make any difference." The lines around Jill's shadowed blue eyes deepened with concern. She touched Noelle's shoulder. "You okay?"

"I'm fine. I just wish you'd called me last night."

"We kept thinking we'd find her quickly. I didn't want to upset you over nothing." Jill frowned and pushed at her short brown hair—which had grown out a couple of inches, and no longer resembled a hard hat as much as it did a lion's mane. "Cecil's still blaming himself for sending her out for the ledger. Silly, I know, but I've struggled with the same problem. We let her go out there after dark."

"Don't be ridiculous," Noelle said. "Nathan told me she was going out there anyway. She's twelve years old, not a little child. Where were you when she disappeared?"

"I'd gone up to our old house to find some other ledgers upstairs." Jill glanced over her shoulder through the screen door, lowering her voice. "We've been entering this year's records on computer and trying to justify them with the records from the accountant—you knew he died, didn't you? Anyway, there's a discrepancy of fifteen thousand dollars, and we can't seem to find it. That's why we asked Carissa to get the ledger from the office at the sawmill. Turns out she had the wrong one, anyway. It was from ten years ago."

"I'll go have a word with Melva, then hit the trail." Noelle gave her sister's shoulder another squeeze, then opened the screen door and stepped inside.

Nathan leaned against the porch railing, arms folded

across his chest in an automatic gesture of self-protection as he watched Jill pace the length of the porch. The chilled morning air hung heavy and thick in the sunlight that gleamed on her dark hair.

"You didn't tell me you were going to get Noelle," she said at last.

He glanced toward the Coopers' open front door. "I wasn't sure she could get away from the store, but I felt she needed to know about Carissa."

Jill's boots made little noise on the concrete porch. She turned to face Nathan across the half width of the house. "I had reasons for not wanting her here. She had a bad time right after the accident."

"Of course she did. The whole family did. Why single out Noelle?" Nathan had to struggle to keep his voice low. "She's a grown woman, and she needs to be treated like one."

"Oh, for pity's sake, I know that, but why should she have to trudge all the way down here when half of Hideaway's already out looking for the child?"

"Noelle is family. She needs to be treated like family, or you'll be wasting your time trying to get her to move back here and work at the clinic."

Jill paused, gazing down the lane again. "Maybe she shouldn't come back here," she said slowly.

This was a drastic about-face. "But I thought you were trying to—"

"Never mind what I was trying to do." Jill stepped to the end of the porch, away from the screen door, and gestured, with a jerk of her head for him to join her.

He obeyed.

"After the sawmill accident, the grief almost killed her," Jill said softly.

"Of course it did. We were all stricken."

"But it was worse for Noelle. She went into a deep depression, had awful nightmares, told me she woke up screaming every night for the first month after the funerals."

"She had a lot of other things on her mind at the time, and besides, she's not the same person she was ten years ago." He hesitated. "Did she say what the dreams were about?"

"She kept reliving the accident, as if she were one of the victims watching the logs tumble onto her. She had to quit her job, which really threw that ex-husband of hers into a tizzy, because at the time they were dependent on her income to support them—and his drug habit." Jill's voice dripped with disdain.

"Did she get professional help?"

"Oh, she went to her family doctor, and he prescribed an antidepressant. She took it for three weeks, then flushed the rest down the toilet. She said it made her ears ring. You know how independent she can be."

"She takes after her sister."

Jill gave him a half-hearted scowl.

"Did the antidepressant help her at all?" he asked.

"Are you kidding? After just three weeks?" Jill snorted. "I even got some of that herbal stuff Pearl's always trying to push off on everyone. Noelle still had the nightmares for a long time afterward."

"She told me a little about that time," Nathan said.

"Now it'll start all over. What's she going to do when she wakes up in the middle of the night and finds herself alone?"

"Jill, Noelle is a big girl. She can take care of herself." He studied Jill's expression for a moment. She didn't look at him, but kept her gaze focused on the trees across the road.

There was something about her behavior that caught his attention. She stood with her shoulders hunched forward, arms crossed, head bowed slightly. What wasn't she telling him? He knew better than to ask.

"You can't shield her from pain by building a wall around her," he said.

"I'm not building a wall, I'm just—"

"You're still trying to be her mother. Stop it, or you'll smother her completely. Let her handle her own problems."

She sighed and shook her head, then turned away from him. "Fine, then you be there for her when her nightmares return."

"She's told me a little about Joel and her marriage."

"Yes, but how much did she tell you? She has a tendency to downplay certain aspects of her life so no one will worry."

"Maybe that's because she knows we tend to worry too much," he said gently. "Jill, you knew Joel a lot better than I did. Do you think his return could in any way be connected to Carissa's disappearance?"

She didn't react, which meant she'd already considered the possibility. "I don't know. As crazy as he got sometimes, I wouldn't put it past him." She turned and looked up at Nathan, arms still folded over her chest. "Maybe we should tell the sheriff to check him out."

"Maybe we should."

Chapter Seven

Noelle felt suddenly overwhelmed. Neighbors and people from the search-and-rescue team filled the Cooper living room and kitchen, occupying every available chair. Most of them had obviously been out all night, searching through the mud and brush.

Noelle waved at several familiar faces as she passed through the living room to the kitchen in the back of the house. She recognized Dane Gideon, the mayor of Hideaway, who also owned the general store and ran a boy's ranch across the lake from town. He sat on the sofa beside some teenaged boys, who looked grimy and disheartened. Perched across from them on a love seat was Taylor Jackson, a tall man with rusty-brown hair, wearing a mud-spattered ranger uniform. Beside him sat Karah Lee Fletcher, a striking redhead, almost as tall as the ranger. She was the newest doctor at Hideaway's clinic.

Noelle had met Karah Lee and Taylor last month at the Hideaway Festival, when Dane Gideon and Dr. Cheyenne Allison had exchanged marriage vows in the park.

Several people called out a greeting to Noelle as she passed, and the evidence of such overwhelming support once again brought tears to her eyes. Here was the real meaning of community. She'd missed that.

She entered the warm, fragrant kitchen to find several locals, including Bertie Meyer and the newlywed doctor, Cheyenne Gideon, preparing breakfast for the searchers. Melva stood with her generous backside to the room, scraping dishes. Bertie and Cheyenne called a greeting to Noelle, and Melva swung around, water dripping from her spatula.

"You came." Her voice trembled; her chin was quivering. Melva's Ozark accent always became more pronounced when she was upset. She dropped her spatula in the sink and grabbed a dish towel as she crossed the room to Noelle. "Jill said not to call you because we were going to find Carissa any minute, but we . . . didn't." Melva's pretty face reddened with an obvious effort to keep tears at bay, and her short golden lashes, uncharacteristically devoid of makeup, glistened, attesting to the fact that she had recently lost the battle.

"Nathan drove to Springfield this morning and picked me up." Noelle wrapped her arms around Melva's plump shoulders and held her, glad, at last, that she'd stopped at the house.

"Tell me she's going to be okay," Melva whispered.

"She is." For that moment she was sure of it. She only wished the moment would last.

Bertie Meyer crossed the kitchen floor and caught

them both in a loving hug. "Honey," she said to Melva, "you know how much we're praying, and I know you believe in the power of prayer."

"I keep trying to believe in it, Bertie." Melva disentangled herself from the two pairs of comforting arms and reached for a tissue to dab at her nose. "I was so sure Carissa was just lost out there in the dark, but now they're talking about horse tracks that shouldn't be there and blood on the sawmill floor and somebody hauling her away." She bowed her head and picked up the dish towel again. "I just don't know."

Bertie shook her head sadly. "I felt the same way when Red turned up missing last year." She paused for a moment, the smile lines around her eyes and mouth giving way to remembered grief for her late husband. "We've just got to give it more time. Melva, I wish you'd eat something. You need to keep up your strength."

Melva grabbed another tissue from the counter and blew her nose. She took a deep breath, visibly composing herself, then patted her ample derriere and glanced over her shoulder at Bertie. "Don't you think I've got enough reserve to keep me going for a few days?"

At least Melva hadn't lost her self-deprecating humor.

"How about you, Noelle?" Bertie asked. "I bet you didn't have time for breakfast before you came down."

"I'll grab something later, Bertie. Nathan and I want to check out a few of our favorite old haunts first, just in case someone's missed something."

Bertie patted her arm. "The way you two young'uns traipsed over these hills and woods when you were growing up, you should be able to find her if anybody can." She jerked her head toward Melva. "See if you can get her to sit down. I'm afraid she's going to keel over."

"I'm not going to keel over," Melva said as she returned to her sink of dishes. She definitely didn't look like her usual groomed self. Her auburn hair, customarily held in place with stiff mousse, fell about her neck and face in charming disarray. She still wore the jeans and long-sleeved man's shirt she had obviously worn into the woods to search for Carissa. The jeans were probably the only pair she owned. Her typical attire was tailored dresses and suits to minimize her voluptuous curves. Now she stood in her stockinged feet, looking vulnerable and lost.

Noelle gave Bertie another hug, then stepped up behind Melva. The way that Melva was plying the spatula revealed her frustration, and Noelle placed an arm around her old friend's shoulders.

"Melva, I heard Gladys has been trying to contact Justin and Carissa." She felt Melva's shoulders stiffen. "Could she have anything to do with all this?"

Melva cast a warning glance toward the others, then placed a half-scraped plate back into the sink and dried her hands. "I wouldn't put it past her." Weary bitterness laced her voice. "Except I don't think she cares enough about Carissa to go to the trouble. That sea turtle wouldn't know a maternal instinct if it bit her nose off, and I wish it would."

Noelle bit her lip to keep from laughing at Melva's colorful phrasing. "Has anyone contacted Gladys about Carissa's disappearance?"

"Cecil tried, but couldn't get through. She's probably just ignoring his calls because she's mad." Again, she glanced toward the others, lowering her voice. "She got the kids all stirred up yesterday morning, calling before they left for school, promising them a cruise with her and her latest lover in the Caribbean. She wants to take them out of school, can you believe that? After she's pretty much ignored them all these years, now she's trying to bribe them like this? We told her no, of course."

"What was Carissa's response?" Noelle asked.

"Oh, she desperately wanted to go, and you know how that girl can wrap her daddy around her little finger. Cecil started to weaken, said maybe they could go on the cruise during Christmas break, and I said, 'Cecil Hanson Cooper, are you crazy? Let our children traipse off halfway around the world with that woman and a stranger?' And of course he had to remind me, real quick, that she *was* their mother." Her light-brown eyes flashed, and the decibel of her voice increased with her words. "What he meant was she's their *real* mother. Like what I wanted didn't count now that Gladys is trying to wiggle her way back into the family and—" She stopped suddenly and glanced around the room.

The others stayed silent, listening.

Melva rolled her gaze to the ceiling in chagrin. "Leave it to me to blast the news to the four corners of the county. Sorry, don't mind me. I'm angry at the whole world right now, and I will be until we find our little girl. And blast it, I don't care what anyone says, she's *my* little girl!"

Noelle gave Melva's shoulders another affectionate squeeze. "You tell 'em, pal!" she said, then lowered her voice. "How badly did Carissa want to take that trip?"

"Very."

"You know how headstrong she is." Noelle felt like a traitor to even suggest such a thing, but maybe her instincts were wrong for once, and this conviction that Carissa was in trouble was pure imagination.

"I know what you're thinking, Noelle Cooper, and don't you start that, too. That's what the sheriff said. Carissa wouldn't just run away like that."

"But if she's angry—"

"Nope." Melva raised a hand to silence Noelle. "I can't believe she'd do that."

"I would have at her age," Noelle admitted.

"But Carissa isn't you," Melva snapped. She paused, sighed, shook her head. "Sorry. I know you and Carissa are close. I just . . . don't ever be a stepmother. The kids are never totally yours, no matter how much you want them to be. Blood relatives always seem to come first, even coldhearted women who should never have been mothers in the first place—although I have to admit that if Justin and Carissa had never been born . . ." Her voice trailed off, and tears once again filled her eyes. "Listen to me jabber on. I know I can't be worrying about something like that now." She squared her shoulders and glanced through the kitchen doorway at the houseful of searchers, still talking, eating, several of them praying at the round dining-room table. She touched Noelle's arm and gestured toward the far-west corner of the kitchen, where the door to Carissa's bedroom was closed. "Come with me," she whispered.

Stepping past muddy shoes, raincoats and umbrellas, they entered the expansive bedroom, which was, as usual, untidy. "She still hasn't learned to make her bed, and I stopped nagging her," Melva said. A chair rail border surrounded the room with horses racing across open prairie, and the curtains had been fashioned from fringed suede the color of buckskin. Noelle knew Melva had spent a lot of time helping Carissa decorate this room with all of the child's favorite things.

Melva closed the door behind them. She stepped to the antique dresser and opened the top drawer. Pulling out a handful of pages from a notebook, she sifted through the stack and tugged one sheet from the others. "Take a look at this. Carissa's always scribbling notes to herself, and you know she's started writing poetry lately."

"She showed me some of her poems a couple of months ago. They're all about her favorite animals and her closest friends. But, Melva, what do they have to do with—"

"Read that one. There's no rhyme scheme, like with her others."

The first words caught Noelle's attention.

Dead silence in the darkness lurks in wait for
    someone,
Maybe me. Maybe you.
It waits, listens, calls
Darkness calls again, deepens with the moonset,
Whispers with its song of longing,
Growing deeper until I go with it,
Until it enters me and controls me,
With the death of the moon,
With the dying moon.

Suppressing a shudder, Noelle handed the page back to Melva. How could a twelve-year-old girl write something like this? Especially when all her other poems reflected the happiness and joy of life that came from her spirit, or her innocent words of wondering about a mother who didn't want her.

"Apparently, she didn't show it to anyone," Melva said. "Because I found it here in her drawer beneath all the others."

"When?"

"Last night, when she didn't return from the sawmill." Wearily, she combed her fingers through her hair. "Okay, the thought did cross my mind that she might have been hiding, and I was looking for some kind of clue about where she might have gone."

Noelle frowned at the poem again. It wasn't reassuring. "You really think Carissa wrote this?"

"It looks like her writing, doesn't it?"

It looked familiar, all right. Sloppy writing ran in the Cooper family. Noelle herself had been cursed with barely decipherable scribbling, just like Jill. But it didn't necessarily have to be Carissa's hand that had written the poem.

Melva put all the sheets back in the top drawer and shoved it shut. "Let's get out of here."

"Wait." Noelle reached out and touched her arm. "You don't think the poem has anything to do with her disappearance, do you?"

"I don't know, but I can't get it out of my mind. Call me superstitious, but too much has happened in this hollow for my peace of mind. Too many deaths, and now this."

"The deaths were accidents," Noelle said. "You're right, you're being superstitious." Maybe.

"I can't help what I feel. Sometimes it seems like this place is haunted or something."

"The only thing we're haunted by is bad memories, and that's bad enough."

"It's almost like this place has some kind of a curse on it," Melva said. "Deaths, divorce, psychological—" She glanced quickly at Noelle, then dropped her gaze. "Anyway, maybe Cecil wouldn't have made some of the choices that he's made if he hadn't allowed his parents to play on his guilt and coerce him into staying here."

"You can't blame a curse for Cecil's choices any more than I can blame a curse for the choices I've made," Noelle said.

Melva sank onto the rumpled bed. "Not completely, I know, but I believe there are influences that affect our choices." She gave Noelle a sheepish glance. "So you don't think I'm crazy with all this talk about some silly curse?"

Noelle sat down beside her. "I know you're not crazy. We've known each other too long for that."

"Gladys skipped out as soon as things got a little tough," Melva said, gazing through the open curtains to the field beyond. "The money ran out, and so did she. That's one reason I hate to see her try to barge back into Justin and Carissa's lives now. They're finally settled and living happily without her. To me, it's just one more curse, especially when the kids are so ready to forgive everything and welcome her back with open arms."

"I don't think that's the case, Melva. You know those kids love you."

"Now that same curse has taken Carissa. And Justin—" Melva clamped her mouth shut.

"What about Justin?"

"Never mind. It can't be the same thing. Surely, surely it can't be the same thing." Melva lowered the curtain. "Let's get out of here."

Noelle glanced at the dresser drawer that held Carissa's papers. If only she could read that poem once more. If only she could look through some more of Carissa's things, maybe she could get a clue.

"Maybe Bertie's right," Melva said, leading the way to the door. "Maybe together, you and Nathan can find something no one else can."

Chapter Eight

"Did you get any helpful information from Melva?" Nathan had to quick-step to keep up with Noelle along the trail past the house.

"I'm not sure. Maybe. It disturbed me."

"Disturbed you how?"

"Carissa was upset with Melva yesterday because Melva didn't want the kids taking a cruise with Gladys and her latest guy. Melva showed me a poem she discovered in Carissa's dresser drawer." She glanced over her shoulder at him. "It was pretty spooky, all about being controlled by some hidden force of darkness."

Nathan broke stride. "*Carissa* wrote something like that?"

"It isn't anything like her other poetry. I know, because she showed me some of her writing when I was in Hideaway a couple months ago. Besides, this poem is so mature. It scares me that Carissa is having thoughts like that. She's not the family member you're counseling, is she?"

"No."

"I still think she might have stumbled onto something dangerous. What about drugs? What if she found a patch of marijuana somewhere? Or what if there's a meth lab somewhere out in the national forest? She could have—"

"It won't help to jump to conclusions like that. The last thing a marijuana grower would want is a search party beating the underbrush through the woods at harvest time, and nobody's turned up any evidence of it."

"But a meth lab?" she asked. "Those can be very mobile."

"But if someone had a mobile lab, why kidnap Carissa? Why not just pack up and drive away?"

"I don't know, maybe because she knew whoever it was, and she could get that person into big trouble." Noelle's pace slowed at a fork in the trail, and she glanced at the old track to the right, now overgrown with weeds, that led to the Cooper cemetery. Miniature cliffs formed a narrow passageway for a short distance beyond the cemetery, not far from the house where Noelle and Jill had grown up. Nathan remembered playing around those cliffs as a kid.

"I'm sure the old house was searched." Noelle took the left fork that led along the hillside and eventually connected with national forest. The "old" house, where Noelle and Jill had spent their girlhoods, was no longer lived in, but the family had kept their bookkeeping files in the attic for years.

"We checked it out," Nathan said, "but remember, Jill said she was at the house last night looking for some old records when Carissa went to the sawmill."

The trail narrowed, and Nathan walked in silence behind Noelle for the next mile or so. Her footsteps were brisk, her head down, and he wished he could get a readout of her thoughts right now. When they were growing up, he'd almost been able to read her mind, but it had been many years since they were so attuned to each other.

They'd been walking silently for ten minutes when they heard voices in a thicket of new growth.

"I told you to stop wandering off on your own." The deep voice, heavy with annoyance, belonged to Cecil Cooper.

Noelle's steps slowed, and Nathan had to scramble to keep from stumbling into her back.

"But we've looked here, Dad. What good's it going to do if we keep covering the same ground over and over again?" It was Justin, Cecil's son. "Why won't you look any place but Cooper land? Melva says—"

"Melva's saying lots of things right now. She's frantic. She's not thinking straight."

"Well, I don't see why we can't split up," Justin muttered. "We could do a lot more if we weren't joined at the hip. You're treating me like I'm Carissa's age, not seventeen."

"You're acting younger than Carissa."

"Dad, you're acting too weird."

Brush rustled at the side of the track, and Cecil and Justin emerged from the edge of the thicket a few yards ahead of Noelle and Nathan.

Father and son looked a lot alike. They both had the same blue Cooper eyes beneath thick, well-shaped eyebrows. Cecil was a big bear of a man with straight, dark-brown hair cut militarily short, a high forehead and a florid complexion that revealed his temper—as it did now. That didn't surprise Nathan, since Cecil and his son hadn't exactly been the best of buds lately.

Justin, as tall as his father, though not as heavily built, showed the same signs of temper. He made no effort to conceal his anger. Eyes flashing blue fire, he started to speak, caught sight of Nathan and Noelle and clamped his mouth shut.

Cecil followed his son's glance, and his expression changed with the suddenness of Ozark weather when he saw his cousin. "So you brought her down anyway. Good going, Nathan." He strode forward and enveloped Noelle in a hug, ruffling her hair as he had done ever since they were kids. "Jill pulled her big-sister act again, or we'd have called you."

"Hi, Noelle," Justin said, his voice still holding traces of resentment from the argument with his father. He hung back, hands shoved into his pockets. "We haven't found a thing. They brought the dogs in and everything, did they tell you? Carissa's not here."

"We're going to find her." Cecil's expression remained calm, though annoyance once more edged into his voice. He turned to Nathan. "You two been to the house yet?"

"We were just there."

"Jill didn't see you, did she?"

"She sure did."

"I bet you took a tongue-lashing," Cecil said.

Nathan nodded.

90

Noelle touched her cousin's arm. "Cecil, Melva said Carissa was upset yesterday."

For a second, Nathan thought he caught a glimmer of . . . what, chagrin? . . . in Cecil's expression. "Let's just say she inherited my temper, but that blew over in a hurry. By last night, she was more interested in digging up information about that report of hers than she was about the call from Gladys. She's talked to all the neighbors, picked Jill's brain, visited with Pearl and wanted to dig through sawmill records. You know how she is when she gets her teeth into something." He shook his head slowly. "Wish I hadn't sent her out in the dark like that."

Justin shook his head. "Dad, she's not a little kid anymore. She's slipped out lots of times at night like that to go on a walk or check on Gypsy. Why would last night be any different?" He shrugged. "Besides, nothing goes on down here in this holler, you know that." He looked at his dad, then down at the ground.

Cecil clamped his big hands on Noelle's shoulders. "We're gonna go to the house for a bite, then hit the woods again. Thanks for coming, Noelle. Just having you here with us again helps." He released her and turned to his son. "Come on, Justin."

Justin nodded awkwardly at Noelle. "Glad you're back, Noelle," he murmured as he followed his father.

Noelle stood watching her cousins leave, both of them silent, heads bowed, shoulders stooped as their long-legged strides carried them toward their home.

"Guilt," she said softly.

Nathan looked at her. "What?"

"Since Mariah and I opened the store, I've read a few books on body language, in order to read my customers better. It could be my imagination, but almost everybody in my family's acting guilty for some reason or other today. It's weird."

"Carissa's missing, and they all feel responsible. Seems natural enough to me."

She turned and continued down the trail. "Okay, one more time, Nathan—who're you counseling? Is somebody in the family crazy enough to want to get rid of Carissa?"

He fell into step behind her once again. "Of course not."

She wished she could catch a glimpse of his expression without being obvious about it. "You sure it's not Carissa you're seeing? Do you think she—"

"No. I told you I'm not—"

"I know, I know. You're not at liberty to divulge that information. So you don't think your sessions have anything to do with her disappearance."

"That's right."

"How can you be sure?" Noelle spread her hands in helpless frustration. "Why can't you tell me who? Maybe if I knew—"

"Will you stop it! If I tell you, you might use the information about who it is to decide where to search for Carissa, and that would be wrong. I didn't bring you here to use your head or to read body language. I brought you here to use that special gift of yours. Tell me where we're going. You didn't hesitate to set off in this direction the moment we left the truck."

She couldn't reply, because she wasn't sure herself. She and Nathan were both intimately familiar with this portion of Cooper land.

"We're going to Bobcat Cave, aren't we?" Nathan guessed.

As young children, they had spent many hours playing in and around Bobcat Cave—until their parents discovered where they'd been and no longer allowed them to run free.

"What good would that do?" she asked. "The entrance is boarded up." Until this moment, she hadn't realized it, but Nathan was right. The cave was where she was going. And she had no idea why.

Carissa awakened to the sound of water splashing down from the cave roof and puddling beneath her cheek. How long had she been asleep?

Was there someone sitting in the dark listening? Someone she knew?

The dripping water sounded like a whispering voice—whispering what? A warning? Or a threat? The way her head roared and throbbed, someone could be calling to her and she might not realize it.

The throbbing in her head grew louder, then softened again. Her stomach felt jumpy and weird, but that could just be hunger. Or fear. She was so scared.

"Please, Jesus," she whispered. She clearly heard a

splash of water in the distance. It sounded like the waterfall down on the creek after a hard rain, or like the splatter of raindrops on the lake during a heavy storm. A pool?

She inched her fingers over the rough rock of the cave floor. When she didn't feel a formation or a drop-off, she crawled forward, moving slowly. The rock turned to clay again. She drew closer to the sound of water, but the splashing distorted the pounding in her head.

She rested her cheek in the cold clay, suppressing a moan. Quiet. She had to try to be quiet.

Her nausea got worse, and she felt weak and shaky. If she could only sprinkle her face with some water and put some on her head, maybe it would help her feel a little better. Then maybe her ears wouldn't roar so loudly.

She crawled forward again, drawing closer to the water, feeling a fine spray as drops hit the pool. It sounded like a whirlpool, and the spray felt good against her skin. She inched closer as the clay turned to slick mud, and the ground grew steeper. She trapped a handful of water and drew it to her face. The icy coldness chased away some of the nausea. She scooped another handful and splashed it on her neck, letting it run down her arms and chest.

The next handful she carefully sprinkled over her head, near the wound, and the next she put on the wound.

That was a mistake. It stung. Badly. A cry sprang from her throat. Sickness gripped her stomach. She clenched her eyes against the darkness lit with flickering bits of flame.

She lost her balance and slid forward. As the darkness whirled around her, she grasped at the soft mud beneath her. Her hands slipped forward and plunged into the water. With a scream that echoed against all the walls of the cavern, she slid, headfirst, into the freezing whirlpool.

When the trail widened again, Nathan drew abreast of Noelle and watched her. Various expressions flitted across her face in a fascinating jumble—anticipation to fear to anger—as she peered into the depths and shadows of the lush green overgrowth of the forest that surrounded the mouth of Bobcat Cave.

Suddenly, with no warning, her mouth flew open and she gasped. Her eyes widened in shock.

"You're doing it again." Nathan reached out and grasped her shoulder.

She didn't respond to his touch.

"Noelle?"

Into the silence, somebody screamed—a young girl's cry, barely audible.

Noelle's eyes met Nathan's in horror. The cry seemed to come from the hillside to their left.

Another scream pierced the air.

"Carissa!" Noelle cried. She grabbed Nathan's arm. "The cave. Come on!"

Chapter Nine

Nathan rushed past Noelle and plunged through a stand of saplings, tripping through undergrowth, scratching his face and clothes on blackberry brambles that seemed positioned to slow them down.

They reached the cave mouth to find it still boarded up. In frustration, Noelle kicked the weathered gray board at the bottom. All of the sturdy two-by-fours had been nailed to a wooden frame that was fastened with concrete nails into a buttress that had been poured around the mouth of the cave to seal it shut. Noelle's grandfather had hired a contractor from Branson to affix the seal two days after the cavern collapse that had taken his daughter-in-law's life and nearly killed Noelle.

Noelle reached for the top board, wiggled the tips of her fingers into the crack between board and concrete, and pulled at it with an angry grunt. "It won't budge. Nathan, help me!"

"Carissa obviously didn't come this way," Nathan said.

"She's in the cave, Nathan. I know it, okay? I can feel it, almost as if I'm experiencing snatches of her thoughts and sensations." Again, Noelle yanked on the top board.

Nathan caught her gently by the shoulders. "Forget it, superhero. If you can't get inside, it's a sure bet Carissa didn't, at least not this way. Even though she's in a cave somewhere, she got in some other way, and maybe it isn't Bobcat."

Noelle whirled to face him, her eyes full of alarm. "The sinkhole. Nathan, what if she's fallen into the sinkhole?"

The sinkhole she referred to was an opening at the top of one of the large chambers in Bobcat Cave, where the ground had collapsed decades ago. Nathan had seen it several times when they were in the cave, but he didn't know how to find it from the surface.

"I don't know how to reach it from out here. You took Cecil on those forays, remember?"

Noelle yanked her backpack from her shoulders and unzipped the bottom pocket. She pulled out two flashlights and a coil of thick yellow nylon cord. She handed one flashlight to Nathan. "Conserve the battery power, because these are all I brought."

He shoved the flashlight into his pocket.

"The sinkhole isn't far from the waterfall that feeds into Willow Creek on the other side of this hill," she said, shoving the backpack at him. "Cecil and I never told our parents about it because we didn't want them to seal it up, too. Your turn to carry."

He took the backpack from her and slung it over his shoulders as he followed her, glad she was finally allowing him to help. Sometimes she carried her independence too far.

She led the way around the right side of the sealed cave mouth, then plunged through another thicket that grabbed at their clothing and impeded their progress up the steep hillside.

The Hideaway peninsula—thousands of acres of land encompassed on three sides by Table Rock Lake—held a multitude of caves within its boundaries, some of which had filled with water when the lake had been built. One section of those subterranean passageways near downtown Hideaway had gone undetected for many years until this past summer, when the heavy weight of a condominium project had collapsed several acres of land after a mild earthquake hit just over the state border in Arkansas. The collapse had endangered lives and destroyed hundreds of thousands of dollars worth of resort investments. Bobcat Cave was part of that same system, but since it was on private land, it hadn't been explored completely.

By the time Nathan and Noelle reached the top of the ridge that overlooked Willow Creek, with Cooper farmland beyond, they were both panting from the exertion. Nathan wished they'd left the backpack at the cave mouth. He was glad Noelle had given it to him, however, when they slid down loose shale and his feet slipped from beneath him. The heavy pack cushioned his fall.

Droplets of rain splashed their faces as they descended the ridge, and by the time they arrived at the gaping mouth of the sinkhole, halfway down, the water had drenched them. Thunder echoed over the hollow, and lightning flashed in the distance. Nathan shielded his eyes and gazed at the sky. If the weather forecast he'd heard on the way to Springfield was correct, they could be stranded in this hollow on the wrong side of Willow Creek, especially since the low-water bridge was already underwater.

"Carissa?" Noelle shouted into the hole. "Honey, can you hear me? Are you in there?"

A scream, high-pitched and frantic, answered.

Noelle tied the rope to a tree nearby and turned to stare at the hole with obvious trepidation.

"I'll go first," Nathan said.

She exhaled with relief. "Heights still get to me."

"You'll be okay. I'll be there to catch you." Nathan lowered himself through the eight-foot-wide entrance, scrambling to remain balanced as his toeholds gave way, and mud and loose rock spilled from the rim of the sinkhole. He reached the cave floor at least fifteen feet below the opening, and then anchored the rope for Noelle.

"It's okay," he said gently. "You can come down."

She came, and her movements on the rope brought a fresh cascade of loose dirt and rocks down on his head and shoulders.

Noelle reached him, stumbled against him. When he caught her to steady her, he could feel her trembling.

"Carissa?" she called, pivoting to shout through the darkness as she brushed dirt from her head and clothing. "It's Noelle and Nathan. Where are you?"

No answer.

Nathan cupped his hands around his mouth. "Carissa!" His loud voice ricocheted back at them from the unyielding boulders. "We're coming for you. Help us! Talk to us!"

There was the sound of splashing water, then, "Help me! Help me, it's cold, and I'm slipping back!"

"Nathan, the whirlpool!" Noelle switched on her flashlight and led the way through an old breakdown cavern, following a precipitous pathway between fallen rocks. She hesitated and looked back at Nathan, checking to make sure he was behind her.

Even in the dimly lit shadows of her flashlight glow, he could see the mounting distress in her eyes. "It's okay, Noelle, I'm here." This was the cave where her mother had died.

Noelle raced up a steep, rocky incline to their left. At the top she ducked to avoid the treacherous ceiling of broken soda straw formations. She obviously knew this cave much better than he did, but that didn't surprise him. Even after their parents had forbidden them to come to Bobcat Cave without adult supervision, Noelle had always been a rebel. Though in their childhood she'd lured him into these mysterious depths a couple of times after the ban, he'd usually obeyed his parents. Time also had a way of softening the edges of memory, and he had forgotten the size of this place.

The stalactites seemed to engulf them, like the gnashing teeth of the monsters that had once inhabited Nathan's childhood dreams about this place after Noelle's mother's death.

"Carissa, keep talking!" he shouted.

"I . . . can't hold on." Carissa's panicky voice echoed

through the chamber, followed by the sound of a splash and another cry. "The water's pulling me!"

Nathan and Noelle reached a sharp drop on the lime-stone path. Noelle's feet slid out from under her, and she scrambled on her backside down the embankment of loose rock. Nathan kept his footing and beat her to the bottom. With the bright glow from her flashlight, he raced ahead, leaped up a shallow limestone ledge and darted around the curve of a tunnel.

"Carissa?" The water dripped loudly into a wide, deep whirlpool. Twenty-nine years ago, this had been the only pool Nathan and Noelle had known about in Bobcat Cave.

Carissa didn't answer.

Nathan pulled his own light from his pocket just as Noelle reached his side, and together they scanned the black pool with its ominous ripples, evidence of the current within.

Noelle aimed her beam toward a section of mud that had collapsed into the pool. There was a clear hand-print. *Carissa's handprint?*

Nathan kicked off his shoes. "Hold the light, I'm going in."

Noelle grabbed his arm. "It's a whirlpool, Nathan. It could suck you under."

"Then it might already be sucking Carissa under." He unhooked Noelle's backpack and shrugged it from his shoulders as he kicked off his shoes.

He jumped into the pool, catching his breath at the icy chill of the water. His feet touched the rocky bottom.

The water reached his chest, and he could feel with his foot that the ledge dropped away. The glow of Noelle's light reflected off the surface of the water, making it difficult to see. There was no sign of Carissa.

"She's below me," Noelle said. "Check beneath this ledge, Nathan."

He didn't question her.

Fighting the numbness brought on by the icy water, he dove into the murky darkness beneath the cave floor, where the light did not penetrate. Sharp, jutting ledges of rock bruised his hands as he groped through the blackness, exploring every niche along the whirlpool's bed for Carissa. His lungs begged for air. Reluctantly, he returned to the surface, gasping for breath.

"She's down there, Nathan. I know she is," Noelle said. "Can't you find her?"

"I will." He dove again, allowing the current of the whirlpool to pull him deeper into the icy water, stroke by stroke, as if he were taking a summer swim in Table Rock Lake. This swim, however, sucked all sensation from his limbs, from his whole body. He struggled to identify what passed beneath his chilled and stiffened hands as he groped along the crevices of rock. He entered the blackness beneath a rocky ledge, but amazingly, as he swam farther, the darkness lifted slightly. The farther he allowed the current to carry him, the lighter it became.

And then he saw her. She was caught beneath a ledge, where the current must have dragged her, her silhouette in sharp relief against the glow of daylight from an opening that spilled the contents of the pool from its lip like a giant teacup. Carissa wasn't moving.

He allowed that same current to carry him to her, fighting his ever-increasing lethargy as he placed his arms around her waist. Battling the pull of the current, he pushed the girl's limp body back toward the glow of Noelle's flashlight, thrusting his feet against outcroppings of rock to gain advantage against the flow. Just as his lungs were about to implode, he thrust Carissa up to the surface, into Noelle's outstretched arms, and came up after her, bursting out of the water with desperate gasps as water poured from his ears.

Noelle heaved Carissa onto her stomach, allowing the water to drain out of her mouth and nose. Nathan pulled himself onto the ledge with difficulty, his limbs almost too chilled to move. He gulped in air, filling his lungs, as he listened for some sound that would tell him Carissa was alive.

"Come on, honey, breathe!" Noelle cried. "Carissa, come on! Nathan, I'm starting CPR." She pulled Carissa on to her back and drew her jaw forward.

He pulled himself toward them and positioned himself over Carissa's chest, but before he could touch her, he heard the sweet sound of her choking, gasping breath.

"Thank you, Lord," he murmured as he knelt over the child.

Noelle slumped against him in relief.

"It's okay, Carissa," he said. "You're safe now. We're going back home."

He felt the young body stiffen. "No. No, I'm not safe there." Carissa coughed harshly, choking and gasping once more. "Don't take me there!"

Noelle gasped at her cousin's words, and at the meaning she accepted with frightening certainty. Carissa was afraid of someone close. "It's okay, Cis. I know. I won't let them get to you."

Carissa's eyes widened, her face pinched and white. She shivered from the chill of the water. "But you d-don't understand, it's s-someone—"

"It's someone you know."

Carissa blinked up at her. "How do you know that?"

"I'm not sure. Do you have any idea who it is?"

The girl shook her head. "I can't remember every-thing that happened, but I *know*—"

"It's okay." Noelle looked at Nathan and felt a deep sense of dread. "We're not going to let anyone hurt you."

Had someone in the family really attacked Carissa? It couldn't be! No, it was someone else Carissa knew. Or maybe she just thought she knew her adversary, some subtle familiarity of voice or fragrance or manner of speaking that might have made her think . . .

Noelle didn't try to analyze the particular fear she'd seen Carissa experience at the thought of home. All of her attention was focused on Carissa, while Nathan dug through the backpack and pulled out a thick quilted jacket. "Honey, what happened?" she asked.

"Someone f-followed me," Carissa said, teeth chattering. "It was d-dark, and I dropped my flashlight. When I ran back to the sawmill, whoever it was chased me, and I fell. My head hurts, and there's a lump back there."

"What happened then?" Nathan wrapped the jacket around Carissa and pulled her close in an effort to instill some warmth into her.

"I don't know. I woke up in this cave."

Noelle aimed her flashlight on the back of Carissa's head. "Do you think the bump on your head knocked you out?"

"I guess it did."

"Do you remember if it happened when you fell, or did your pursuer strike you?" Nathan asked.

"I think I fell, but I'm not sure."

Carissa's dark, wet curls covered any wound. Noelle probed gently, and Carissa tensed.

"It still hurts, doesn't it?"

Carissa nodded. "I've got a headache."

"Did you get any sense about who it was that chased you?" Nathan asked.

"One of the family?" Noelle asked, and felt Nathan's startled gaze on her.

"Maybe," Carissa said, her voice softening with surprise as she looked up at Noelle. "There was something familiar . . . but I can't remember what it was." She shivered again as she grasped Noelle's arm. "Whoever it was will try again. They were looking for me here, and I hid. There were . . . whispers."

"Whispers," Noelle repeated. "More than one person?"

Carissa frowned. "I don't know. I don't think so."

"It's okay," Nathan released her and put on his shoes while Noelle ran a quick neurological test on Carissa.

Considering what the child had been through, she was doing well. Though she'd experienced a loss of consciousness earlier, she was now alert and oriented times three.

Nathan got to his feet and reached down for Carissa. "Come on, I'll carry you and let Noelle get her backpack. I have a feeling you're lighter than the pack."

"But where will we go?" Carissa asked.

He lifted her into his arms. "We need to get you to the clinic, first of all."

"Since both doctors and Jill were at your house when we came through," Noelle said, "we shouldn't have any trouble getting you examined. Then we'll take you on to a hospital if necessary."

"If the creek doesn't rise," Nathan drawled. "The CT truck is in town today, and if we can get there before it leaves, there's a chance we won't have to take you on to the hospital."

"CT?" Carissa asked.

"It's a huge machine that's used to take pictures of your brain and make sure it isn't wriggling out your ears," Noelle said.

Carissa sighed and gave Noelle a long-suffering look over Nathan's shoulder. "You don't have to talk to me like a kid anymore, Noelle. I know what a CAT scan is, I just wondered if I'd have to have one now, since I'm doing better."

"We don't want to take any chances," Nathan said.

They scrambled up the steep incline as thunder rumbled aboveground.

"Did you bring your cell phone in that backpack of yours?" Nathan asked Noelle.

"Yes, but it won't work down here." She pulled it out to prove it. "See? Nothing. The sinkhole's just ahead. All we need to do is—" She stopped and stared upward, where they had left the rope dangling from above. The rope was gone.

"Nathan."

"I can see."

"What happened?"

"I'll give you one guess."

Carissa shivered again, and from her peripheral vision, Noelle saw Nathan lay his hand against the side of the child's face.

"We need to bundle her up," Nathan said. "Her skin's still icy."

"Would you t-two stop talking about me like I'm a little kid?" Carissa snapped. "I mean it. I'm almost thirt-t-teen."

"Yes, and you're injured and half-drowned. Give us a break. We're doing the best we can." Noelle felt Carissa's face for herself.

"So why have we stopped?" Carissa asked.

Noelle sighed and pointed to the light coming down

through the opening of the sinkhole. "Because that's the way out, and our rope is missing."

What have I done? They're buried down in that cave unless they can find their way to the other end of the cave system, and I don't think that'll happen. No one knows about the new collapse since that little earthquake we had this summer.

What about the search dogs? They're new. They sure can't seem to find Carissa's scent, but they could get lucky. I wonder if there's some way to confuse them . . . maybe to scatter Carissa's scent and Noelle's and Nathan's.

I can't grieve. This is the way it has to be. If they knew about me, they could lock me away forever.

Got to be strong. I can't let myself doubt now.

I have to believe this is the right thing to do or I couldn't live with the past.

Chapter Ten

Noelle climbed onto a ledge above Nathan's head and aimed the beam of her flashlight toward an intimidating wall of boulders, trying unsuccessfully to push away her memories. This was the rockslide that had killed her mom.

"Noelle, what are you doing?" Nathan objected. "I told you I'd do the climbing."

No time for memories. "Come up and give me a

boost, Nathan, and I'll see if we can get through this way."

"I thought you were afraid of heights."

"I'm more afraid of what's going to happen to Carissa if we don't get out of here quickly. She's already in danger of aspiration pneumonia, and that lump on her skull worries me."

He joined Noelle on the ledge. "Then let me do the climbing. Give me the flashlight and—"

"No macho stuff, okay? Use that common sense you were bragging about earlier. I'm lighter." She took a step up without his help, reminding herself not to look down. If she could just focus on this pile of boulders . . .

"At least give me your flashlight and I'll hold it for you," Nathan said. "You need both hands to climb or—"

"You are not getting this flashlight. I need it to see where I'm going." She took another step up, then another, then stopped and aimed her light past the pile of rocks. More rocks. She groaned.

"Let me guess. Can't get out?"

Noelle grimaced at the "I told you so" inflection in his voice. "That's right. It also means no one came in this way."

"We knew that," he drawled. "The seal at the mouth of the cave made it obvious."

"Yes, of course, but I thought if we could just reach the mouth, we might be able to knock enough boards away to get through from this direction. I mean, think about it, Nathan—twenty-nine years ago the collapse didn't block the entrance completely. This was the way they carried . . . carried Mom out."

"So it looks as if there's been another collapse since then."

"Yeah. Maybe it happened when the condominium came down in town this summer. This is just another breakdown cavern now. But like I said, there's got to be another entrance, or Carissa wouldn't be here."

"She could have been lowered through the sinkhole."

"Did you see any disturbance around the sinkhole when we arrived?"

"No, but—"

"Exactly. We would have noticed something."

"Okay," he conceded with obvious reluctance. "Unless he went to a lot of trouble to cover it up."

"How do we know it's a he?" She aimed the beam of her light against the opposite wall in search of some evidence of another entrance, then played the beam to the left. Nothing. She started to turn and climb down when a rock dislodged beneath her foot. She stumbled and lost her balance, flying headlong at Nathan, with a shriek that echoed from the walls around them. He caught her, then stumbled and fell beneath her on the ledge with a loud grunt of expelled air.

"Noelle!" Carissa cried from the darkness.

Noelle scrambled to her feet, unintentionally gouging Nathan in the ribs with her elbow. He grunted again.

"Yeah, Cis, we're okay," she called. "Nathan, I'm

110

sorry. Did I hurt you?"

"No, I'm fine," he drawled. "Women are always finding new ways to throw themselves at me." He swung his legs over the side of the ledge and jumped down, then reached up to help her.

She hesitated. "You're sure? I hit you pretty hard."

"Would you come down from there before you fall again?"

She leaned toward his outstretched hands and allowed him to lower her to level ground. His hands were gentle and his grip strong. For a moment, all she wanted was to remain within the reassuring circle of that grasp.

Reluctantly, she stepped away. "Now what do we do?"

"We find another way out of here." He brushed himself off. "Remember when we played here as kids? We turned out our flashlights and sat in the darkness, waiting for our eyes to adjust so we could see if any light came in."

"I remember," she said. "We saw light reflecting around the whirlpool, but we never found any opening big enough for us to fit through."

"If there's been a shift major enough to cause another rockslide, it might have affected other parts of the cave system, but we don't have time to go spelunking in a major way. We could encounter fifty dead ends before we found anything worthwhile."

They skirted a limestone column to find Carissa still bundled up in the quilted jacket and the thick chamois shirt Noelle had been wearing over her T-shirt. The fact that the usually inquisitive, active child hadn't moved since they'd left her attested to her misery. She needed more medical care than Noelle could give her in these conditions.

Nathan sank down beside Carissa on the slab of stone and patted the spot beside him for Noelle. "I know we were kids when we were here last, so things might look different to us now. The whirlpool seems a lot broader than it was years ago. It looks like it may have undergone a lot of erosion."

"That makes sense." Carissa leaned against Nathan and tugged at his arm until he got the message and wrapped it around her. "I overheard Dad saying we've had more flooding in Cedar Hollow in the past ten years than he'd seen since he was a kid. That would cause the erosion."

Noelle leaned against Nathan's other side for warmth. "Cis, you're sure you can't remember which way you came through the darkness to the whirlpool?"

Carissa shook her head. "I can't remember because I couldn't see anything. The only time I did was when that whisperer came looking for me."

Nathan wrapped his other arm around Noelle. "When I was searching for Carissa in the water, I wouldn't have found her if not for the light coming from the other side of the cave wall. It looks like that might be a way out."

"I am *not* going back in that water," Carissa said.

"You wouldn't have to," Nathan said. "Only one of us

would. Face it, you two, I'm the only one who saw the light."

Noelle snorted at the bad joke. "Bad idea. It's too dangerous."

"Can you think of a better way to get us out of here?"

Noelle looked into Carissa's eyes. "I wish I'd thought to pack a thermometer in my kit."

"It's no big deal, okay?" Carissa said.

"You could develop pneumonia from inhaling the water," Nathan said. "Noelle, are either of these flashlights waterproof?"

Noelle glanced down at the flashlights that she and Carissa were holding, then frowned at Nathan, feeling fresh alarm. Plunging beneath that whirlpool a second time would be a dangerous move. But what other options did they have? Eventually, the others would realize they, too, were missing, but that could take hours. Carissa needed medical help soon.

She held out the red flashlight in her hand. "This one's waterproof."

He took it. "Thanks."

"You're really going to do it?" Carissa asked. "You're going to try to get out that way?"

He stood. "The water must flow from this cave into the creek, and there was enough light for me to see you clearly, even though it's cloudy out. So maybe I can fit through the opening and double back—"

"Are you forgetting the waterfall?" Noelle asked.

"And are you forgetting our dilemma?" Nathan countered quietly. "Willow Creek is deep, and you know it, because we swam in it plenty of times."

"Sure it's deep and it's cold and—"

"If I can just get through that opening—"

"What happens to Carissa and me if you drown?" Noelle asked.

"Thanks for the vote of confidence."

Noelle sighed, wrapping her arms around Carissa's shoulders, drawing comfort from the contact. "I don't like this."

"Me neither," Carissa said.

"Have a little faith, will you?" he said.

Noelle glared at him.

"You two stay here by the sinkhole, because that's where I'll come to as soon as I can find a way to pull you out of here." He stuck the flashlight into his pocket. "Relax, Noelle, I made it back to the surface with Carissa a while ago—I can make it back alone if I can't get through. I'll see you in a few minutes, one way or the other."

"Promise?" Noelle asked.

"Cross my heart and hope to—"

"Don't say it. Just get back here."

"I'll be okay."

This time the depths of the pool looked different. The water numbed Nathan's arms and legs more quickly as he forced his way down through the tunnel where he had found Carissa. The current grabbed at him, wedging him between two outjutting elbows of limestone before he could fight his way around them. He pushed against the rock and freed himself, then returned to the surface to catch his breath before making another attempt.

He was quickly chilled, and his movements were awkward. He wouldn't be able to withstand the cold much longer before he lost the ability to propel himself forward. But he had to get Noelle and Carissa out of this cave.

He plunged once more into the depths of the pool and under the ledge where Noelle had crouched, insisting Carissa was beneath her. This was the way, wasn't it? He couldn't afford to get turned around. If he did, he could drown before finding his way to the surface.

His confidence waned as he swam several more yards without a glimpse of light. Should he try to turn around and go back? He was running out of air. Quickly.

He peered hard into the darkness and followed the current forward a few more feet. Then he saw the reflection of daylight ahead, the light brightening as he kicked his way toward it, shoving hard with his hands against the rough surface of the underwater tunnel.

The sides of the tunnel drew in closer around him. He caught a glimpse of blue sky and kicked hard, pushing himself forward. Something caught his shirt, holding him fast. He tried to jerk away. His lungs begged for air. He looked down and saw a sharp rock poking through the sleeve of his shirt. He ripped free and propelled himself forward only to feel the stones converge around him, hugging his shoulders tightly in their grip.

His lungs screaming for oxygen, he grabbed at the

largest rock and wrenched at it until it loosened and gave way. The force of the water behind him swept him forward, wedging him even more tightly in the mouth of the cave. Thankfully, his face broke surface. He sucked in several deep lungfuls of air.

Spluttering and choking, he wrenched at another rock until it, too, gave way. The force of water behind him shot him forward, up and out into nothingness for a few heart-stopping milliseconds. Then his body bounced and splashed painfully down the waterfall on the hillside until he plunged into a shoulder-deep pool.

Coughing, gasping for precious air, he crawled onto the brush-covered bank of Willow Creek and collapsed, feeling the warm spatter of raindrops against his icy skin.

But there wasn't time to rest. He had to get Noelle and Carissa out of the cave, fast. Could he do it alone?

He dragged himself to his feet and crashed through the brush toward the road. It would take him at least twenty minutes to climb back up to the sinkhole and look for the rope that probably wasn't even there, and he couldn't afford an extra twenty minutes. Cutting across the hollow and getting a rope from his truck would be faster.

He glanced back up the hill to memorize the location of the opening, then broke into a jog.

A decayed old military green backpack leaned against a boulder in a dark, secluded corner of the cavern beneath the sinkhole. Noelle felt a chill scatter across her shoulders and down her arms as the beam of the flashlight danced over the familiar pack. She picked it up and carried it back to the natural shelf of limestone where Carissa sat, her hunched silhouette visible in the light coming through the opening above her head.

"What's that?" Carissa asked as Noelle sank down beside her.

"It was my grandfather's backpack when he was in World War Two."

"My great-grandfather?"

"No, this belonged to my mother's dad." Noelle felt Carissa's face and neck. Her temperature was rising with disturbing swiftness, and her breathing sounded slightly labored. She needed medical attention as soon as possible.

"What's it doing down here?" Carissa asked.

"My mother used to bring it when she took Nathan and me on hikes. How are you feeling?"

Carissa shrugged with typical adolescent nonchalance. "Fine. Is this the cave where your mother was . . . where she died?" she asked gently.

"That's right. There was a rockslide, and—"

"I remember. You told me about it, and I've put it in my family history report for school." Her voice sounded hoarse, and she paused to catch her breath. "I found a police report on the accident up in the attic of your old house. It said a fault line runs through this place."

"That's right."

"Is that like the San Andreas Fault in California that

causes earthquakes?"

"Yes."

"The report said that the geologist who investigated didn't think the accident was caused by a shift."

"Maybe he didn't know what he was talking about." Noelle heard the sharpness of her words. *Oh, Mom, if we'd only known.*

"So what do you think caused the rockslide if it wasn't the fault line?" Carissa asked.

"No one ever said for sure. My dad thought it was just a freak occurrence, and he refused to discuss it."

"Why?"

"My father wasn't much of a talker. He loved Mom very much, and I don't think he ever got over her death. He was a typical Cooper male, a strong, silent leader of the family."

"Like Dad." Carissa sighed and leaned against Noelle.

Noelle placed an arm around the girl and hugged her close. "I heard about your mother's phone call yesterday."

"Melva nearly had a cow."

Noelle grinned at the vernacular that Carissa had obviously picked up from Jill. "I also heard you were upset about it."

"Wouldn't you be? I mean, she's my mother, and I don't think anyone has a right to keep a kid from seeing her mother."

"Put yourself in Melva's place. You know how much she loves you."

"Yeah, I know," Carissa said. "Melva loves me and all that." She fell silent.

"Carissa?"

"Um-hmm?"

"The person who chased you . . ."

Noelle felt Carissa's body stiffen with wariness. "Yeah?"

"You still can't remember what was familiar about this person?"

"No."

There was a long silence, then Carissa pulled Noelle's arm even more tightly around her. "I'm scared."

Noelle wrapped both arms around her. "I know." *So am I.*

At that moment, there was a distant shout, a familiar voice. Nathan had made it through.

Chapter Eleven

This can't be happening! How did they get out? No one knows about the other entrance—no one! And there was no way they could've climbed out through that sinkhole.

I've got to settle down—can't panic or someone will notice, especially now.

They'll tell. The sheriff will be nosing around all over the place. This is bad.

Dr. Gideon has called Dr. Fletcher at the clinic, and they're ready for Carissa. No one in the family wants her to go to the hospital if they can keep her near home. She'll have good care here. Dr. Gideon was an ER doctor before she came to Hideaway, and Dr. Fletcher has proven herself several times since she arrived to work at the clinic in June.

I can't tell if I'm more relieved or scared. I can't afford to feel anything. Emotions always lead to danger. I love Carissa, but she's more of a problem than ever. Problems have to be solved. Better late than never.

And now . . . Noelle. She's watching. That light of knowledge is back in her eyes. That makes her more dangerous than Carissa.

It was one thing for Carissa to go digging in the old attic. Those old records just need to be buried or burned. But Noelle doesn't need those records to know what she knows.

Noelle stood with family and friends beneath the shelter of the porch and watched through the rain while Jill and Cheyenne Gideon loaded Carissa into Taylor Jackson's Jeep. Cecil and Melva squeezed into the back seat. Melva was jubilant, and although Cecil's response was more understated, Noelle could tell he was deeply relieved. Jill was ecstatic, and Pearl was going around thanking all the neighbors and friends who had gathered to search, hugging and congratulating them on their efforts and reminding them that they were heroes.

Could one of those people just be playing a part?

Everyone had been told only that Carissa had fallen in the sawmill last night and awakened alone in the cave this morning. The girl had begged Noelle and Nathan not to say anything else yet. Noelle agreed. There would be questions later, but for now the relief was so great to have the baby of the Cooper family safely home that answers could wait. Soon, the truth would have to be told.

Although she had reassured Carissa over and over that she would be safe in the company of *several* family members, especially with the doctors in attendance, Noelle still felt an aching need to go with her young cousin. But she couldn't. Not now. The more she thought about it, the more she wondered if this whole ordeal could be connected in some way to the sawmill and possibly to the ledger that Carissa had been carrying last night. Whatever was behind it all would have to be discovered before Carissa could be safe—maybe before any of the Coopers could be safe.

Cecil opened the back door of the Jeep and leaned out, holding up a hand to shield his face from the downpour. "Justin!"

The teenager stepped out through the screen door onto the porch. "Yeah, Dad?"

"You follow us in my car, you hear? No side trips. Come straight to the hospital."

"I will, Dad." Resentment conveyed itself well in those three words.

"I mean it," Cecil called sternly. "Be there within ten minutes of the time we get there. Noelle, you didn't drive down, did you?"

"No, I rode with Nathan."

"You can drive Melva's old beater, if you need to. The keys are on the kitchen counter by the sink."

"Thanks."

Justin shook his head as the Jeep took off. He glanced at Nathan. "If there'd been room, he'd've dragged me with them."

"Give him time to come to grips with everything," Nathan said quietly.

"How much time does he have to have? He's like a prison guard."

Noelle raised a brow at this exchange, but neither Nathan nor Justin seemed interested in explaining anything to her.

Justin glanced at her briefly. "Looks like you'll want to clean up and change before you come into town."

"I've got some clothes in Nathan's truck," Noelle said.

"Nathan, you can put on some of my things until you can get home to change," Justin offered. "You're a mess."

At that moment, a loudly outraged gander heralded the even louder rattle of a tailgate as Pearl drove her ancient rattling Chevy pickup through a flock of geese on the road. She stopped in front of the house with a squeal of brakes. "I'm goin' on in. Anybody want to ride with me?"

Jill stepped out of the house with her purse on her shoulder. "Thanks, Pearl, but I'll drive myself. Everybody's welcome to stay at my house in town tonight, if Carissa has to stay at the clinic, which it looks like she will. I daresay the creek will be rising in the next few hours, and no cars might be able to get back over the bridge, anyway."

"Not enough rain yet for that," Pearl said. "Besides, I reckon this old truck'll make it. Never failed me yet." With a wave, she disappeared down the misty, tree-lined lane, splashing mud in every direction.

"I'd better get going," Jill said. "Melva'll be a nervous wreck at the clinic." She put her arms around Noelle and held her tight for a moment, then kissed her on the cheek. "I'm sorry, honey, I was wrong. I should have called you sooner." She drew back and searched her sister's face. "I was just worried about you."

"I understand that, but it's time to stop trying to shelter me."

Jill nodded, wearily rubbing her eyes. "I'll try. That's about the best I can do."

Noelle watched her leave in her big, black Chevy Suburban. Several others left as well, sliding over the increasingly muddy track until it resembled a hog wallow.

Justin stepped into the house, then reappeared on the porch with a set of keys in his hand. "Nathan, we got a call from the sheriff's office a little bit before you came in with Carissa. That was human blood they found in the sawmill, all right. Guess it was Carissa's, huh?"

"Looks that way," Nathan said.

"Melva fainted when they told us. Did Carissa say why she fell?"

"She tripped over something," Noelle said.

Justin's heavy brows lowered over his blue eyes, as cloudy now as the stormy sky. "You're saying she hit her head so hard she just wandered away and got lost after she came to?"

Noelle squirmed inwardly at the doubtful tone of his voice. "We're not sure exactly what happened yet. Carissa doesn't know, and we don't want to jump to any conclusions." She hated lying to family. For now, however, she didn't know whom she could trust.

Justin headed for the steps of the porch. "Guess I'd better get or Dad'll have my hide. I'll take you to the sawmill so you can get your truck, Nathan."

"Don't worry, son," Nathan said, joining Justin to walk to the garage, "your sister's okay now." He put a hand on the boy's arm. "It'll be okay."

Justin went down the steps in silence, then just as thunder rumbled, he said something softly to Nathan. Noelle didn't catch his words, but she read frustration in the slump of his broad shoulders and his downcast eyes.

Nathan patted him on the arm again, and the two of them quick-stepped through the rain and entered the garage together.

Noelle watched them drive away. She waved at the remainder of searchers as they drove from the field where they had parked.

She pulled her cell phone from the side pocket of her backpack and hit speed dial for Hideaway Clinic. On any other day, Jill would be manning the telephones between patients—the clinic was woefully understaffed, and they'd been searching for quality help since early summer.

The harried voice of Dr. Karah Lee Fletcher answered at last, and Noelle relaxed. Of course, Jill hadn't had time to reach town yet. Still, Noelle felt like a traitor to her family. How could they ever forgive her if they found out she was micromanaging behind their backs to keep them away from Carissa?

And yet, how could she take a chance with Carissa's life?

"Karah Lee, this is Noelle Cooper."

"All right!" came the warm, rich tones of Karah Lee's voice. "The rescuing heroine. I heard you and Nathan found her."

"That's right, but I'm afraid it isn't over yet," Noelle said. She braced herself. How much could she say without sounding like an alarmist?

There was silence at the other end, and Noelle could picture the tall redhead holding the phone, frowning in confusion.

"Carissa needs your constant supervision at the clinic, and not just to watch for pneumonia," Noelle said. "I know this could get sticky, but please don't leave Carissa alone with anyone, even family members. If you and Cheyenne could keep an eye on her until Nathan and I get there—"

"Okay, Noelle," Karah Lee said with a cautious drawl, "what're you trying to tell me? Are we going to have to call Social Services? Because if someone attacked—"

"The only injury Carissa received was the bump on the back of her head, which apparently happened when she tripped and fell in the sawmill, though I can't say that for sure. We can't prove that anyone attacked her. Please don't say anything to the family about this yet, because by all appearances, Carissa became disoriented, wandered from the road and got lost."

"What do you mean, 'by all appearances'?" Karah Lee asked. "Is something going on we don't know about?"

Noelle repeated what Carissa had told them about the whisperer.

"So she really was abducted!" Karah Lee exclaimed.

"It looks that way. Someone also removed the rope we used to climb down into the cave when we were searching for her. Nathan took some creative measures to get us out. We're going to call the sheriff and tell him about it, but we think it would be best if we didn't alert the rest of the family to the situation just yet."

"Okay." Still that hint of caution in Karah Lee's voice, as if she were trying to decide whether she really was talking to Noelle or if this was a crank call.

"If you can just tell Cheyenne what I'm telling you," Noelle said, "and then make sure Carissa isn't left alone with anyone, including any family members, until we can get this thing sorted out, Nathan and I would appreciate it. I wish I could tell you more, but right now we don't have all the facts, and we don't want to go around accusing innocent people. Everyone's been through enough."

"Hold it. You said *any* family member?" Karah Lee said. "But Jill's a family member."

Noelle swallowed and offered a silent apology to her sister. "I know," she said softly. "Even Jill."

"You're right. This could get sticky."

"I'm sorry. I'll try to explain the whole thing later, if I can. Look, Karah Lee, I understand that you don't know me very well, but you do know Nathan, and you must realize that he can be trusted. He'll tell you the same thing I'm telling you."

"But to suspect Jill—"

"I know you're friends, and I'm sorry. I'm hoping all this can be cleared up quickly, and Jill won't even have to know about it. I'm sorry to put you in this position."

"I'll talk to Cheyenne about it when she gets here," Karah Lee said. "I could call Bertie Meyer to come across the street and sit a spell with Carissa. And Blaze threatened to skip school today and come in. He always keeps a close eye on things."

"Blaze?"

"You know Blaze Farmer, our tech? He lives across the lake at the boys' ranch—though really, he spends most of his time here. Great kid, though don't you dare tell him I said so." Obviously, Karah Lee was warming to the idea of subterfuge. "No, wait, hold everything. Why didn't I think about this? Fawn can be on standby if I get busy with patients."

Noelle had met Fawn Morrison in September, at Cheyenne and Dane's wedding. Earlier in the summer, Fawn had been a homeless, streetwise seventeen-year-old who had somehow managed to attract the attention of an organized crime syndicate and had successfully fought back, with the help of her new friends in Hideaway. Now she was no longer homeless. She lived with Karah Lee at the Lakeside Bed and Breakfast, down the block from the clinic.

"Thank you," Noelle said. "From what I know of Fawn, she'd make a good bodyguard."

"You'll let me know as soon as you find out something? Jill's going to be suspicious, you know."

"I know."

"And I don't like crossing her."

"Believe me, neither do I." Worse, this would hurt Jill, when all she'd ever done was take care of other people. "Nathan and I will be there as soon as we can figure a few things out here at the house."

Oh, how she prayed they would figure it out soon.

Chapter Twelve

Nathan pulled his truck up to the front gate of Cecil's house and slid to a stop in the mud. Hypothermia was setting in, and he shivered, still chilled to the core. It would be a relief to change into dry clothes.

Noelle was standing on the porch where he'd left her, cell phone in hand, staring into the distance toward the sawmill. He knew this whole ordeal was hurting her deeply. It hurt him, too. He'd known the Coopers all his life, and he hated to see how the fabric of their family had been torn apart throughout the years. And now this. *Oh, Lord, protect this family and bring healing to this hollow.*

He strolled up the sidewalk to the porch and held up Noelle's overnight case. "I'll carry this inside so you can change before we leave."

"Thanks." She followed him through the screen door into the house. "Nathan, did you notice who was here when you came back for the rope?"

"I didn't come back here, I went to the truck. Did you get any sense of who Carissa might have seen?"

"None."

"You've been on the telephone?"

"I called the clinic and asked Karah Lee not to leave Carissa alone with anyone, including family."

He grimaced. "What was her reaction?"

"I think, at first, she thought I was wacko, but she's going to call in reinforcements."

He nodded. Karah Lee Fletcher wouldn't back down from anyone if it involved the safety of a patient, as she had proven this summer when she'd confronted a killer, an amazing story that everyone in Hideaway was still talking about. With her size and voice of authority, Karah Lee could be intimidating. Nathan just hoped it didn't become necessary for her to display it again. "They'll be checking Carissa out for a while. Cecil will be livid if he discovers there's a conspiracy going on to keep him from his daughter."

"I know," Noelle said. "And Jill's going to wonder why she isn't allowed to attend Carissa. We'll need to explain everything to everyone, but first, can we search around the sawmill before we go into town?"

"Don't you think we should talk to the authorities before we do anything else?"

"This may be our only chance to check it out with everyone gone." She handed him her cell phone. "You know, you might want to get one of these. They come in handy."

"I have one, I just allowed the battery to run down and haven't taken time to recharge."

"Who're you going to report this to?" she asked. "The sheriff?"

"No, I think the rangers are the right authority for this. I'll talk to Taylor Jackson. The abduction took place on land bordering national forest, so he'll need to be on the lookout for anything unusual. He can tell the sheriff's office. I trust him to be discreet."

"Okay, you call while I change."

He glanced down at the extra backpack that Noelle had carried with her from the cave and deposited in this room. In all the excitement of Carissa's rescue, no one else had noticed it, but Nathan had recognized it the instant he saw it emerge from the mouth of the sinkhole on the end of the rope—Noelle had sent it up before she came out herself.

"I see you found your mother's backpack," he said.

She nodded. "I wondered if you would remember. We were planning a surprise birthday party for you in the cave, because we knew you loved that place. My Mom and I packed it with food and presents."

He did remember. Noelle's mom had died on his eighth birthday.

"I baked the cupcakes myself," she said. "It was all my idea. We were going to have the picnic and the gifts all set out and waiting. It was going to be so much . . . fun." Her voice quivered, and her eyes glazed with tears.

For a moment, Nathan recalled the shock of that day, when he'd entered the cave to find all those rocks and boulders scattered where they shouldn't have been, the unexpected, heavy smell of freshly disturbed earth, and the air thick with dust. "I almost left before I found you, but then I remembered that you'd told me you and your mother were going to be there. So I wondered if you were somehow playing a joke on me." Even at that age, she'd been a tease. "You still don't remember, do you?"

Noelle's lids fluttered downward; she shook her head.

"I found you under your mother's body. You were both half concealed by a rockslide. At first, I thought both of you were dead." How many times had he relived that day? "But when I touched you, you started screaming." He swallowed hard. "I tried to pull you out, but I couldn't. I had to run back to Cecil's house, to get help, and as I ran from the cave your screams followed me. Later, when it was over and you were back in your house with your dad, you were silent and in shock. You didn't talk for three days. I never forgot those screams."

Noelle pressed her lips together, obviously fighting tears. "I hope I never remember."

He gestured to the pack. "Then why drag that out of the cave? It's bound to trigger emotions."

"It was Mom's," she said simply. "The cave was sealed before I could ask to go back and get the pack. After Cecil and I found the sinkhole, we explored other parts of the cave—you know, it goes back into the hills for a couple of miles—but I could never bring myself to return to the site of the collapse." She lifted the bag and slung it over her shoulder. "Nathan, do you mind if we keep this in your truck? I don't want anyone messing with it until I've had a chance to go through it. It contains some of the last memories I have of my mother."

"Get changed and we'll take it with us. I think you're right, it's time we did some investigating."

Noelle inhaled the mingled scents of rain, moist earth, freshly sawn logs and the ancient grease that kept the gears of the sawmill running smoothly. The smells brought back memories so powerful she could almost hear the whine of metal teeth ripping into fragrant wood. She walked along the outer wall of the enormous building that hovered in oppressive silence.

Nathan followed, then stepped past her to force open the heavy wooden door to the office, which always swelled and stuck during humid weather.

She hesitated on the threshold, peering into the gloom. "I haven't come in here in years. Every time I do, I think about the accident."

"So do I."

She glanced up at him. "Yeah, I guess you would."

He had returned to Hideaway to begin his young pastorate only a year before Noelle's father and grandparents had been crushed by falling logs on the floor of the sawmill. As a clergyman close to the family, Nathan had conducted the triple funeral for Joseph and Anna Cooper and Noelle's father, Frank.

In one wall of the cedar-scented office was a soundproofed, sliding glass door that opened onto the cavernous operation room of the mill, where the huge machine, the shining, deadly-looking saw with teeth as long as a man's fingers, waited in silence.

"Have you been in here since the accident?" Noelle stepped into the workroom.

"A few times, but like you, I've avoided it as much as possible."

"Cecil told me about the accident after the funeral. He said he was just leaving the mill for the day when he heard the crash. He ran back inside and saw the pile of logs beside the flatbed trailer. He'd searched for Dad and Grandma and Grandpa . . . until he caught sight of Grandma's hand sticking out from beneath a cedar log."

"That memory must haunt him," Nathan said.

"Yes, but you know Cecil. The ultimate tough guy. Never let 'em see you sweat, and all that garbage."

"Runs in the Cooper family."

She glanced at him. "Dad was the same way. So was Grandpa, and Grandma worked right alongside the men without complaint."

"So did Pearl, when she wasn't keeping the books."

Noelle shuddered again at the memory of the accident, then returned to the office. Ancient metal file cabinets lined the west wall, between the two desks. On top of the far cabinet lay a thick black ledger, caked with dried mud, its pages crinkled from water.

"This was what Carissa was carrying?" she asked. "An account ledger?"

"I think that's it. Someone must have found it in the driveway and put it there." Nathan glanced back into the workroom through the open office door, while Noelle paged carefully through the book.

"It's an old one," she said. "The last entries are dated . . . ten years ago." She turned another page. "The last date entered was the day of the accident."

"Carissa was researching family history for her school report, remember? I'm sure she was searching for details about the accident. In fact, knowing Carissa, she'll continue with that report as soon as she recovers. Prepare for an interview. I've already had mine."

"What kind of interview?" Noelle asked.

"You know, questions like: 'Were you here the day the tornado hit?' Or: 'What were you doing the day of the accident at the sawmill?' "

"We talked about Mom's death while we waited for you in the cave. Do you remember much about the sawmill accident?" Noelle asked. "You and your wife were at Cecil's when I arrived, and it was such a comfort to see you there."

He looked over at her and smiled. "Thank you. That means a lot. I remember feeling so helpless, so young and inept at the time."

"You were always mature for your age. You handled it well."

"There seemed to be an undercurrent of tension among the Cooper clan."

She remembered that, too. In fact, she had felt such an overwhelming sense of oppression during that whole time that she'd fled back home to Springfield almost immediately after the funeral. The nightmares that had plagued her afterward, and the depression she'd battled, had been horrendous, and she'd lost considerable confidence in her ability to cope. That was around the same time she was discovering marital bliss wasn't so blissful. Actually, being married to a drug-and-wife-abuser was a frightening, imprisoning and ongoing nightmare.

"I picked up on some kind of undercurrent of tension, too," she said. "I didn't know what it was. Cecil wasn't speaking to anyone. Pearl only came out of her house to attend the funeral, and Jill seemed as mystified about the whole thing as I was." Noelle dusted chunks of dried mud from one of the pages of the ledger. She had known she wouldn't be able to return here without dredging up old pain.

Nathan peered at the open ledger. "This doesn't look like Cooper writing—it's too readable."

"Thanks a lot."

"The truth hurts."

"Well, it isn't Cecil's writing, because he didn't keep the books. Aunt Pearl and Grandma did. Then, around the time of the accident, Melva was hired." Noelle looked up at Nathan, then back at the book. "If Carissa was carrying this last night and someone was trailing her, is it feasible that her pursuer was after this ledger?"

Nathan circled the desk and joined her at the filing cabinet. He thumbed through the last pages of entries. "If that was the case, don't you think the ledger would have been taken? And besides, what possible threat could ten-year-old accounting records pose for anyone?"

"I don't know."

Nathan continued turning pages until he reached the cardboard backing of the binder. "Here's something. Look at this."

The remnant of a ledger sheet was caught on the bottom ring; someone had ripped out the sheet and left behind a small piece of the page.

Noelle carried the book to the window for better light. She shuffled through the pages once more, slower this time.

"This isn't a full ledger. It could hold three times as many pages."

"Maybe someone started a new book. You know— new managers taking over for your dad and grandparents, new ledgers."

Noelle frowned, holding the book closer to the light.

"What is it?" Nathan asked.

"Impressions. The last page is blank, but there are indentations from writing on this end piece of cardboard. What does that suggest to you?"

"Someone's removed incriminating evidence?"

"Yes, and it would be financial in nature," she said.

"Embezzlement?"

"Any discrepancies would have been caught by the accountant at the end of that year."

Nathan looked at her. "You mean Harvey Sand?"

She felt a frisson of startled dread. "Oh, Nathan."

"The sheriff's still investigating Harvey's accident, which means the authorities aren't convinced it was accidental."

She closed the book. "Let's not jump to any conclusions, okay? This could all be a big coincidence."

"Jill told us that this wasn't even the ledger she and Cecil wanted. They needed a ledger from this year to understand a fifteen-thousand-dollar discrepancy on the computer. Look, I know you want to protect your family, but—"

"I'm not trying to protect anybody, I just don't want to jump the gun. Cecil and Jill have been entering a lot of data into the new computers, and maybe there was a glitch or something. Just because Carissa was abducted when she was running that errand doesn't mean that she was carrying evidence."

"But do we really want to take a chance?" Nathan asked gently. "This person is dangerous, whoever it is. I really, *really* hope it isn't a Cooper, but we can't take any chances with Carissa's life."

Frustrated and spooked, she combed her fingers through her hair. "I don't see any box of files in here, so someone probably took the records that Pearl told us were delivered from Harvey's office to the attic in the old house for storage." She peered at the open book, frowning. "Please tell me you don't see a connection between Harvey's death and Carissa's abduction."

"I'm sorry. It may be nothing, but I'm not willing to let the idea go until we can be sure, and neither are you. Even if we didn't trust Carissa's word about her abductor—which we do—someone was serious enough about stopping us to remove that rope from the sinkhole."

"We need to ask Carissa about her research for that report," Noelle said.

"I'd also like to find out what Harvey knew."

Noelle returned to the entrance of the mill, which was dimly lit by windows high on the walls. This was where, many years ago, she had last heard her mother laugh. If Noelle closed her eyes, she could almost hear that sweet voice again, filled with tenderness, calling to her from the office door:

"Go on, honey, run outside and play. I'll be finished here in a minute, then we can get Nathan's cupcakes from the house."

"Oh, Mommy, the cave. Can we have our party at our place in the cave?"

Gentle laughter. Then: "We'll go there as soon as I'm finished helping with these records."

"Can I call Nathan now?"

Noelle opened her eyes.

Nathan came up beside her and put a hand on her shoulder. "Memories?"

She sighed and nodded. "This mill always frightened

me. I think it was all the noise."

The sharp fangs of the huge, round saw, as high as her chest, jabbed at the air. A sickle-shaped cant hook that was used to roll the heavy oak, walnut and cedar logs rested on the corner of a flatbed truck. Noelle looked at the hook for a long moment. The very sight of that tool made her shiver, but then this whole place made her uneasy, as if something lingered here that threatened to crash through her memories, something she did not want to remember. But the threat of some terrible revelation hung idle; all she remembered was the very loud and continuous activity that always filled this huge building.

She could almost hear the deafening whine of the saw and almost smell the dusty-tangy sawdust shavings that floated through the air when the mill was in operation.

The huge contraption that her dad had invented, the sawdust drag, wound around the room's circumference from directly beneath the saw to the vent that released the sawdust outside into drifts. The drag looked as it always had, a large chain, with cups that scooped the dust efficiently from beneath the huge metal saw. Noelle remembered, as a child, always being afraid of that drag, terrified that it would reach up and grab her when she stepped over it.

Now she walked out onto the concrete work floor. "Where's the light switch?" she asked, looking around the office door frame.

Nathan joined her. "On the other side of the building, near the entrance that the employees use. Cecil had it placed beside the power switches for the equipment."

"Do you think something could have been going on here at the mill that someone tried to hide? Some kind of illegal operation?" Noelle asked.

"What, for instance?"

"Beats me. That's why I think we need to see those records that came from Harvey's office."

"If we can find them."

Noelle gave the mill one last sweeping look, then went back into the office. "We really need to talk to Carissa. She might know where the records are. Let's get to the clinic." She placed the ledger back on the metal file cabinet, then turned to give the office one final glance.

She couldn't help feeling frustrated, as though some solution lay within their grasp, if only they could find it.

Chapter Thirteen

The waiting room at the clinic in Hideaway was generously proportioned. As Nathan led the way inside, he saw the Coopers and several other patients, all looking tired and grumpy, no doubt waiting long past the scheduled times for their appointments.

A sense of chaos buzzed through the atmosphere; a child cried out from a treatment room; the telephone rang insistently. Jill opened the door from the treatment area and called a patient, while Blaze Farmer manned the desk and grabbed the telephone. Karah Lee raced to the computer station behind Blaze and clattered the keys without sitting down. She looked tired, and her short red hair hung limply over her forehead. She'd been up most of the night, helping with the search for Carissa.

Blaze completed his call and waved at Nathan. "We were all wondering when the heroes would get here." Although his light-blue scrubs looked crisp and clean against his ebony skin, his dark-brown eyes showed fatigue, and his short hair could use a comb. Like all his colleagues, he had rushed straight to the clinic from Cedar Hollow.

As Noelle joined her family at the far end of the waiting room, Nathan strolled to the reception desk. "Skipping school?"

Blaze grinned. "Any chance I get. Karah Lee and I've been trying to reschedule appointments and juggle patients since we got here, and now it sounds like everybody in Hideaway's trying to call and see how Carissa's doing."

The telephone buzzed once more, and Blaze answered, freeing Nathan to join the family in the waiting room, in a corner area, where two short sofas faced a row of chairs along each wall. Noelle had chosen a chair between Pearl and Cecil, near a rack of children's books and magazines.

Cecil and Justin sat hunched forward, elbows on knees, like twin replicas of Rodin's "Thinker."

Cecil straightened in his chair as Nathan approached.

"They're giving Carissa a thorough going-over," he said.

"Going to use the CT scanner and everything," Melva added. "But both doctors checked her over, and Carissa seems to be doing okay, except for that nasty bump on the back of her head and the fever."

"It's coming down, though," Cecil said.

Melva rested her hand on Justin's shoulder, as if to reassure herself that her stepson was okay. "That's what Karah Lee told us a minute ago," she told Nathan. "Jill's all gripey because Cheyenne won't let her take Carissa over to the CT scanner."

Hideaway Clinic was not officially a hospital yet; it was designated a rural clinic. The director, Dr. Cheyenne Gideon, had seen to it that the facility was well-equipped for most emergencies. Nathan had always been impressed by Cheyenne. Cheyenne had recently announced her plans to seek a hospital designation.

Hideaway's population increased fourfold during the summer months, just as neighboring Branson's popularity increased. Like Branson, Hideaway was quickly becoming a tourism boomtown, and for the past couple of years, both towns' tourist populations had continued into the autumn months. The clinic needed more staff. Even Nathan helped out from time to time when he could, using his emergency medical training to full advantage.

The door to the exam rooms swung open, and Nathan caught a glimpse of Karah Lee racing down the hallway, clipboard in hand.

Jill's voice carried through the reception window. "I don't know why I can't stay with Carissa. You know she's scared—all that CT equipment can be overwhelming for a kid."

"Taylor will keep her calm," Nathan heard Cheyenne answer softly.

"Taylor's a good paramedic, but you're letting him attend Carissa instead of her own flesh and blood."

"It isn't a good idea for a doctor or nurse to treat a family member," Cheyenne said. "Besides, I need you here." Cheyenne looked out the reception area window, and her gaze stopped at Nathan. She gave him a brief nod.

He nodded back. Good. She was keeping Carissa safe. Taylor Jackson was a ranger as well as a paramedic, and he would keep close watch on Carissa. He helped out here at the clinic often between his ranger duties. Word around town was that Taylor was being groomed to direct the ambulance service—when and if Hideaway's city council agreed with the mayor that it was necessary.

"I hope Carissa will be okay during the CT scan over there in that big old truck," Melva said.

"She'll be fine," Cecil assured her. "It takes more than a few X-ray machines to scare my girl."

The CT unit was brought to Hideaway once a week via a tractor-trailer unit—a godsend for this community.

Nathan glanced toward the door. He needed to check

on his pharmacy, to make sure the pharmacist filling in for him wasn't having any problems. Nathan looked at Noelle, talking softly to Pearl about the older woman's latest crop of herbs, then he glanced at Justin, who was staring at the floor, apparently deep in contemplation. The boy's lips moved from time to time, as though he was reciting something in his head and couldn't disconnect the link between his thoughts and his mouth.

Justin was a brilliant kid with uncommonly intense focus . . . something that had been causing him a lot of difficulty lately.

"Noelle." Cecil's deep voice rumbled softly, his gaze on the floor as if he were intensely interested in the pattern of the carpet. "You want to tell me again how you two found Carissa so fast?"

"Nathan and I were close to the cave when we heard her scream."

"So you're saying it was all coincidence." Cecil didn't sound convinced.

"We were in the right place at the right time to save Carissa," Nathan said. "You know I don't believe in coincidence."

Cecil broke his staring match with the floor long enough to meet Nathan's gaze. "You're a pharmacist now, pal. You don't have to play preacher with me anymore."

"Cecil," Melva warned.

"What?" he snapped, showing the first signs of irritability due to weariness.

"What on earth was she doin' in Bobcat Cave in the

first place?" Pearl grumped. "I can't figure it."

"Simple," Melva said. "She lost her flashlight, got lost, wandered from the road."

Pearl patted her chest, then reached up to push her thick, coarse gray hair from her forehead. "What with the only usable entrance sealed shut, only way Carissa could've gotten into that cave would be to fall through the sinkhole the same way Noelle and Nathan climbed down, and if she'd done that, she'd be a lot worse off than she is."

"We don't know how she got in." Melva's voice also took on an edge of irritability. "Nobody will even let us in the room with her. It's like they think we're going to contaminate her or something."

"Carissa's been through a difficult ordeal," Nathan said. "I'm sure they just want to keep her calm."

"By keeping her family away from her?" Melva complained. "You'd think they'd realize having her loved ones around her would make Carissa feel better."

"Not the way we've all been griping at each other lately," Justin muttered. "That'd make any bratty little sister get lost for a while."

"Watch your mouth," Cecil growled.

"Justin, our disagreements have nothing to do with what happened," Melva said. "Carissa was knocked out and she got lost. That's the only explanation. She wouldn't run away over the silly little argument we had about that . . . that woman."

Justin gave his stepmom a dark look. "She *is* our mother."

Melva's expression froze. Obviously, Gladys was a touchy subject with this family. Why, Nathan wondered, couldn't Gladys remain out of the Coopers' lives, now that she'd abandoned her responsibilities and gone off for more moneyed pastures?

Cecil leaned close to his son. "Give it a rest. We're not at our best right now, and talking about your mother can only make things worse."

"Dad, all I was saying was that Carissa sure doesn't need us all in there snipping at each other."

"Point made."

"I don't suppose you've reached Gladys yet about all this, have you?" Melva asked her husband.

"No, I haven't called her again," Cecil said. "I'm not any crazier about talking to her than you are, believe it or not."

Melva's cheeks grew pink. She folded her arms over her chest and glanced at Noelle. "No matter how much a stepmom loves her stepchildren, their blood mother just has to say 'Boo,' and they forget you like an old ghost."

"That's not what this is all about," Justin complained. "Why do you have to be so sensitive? All I'm saying is that maybe my mother would want to know that her own flesh and blood nearly died in some godforsaken cave in Cedar Hollow."

Nathan glanced at Noelle. He could read the sorrow in her face as plainly as if she'd spoken.

Fresh grief caught Noelle like a vise around her heart.

Whether or not a family member was involved, *someone* had endangered Carissa, had terrified her. A child never completely overcame such a dreadful feeling.

Carissa's own mother had rejected her, and now this.

Noelle shot Cecil a surreptitious glance, then her gaze traveled to Melva, who sat glowering at the floor, her face devoid of makeup, the fair skin puffy around her pretty eyes and nose, and red from crying. Justin stared at the floor as well.

Noelle was aware of a slither of unease trailing down her spine. She could not overcome a sense of foreboding, as if the threat had become a living, breathing presence, radiating around them all. Why did the Coopers suddenly seem to be the targets of some sinister force? Noelle wanted to wrap her arms around them all, protect them, tell them everything would be okay, but she couldn't be sure. It seemed the Coopers had inherited more than their fair share of suffering. Maybe Melva was right. Maybe there was a curse of some kind on them. But a curse from where?

She was sensing guilt and high levels of anxiety among her family, emotions she picked up easily by reading body language, emotions understandably created by the stress over the things happening in the Coopers' lives. Noelle had always been able to read the emotions of her loved ones with a simple glance or by an inflection of voice.

Justin yawned and stretched, then stood and dug into the pocket of his jeans.

"Where are you going?" Cecil asked.

"To get a soda. I've gotta have something to keep me awake. Want one?"

"Not yet." Cecil put a hand on his son's arm, holding his gaze. "Wait a while. We'll both go as soon as the doctor tells us how Carissa's doing."

Justin scowled and sat back down, his long face set in lines of brooding. His heavy dark brows, so like his father's, drew low over his eyes.

Noelle watched father and son. Cecil acted as if he didn't trust Justin as far as the foyer, which was in plain sight. Or maybe Cecil just needed to be in control right now, with so much of his life seeming out of control since last night.

She glanced at the others. No one else seemed to think the exchange was unusual. Of course Cecil was worried, after what had happened to Carissa.

She gestured to Nathan. "I feel like stretching. Want to come?"

He nodded. "Anyone besides Justin want a drink?"

"All I want's out of here," Pearl said. "How long are they gonna take with Carissa?"

"We'll have to wait and see." Noelle reached into her jacket pocket to make sure she had change, then stood and preceded Nathan from the room into the cooler, fresher atmosphere of the foyer.

Instead of stopping at the vending machines, however, they stepped out onto the sidewalk. Noelle gazed across the street toward the manicured lawn where a gazebo was encircled by a bed of red, yellow and bronze mums edged by blue, purple and white clumps of pansies. The colors were vivid in the dim light of the rainy afternoon.

The broad sweep of lawn ended at the community boat dock on Table Rock Lake. The lake reflected the dullness of the sky, but across the water, in the rocky bluffs, more colors were threaded through the trees. Red-orange maples blazed like torches, while purple asters and goldenrod bloomed in random patches against the gray of the limestone cliffs. Nathan stepped up behind Noelle. "You miss this town when you're gone, don't you?"

She nodded and turned to stroll along the sidewalk. In spite of the weather, the street was lined with cars as tourists visited the shops in this town square—she had always loved the way the handsome brick storefronts faced out to the streets that encircled them, rather than facing in around a courthouse or village green.

Several sightseers had taken shelter from the rain beneath the dark green awnings that protected the sidewalk around the square. Hideaway boasted a strip of some of the most lively antique trading stores in the Ozarks.

"When did they put up the awnings?" Noelle asked.

"Two weeks ago. The mayor insisted that they be in place for the fall rains. He didn't want anything to interfere with commerce during the biggest tourist season."

Noelle and Nathan strolled past the bakery to the general store. As they turned, in silent agreement, to enter through the old-fashioned glass doors of the store,

Noelle paused and glanced at the big black tractor-trailer rig across the street in the paved parking area east of the square. The CT unit.

Nathan casually placed an arm around her shoulders. "Carissa will be okay. Taylor won't let anyone past her. And don't let Melva's tirade about Gladys get to you."

"I agree with her completely. Melva's been there for the Coopers all these years—not just for Justin and Carissa, but for Cecil, for the sawmill. It isn't fair that Gladys can just come barging back and expect a warm welcome. You know Melva, and this will hurt her deeply."

As Noelle followed him inside and listened to the echo of their footsteps on the refinished hardwood floor, she thought about Melva. Even as a child, Melva Hawkins had struggled with a weight problem, and although she was two grades ahead of Noelle and Nathan in school, she'd spent more time with Noelle than with girls her own age.

Noelle had never made fun of Melva's weight. Neither had Cecil. He had, in fact, gone out of his way to be kind to Melva and defend her against tormentors— and Cecil Cooper had the brawn to do the job. It had been only natural that Melva would develop a crush on him. At the time, the feelings had not been mutual. It wasn't until Gladys abandoned her family, breaking the hearts of her husband and children, that Cecil's priorities changed. He took another look at his former classmate—who now worked in the office of the sawmill and was obviously crazy about him and his children.

Not only was Melva pretty, she had adored him since high school. And at last, he was smitten, too.

Melva had struggled hard and waited a long time for the family she had now. She wouldn't give up without a fight. Noelle didn't want her to.

Chapter Fourteen

Nathan made a cursory check of his small pharmacy at the back of the general store. Though business was brisk, his colleague assured him that he could do without him this afternoon. When he returned to the front, he found Noelle waiting, holding a small grocery bag.

She held it up as he approached. "Hungry?"

"Starved."

She handed Nathan a candy bar and soda as they stepped back onto the sidewalk.

"I thought health-food enthusiasts didn't do junk food," he said as he accepted her offerings.

"This isn't junk food. Today, it's comfort food." She sank down onto a carved wooden bench in front of the bakery, and he joined her, understanding her need to avoid the clinic waiting room for a few moments.

Nathan unwrapped his candy. "Dark chocolate. You remembered."

She held up her bar. "My favorite, too. I think we were together so much growing up, it's almost like we developed the same tastes by osmosis."

He took a bite of the creamy, rich dark chocolate and relished the exquisite taste for a long moment. Comfort food, indeed.

"So, are you going to tell me what's going on with Justin?"

He paused with the candy bar halfway back to his mouth. "You sure know how to ruin a guy's appetite."

"He's the one you're counseling."

"I told you I can't divulge—"

"It is Justin, isn't it?" she said.

He didn't reply, but she was watching him closely. She knew.

She put her hand on his arm. "I understand about the need for professional confidentiality, both as a former pastor and in your present—"

"If you understand, why do you keep bugging me about it?"

"Because there's a terrified child who is convinced someone close to our family—maybe even *in* our family—tried to kill her . . . and tried to kill *us*. As a professional, you are required to report any suspicions to the police."

"I told Taylor everything we know."

"But you didn't tell him about this."

The lack of sleep was getting to him at last, because he had to bite back an irritable retort. "There's nothing to tell," he said quietly. "I've attempted to explain to you that there is no connection." He rewrapped the remainder of his candy bar and slipped it into his pocket. His appetite, even for dark chocolate, had disappeared.

"It is Justin," she said. "The conversation between you two earlier today, the concern I see in Melva's eyes when she looks at him and the tight rein Cecil puts on him. For a while I thought maybe Cecil was the one with the problem, he's acting so paranoid. But it's Justin."

Nathan closed his eyes and gave a slight nod.

Noelle expelled a quick breath of air. "Why is Cecil keeping such a close watch over him? Has he gotten into trouble at school?"

"No, nothing like that. He's a good kid, Noelle, you know that. How can you suspect him?"

She sank back on the bench. "I'm just trying to make sense out of everything that's happened. I can't help wondering about all the veiled remarks about him."

"What Cecil thinks doesn't matter here. He's one of those people who believe a psychological or emotional disorder qualifies a person for a mental institution. He couldn't be more wrong, especially with this particular problem."

"What problem is that? Depression? Justin sure acts depressed." At Nathan's interested glance, she continued. "I've had some experience with that."

"Depression is only a symptom in this case."

"A symptom of what? Is he psychotic?"

"No, he isn't psychotic. Noelle, you're going off on a tangent here."

"Okay, if he isn't psychotic, then it's some kind of neurosis." She held up a finger. "Not depression, so maybe it's bipolar disorder."

He gave up. She was going to find out one way or another, and the sooner he could convince her that Justin was not a threat to his sister's safety, the sooner they could get on with other matters. "Okay. Have you ever had a song get stuck in your head that you couldn't stop singing under your breath? Or have you ever become so focused on some stressful event that you couldn't stop obsessing about it?"

She looked up at him, and her expression cleared. "Obsessive-Compulsive Disorder. OCD."

A lifetime of uncomfortable memories replayed themselves in Noelle's mind as too many pieces of a long-ago puzzle fell into place. Why hadn't she seen it? "That's a disorder that runs in families."

"Yes, but you know OCD isn't some dangerous mental illness. It isn't anything that could threaten Carissa's life."

"It can manifest itself in a lot of different ways."

"It's limited," he said. "Most sufferers lead normal lives. In fact, they don't even realize they have the disorder, because it's all they've ever known."

"Or they cover it up out of self-preservation," she said.

"But they aren't crazy."

"Define *crazy*," she said. "I do know that they wonder if they're losing control."

"*How* do you know that?"

A gang of senior citizens armed with photography equipment trooped past. When they were out of earshot,

Nathan said, "I've thought about the possibilities ever since Carissa disappeared last night. The OCD sufferer is always totally aware of what is going on around him. His thinking is clear, but he doesn't *think* it's clear. Big difference there, you know. He can't stop his particular compulsion or obsession."

"What if that compulsion is abducting children?"

"Absolutely not in the realm of possibility. If it were, you'd be getting into psychosis."

"Okay," she said, "the compulsive sufferer gets a compulsion to clean or to check and recheck everything he does, as if he's afraid to trust his own short-term memory. Or he's compulsive and he has to take a certain number of steps through his yard to his house, and if he doesn't take the right number, he has to go back and do it over again, or he has to make sure his house is in perfect order, or he can't bring himself to throw away a book or a newspaper or old mail."

"Exactly. Frustrating, painful compulsion. But not dangerous."

Obsessive thoughts. Obsessive fears. It ran in families. "But I've never seen Justin behaving that way," she said.

"He's apparently always had the tendencies, but ever since the collapse of that resort condominium this summer, he's been having increasing problems. He was spending the night in town with a friend when it happened, and they had to evacuate the house. Since then Carissa's noticed how often he goes through the house, checking the windows, turning out lights, circling the yard to make sure the gates are fastened."

Oh, poor Justin. "Carissa told Cecil and Melva about it?"

"Yes, she was getting worried about him. Of course, when they confronted Justin about it, the difficulties just got worse. Melva took him to the clinic, and Cheyenne put him on medication and recommended counseling. She asked me if I would have some sessions with him, because she knew Cecil wouldn't stand for his son seeing a 'shrink.'"

"That's my dear cousin. He believes in willpower and doesn't trust therapy."

"Cecil discovered what Melva had done and put a stop to it."

Noelle took a sip of her diet soda and stared toward the lake, at the boat dock, which looked deserted in the rain. "So Justin is no longer taking medication or getting any counseling?"

"That's right."

"After this is all over, I'll have a talk with Cecil. Sometimes he'll listen to me. Justin needs help."

"I've already tried talking to Cecil."

She grinned up at him. "You don't have any feminine charm."

He returned the grin. "Thank you. Are you staying at Jill's tonight?"

"I'll probably stay with Carissa at the clinic, if Cheyenne decides to keep her there, which I hope she does. Carissa was sounding bad and running a fever before we left the cave. She could easily develop pneumonia. And I want to get this thing figured out while Carissa's someplace safe," she said. "It's as though our family is under some kind of evil . . . I don't know . . . curse or something."

Nathan frowned at her. "What makes you say that?"

"Isn't that how it seems to you? All the deaths and disasters and now Carissa?"

"I remember my grandmother mentioning a Cooper curse," Nathan murmured.

"What about it? What did your grandmother say?"

He sighed. "She was talking about your mother's death. She told me the Cooper curse had done it."

"How?"

"She wouldn't say. Grandma loved old wives' tales, scary stories. She was the most superstitious person I ever knew. That stuck in my mind, though, about the Cooper curse, especially after the accident at the sawmill."

"I'm not superstitious."

"Neither am I."

"But I do believe some superstitions might be based on fact somewhere along the line."

"I know," Nathan said. "But everyone thought the death of your father and grandparents was an accident at the time."

"What do you mean 'at the time'? What about now? Do you have doubts now?"

He hesitated. "I've always had doubts. It was such a stupid accident, one that was so unlikely for your dad because he had checks and double-checks on all his equipment. I even suggested my doubts to the sheriff then, but he just laughed at me. He didn't know Frank Cooper the way I did."

Noelle glanced up at Nathan. Spending time with him, talking with him, was making her feel better, much better. That surprised her. She studied his face, the strong jaw, the high cheekbones, the warmth and compassion in his green eyes. She truly liked this man—a lot.

He seemed to grow aware of her interest and returned the scrutiny. "What's on your mind?"

She felt a quickening of her heartbeat. What kind of friendship did they have now?

As if reading her thoughts, he reached out and touched her arm. His fingers gently caressed her skin, while his gaze caressed her face. His smile slowly changed, growing more thoughtful, more serious. "I missed you these past years," he said. "More than I would have thought possible."

Another group of camera-laden senior citizens blazed by them on the sidewalk.

"I missed you, too," she said. But she didn't feel comfortable going further. Not yet. Not with all the unanswered questions hanging over their heads. "Let's get Justin's soda to him before it loses its cool."

Chapter Fifteen

Carissa Cooper jerked and cried out. Her eyes flew open. A steel bed railing met her gaze, and past that, a window overlooking a familiar garden, bursting with autumn colors. It was okay. She lay safe in a bed in a new addition at the clinic. She'd been so tired, she'd fallen asleep as soon as Taylor had brought her back from the CT truck.

Someone touched the side of her face from behind her, and she flinched. The hand felt cool and dry, and Carissa recognized Melva's chubby fingers, with peach nail polish.

Melva stepped around the side of the bed. "Awake, sweetheart?"

"Yeah." Although she was still groggy, she noticed the green-and-black plaid workshirt her stepmom wore. It was Dad's. And her hair was out of place. And she wasn't wearing any makeup. Wow. "You okay, Melva?"

Melva chuckled gently. "I'm supposed to be asking you that." She leaned in close, as if she wanted to take Carissa in her arms. "How about it? Head still hurt?"

"Some."

Melva took Carissa's hand and squeezed it. "You're not shaking the way you were. And you don't feel as feverish. You were so hot." She turned to look at someone out of Carissa's range of vision. "Doctor, what did you say her temperature was when you checked it last?"

"It's only about a hundred and one now," came the rich, comforting voice of Karah Lee Fletcher.

Carissa peered around the end of a privacy curtain and saw the doctor sitting at the far end of the long room, hunched over a desk. She looked like she was going to be staying around awhile. *Thank you, Jesus.*

Not that she was afraid of Melva . . .

"What do you remember, sweetie?" Melva's hand tightened on Carissa's. "Can you tell me what happened?"

"I already told you what I remembered." She didn't want to lie to Melva. In the first place Melva would catch it immediately. In the second place, it bugged her to lie. It wasn't a Christian thing to do. But right now she couldn't say anything.

She looked up into her stepmom's round face and those brown eyes that always seemed to see what she was thinking without a word being said. What was it that had been so familiar about that person last night? It all seemed like a dream now. A horrible dream.

Melva wiped the perspiration from Carissa's forehead. "We can't understand why you went back to the sawmill. Did you hear something? Or maybe you—"

"I can't remember it all."

"Yes, but anything you might be able to—"

"I might've heard something." Carissa said it before she could stop herself, and she saw the startled expression on Melva's face.

160

"What did you hear?" her stepmom asked slowly.

The redheaded doctor across the room looked up from her work and frowned at Melva.

Carissa swallowed past a dry throat. "Could I have some water? I'm pretty thirsty."

The doctor got up and crossed the room. "Of course you can." She reached for a pitcher on the bedside stand.

"Carissa," Melva said in her "take no prisoners" voice, "what did you hear?"

"Oh, you know, the wind on the trees or something," Carissa said. "And I thought I heard a horse. Did Gypsy jump the fence again?"

Melva's eyes narrowed slightly. "She was where she belonged when I looked this morning."

Karah Lee leaned over, stuck a thermometer in Carissa's ear, pulled it back, looked at it, and nodded. "Even better. Bertie's keeping something warm for you over in her kitchen. You want us to call her and have it brought over?"

Okay, this was getting better. "Black walnut pie?"

Karah Lee laughed. "How about saving that for dessert? She made you some chicken and dumplings. She said it was your favorite."

Carissa nodded. Bertie Meyer's cooking had made the Lakeside Bed and Breakfast famous.

Karah Lee stepped to the open door and leaned out into the hallway. "Hey, Blaze, will you call Bertie and tell her she can bring that food over for Carissa now?"

"I can do that," Melva said. "I'll just walk down to the Lakeside and—"

"Nope, that's okay," Karah Lee said as she stepped back over to Carissa's bedside. "Fawn is home from school by now, and she's helping out in the kitchen today."

"All right!" Carissa said. "Fawn is so cool." And Justin had a huge crush on her, which Melva would never find out about, because if she did, Justin would freak for sure. He'd gotten so secretive lately.

While Karah Lee listened to Carissa's breathing with a stethoscope, Carissa avoided looking at Melva. Sometimes, Melva overreacted to things. Like yesterday with Mom and the problem with Justin. Melva had gotten way too freaked about the problem with Justin, and so had Dad. Why couldn't they treat Justin normally anymore? It wasn't as if he'd become a different person. He was still Justin, only weirder.

"Is anybody else here?" Carissa asked when Karah Lee completed her exam. "Is Noelle here? Or Nathan?"

"The whole family's here, honey," Melva said. "Daddy and Justin, Pearl and Jill. They're waiting to see if you're going to be okay, but they didn't want to disturb you while you were sleeping. You want to see them, don't you? The doctor said you could—"

"No!" The sharp reply seemed to carry through the room and out the door, and Melva got that hurt look on her face. Carissa hadn't meant to say it so loudly, but she couldn't help it. She'd promised herself she wouldn't let on that anything had happened. Before she could think what to say, someone knocked at the open door.

"Can we come in?" It was Noelle.

When she and Nathan entered the room, Carissa sank back against her pillow with a sigh. *Thank you, Jesus.*

Nathan followed Noelle into the large hospital-style room, which had only recently been completed by the contractor. He heard the deep tone of Cecil's voice coming through the door of Cheyenne's office. The sheriff had arrived in the waiting room moments ago, wearing a freshly pressed uniform and carrying a clipboard and a tape recorder. He was questioning Cecil now. Justin, Jill and Pearl were scheduled to speak with him next.

Greg was a conscientious sheriff, and he could be trusted to be discreet, but he would also be thorough. He had already spoken with Nathan and Noelle privately. Soon, he would need to interview Melva. Taylor Jackson, the ranger, was already out at Cedar Hollow, following up on Nathan and Noelle's story.

This room had all the amenities of a hospital ward with three beds. Currently, only one bed was occupied, but Nathan had overheard Blaze mention that they were expecting another overnight patient later in the day.

Carissa, the lone patient, looked better than she had when they'd last seen her. Her face was still flushed with fever, but her eyes held a livelier expression, more typically Carissa.

Melva gave them a tired grin from Carissa's bedside. "Hey, you two."

"Is this a bad time?" Noelle asked.

163

"Nope, I was just trying to get this child to spill more details. I think she's had too much sleep and she's acting a little hyper."

"Noelle, where've you been?" Carissa asked.

Noelle stepped to Carissa's bedside and grasped the girl's outstretched hand. "Talking with the sheriff."

Melva yawned and stretched. "I think I'll get some fresh air before my interview. You two going to be here a few minutes?"

"Yeah, why don't you go to Jill's and get some rest after the interview?" Noelle suggested.

"I don't want to leave Carissa alone."

"We'll make sure she isn't alone," Nathan said. "You haven't had any sleep, and Carissa's safe now."

Melva hesitated in the doorway. "Maybe I *should* lie down for a little while." She looked down at her clothes. "And I could use some freshening up, if you know what I mean." With a final fluttering of her fingers toward her stepdaughter, she turned and walked down the hallway.

Nathan strolled over to the door and closed it quietly. "Thanks for watching her for us, Karah Lee. I know you had other work to do."

"Not a problem." The tall, redheaded doctor washed her hands at the sink in the corner of the room, and tugged two paper towels from the dispenser. "When do I get in on the mystery?"

Carissa sat up in bed. "Mystery?"

"About what happened to you last night." Noelle leaned over the bed and gave Carissa a quick hug. "I

164

can see you're feeling better, so we need to talk."

"Mind if I hang out and eavesdrop?" Karah Lee asked.

"Only if you promise not to tell what you hear."

"Promise." Karah Lee grinned. "You know, patient confidentiality and all that. Can I tell Taylor?"

"I wish you would." Nathan pulled a chair over for the doctor. He'd become accustomed to this woman's frankness, and he trusted her instincts.

"You should've seen them today, Karah Lee," Carissa said. "I thought I was dead. I mean, I was drowning, and the water pressure was pushing me against this rock so I couldn't swim out, and then somebody grabbed me and I thought it was the whisperer and that the whisperer was going to kill me, and—"

"Whisperer?" Karah Lee held a hand up to break the flow of Carissa's rapid-fire words. "What whisperer?"

"Her abductor," Nathan said. "What have you told the others, Carissa?"

"What others? I haven't seen any others, except Melva, and all she knows is that I fell and hit my head at the sawmill, then woke up in the cave."

"That's all?" Nathan asked.

"No." Karah Lee leaned forward with her elbows on her knees. "Carissa, you just finished telling Melva you heard something."

Carissa grimaced. "Yeah, I know. I blew it. Now she's going to be all, 'Oh, my poor baby, somebody chased you in the dark,' and she'll worry and check on me all the time, and she'll never let me out at night again until I'm, like, twenty-five."

"You mean like a real mom?" Noelle asked dryly.

Carissa dimpled. "Yeah, like that."

In spite of the seemingly lighthearted chatter, Nathan could tell Carissa was still spooked. She held tightly to Noelle's arm with both hands. Her eyes were a little too bright, her movements a little exaggerated. False bravado.

"Just go over it one more time for us," Nathan said.

"The truth or the story we're telling the others?" Carissa asked.

"The truth. We'll tell the others about it soon enough."

"Okay, fine." Carissa gazed toward the ceiling, and recited in a singsong voice, "Someone chased me in the dark, then I fell and hit my head, and whoever it was took me to the cave. And you know what happened after you found me. Somebody pulled the rope out of the sinkhole so we'd starve to death in the cave and our corpses would rot and—"

"Okay, I get your drift," Nathan said.

"Nobody would've come looking for us there and there's no way they would've heard our screams before we became too weak to scream. We'd've suffered for weeks before we finally died."

Nathan saw Noelle wince. Carissa was having decidedly morbid thoughts. She was going to need some generous doses of healthy reassurance after this ordeal.

"We're trying to play detective, Carissa," Noelle said. "And we're doing all we can to make sure this doesn't happen again. Help us all you can, okay?"

"Okay." Carissa settled her head back onto the pillow, then winced in pain and sat up again. "That pillow hurts the lump on my skull."

Noelle pressed the button to raise the bed into an upright position. "That better?"

"Yep. Karah Lee says I'm probably going to spend the night here." Carissa glanced at the doctor. "What if someone tries to get to me again?"

"We won't leave you alone," Karah Lee said. "There's always a doctor or nurse here if we have patients in the ward."

"But you can't stay by my bed all the time."

"Noelle or I will take turns sitting with you tonight, so no one will have another chance to hurt you," Nathan said.

"Carissa," Noelle said, "we need to know more about last night, before you heard anyone. I know your dad wanted you to fetch a ledger at the mill."

"Right, because they couldn't find some information they were trying to enter into the computer, and the books weren't balanced or something. I wasn't paying that much attention because I was still mad about Mom, and I was trying to get more information for my report—you know, the one I told you about? I guess I got the wrong ledger, anyway. They wanted one from this year."

"So that's it?" Noelle asked. "They just sat around the living room twiddling their thumbs while you walked to the sawmill alone in the dark?"

"No, I think Jill was going to the old place to see if she could find some records in the attic. Dad was heating up the calculator." Carissa glanced toward the door. "Nobody wants to tell me what's wrong, but there's money missing."

"Any idea how much?"

Carissa shook her head. "I heard Melva and Daddy yelling at each other a couple of weeks ago, after Justin and I went to bed. You know, Aunt Pearl told me once that Melva doesn't always keep the books exactly straight. She thinks Melva ought to keep a double check on herself to see where the money goes. Melva says Pearl's always picking on her, and that she'll never be able to do it the way Pearl did." Carissa made a wry face. "Anyway, they're trying to keep Pearl from finding out about this missing money, because she'll freak."

"Where was everyone else when you left for the sawmill?" Nathan prompted.

"Justin was supposed to be doing his homework in his room. Takes him so much time, because of his—" she glanced at Noelle, then Karah Lee "—his problem. He keeps checking his work. But he's getting great grades. I'd get great grades, too, if I checked my work fifteen or twenty times."

"What about Melva?" Nathan asked. "Where was she? And where was Pearl?"

Carissa shrugged. "Melva went to bed with a headache before I went to my room, and you know Aunt Pearl. She goes to bed when the geese go to roost,

I think. Anyway, she doesn't go out after that."

Noelle leaned forward and adjusted the blanket over Carissa's arm. "Honey, this morning before we found you, Melva showed me a poem that she had found in your bedroom. It was in free verse about silence and darkness and the dying moon, nothing like your usual poetry. I know this probably has nothing to do with what happened to you last night, but Melva seemed to think it might be connected."

Carissa frowned. "I didn't write any—" Her brow cleared. "Oh, that. You mean that scary-weird poem? I didn't write that. I found it up in the attic in the old house with a bunch of your school papers and report cards. I thought you wrote it."

Noelle shook her head. "Not me."

"That old house might be where the records from Harvey's office are stored," Nathan said. "Did you look through those, Carissa?"

"Yeah, after they delivered them at the sawmill, but I didn't find anything I could use. It was just a bunch of numbers. I'm looking for the good stuff, like the stories about things that happened. My social studies teacher told me I could probably get written reports from the claims adjuster with the insurance company and the police and newspaper articles. I thought maybe somebody in the family might've saved some of that stuff."

"Can you remember if you saw the accounting records up in the attic when you went back?" Noelle asked.

"Yeah," Carissa said. "I tripped over the box and bruised my shoulder, and Melva got all freaked and told me to be more careful, and I sassed her and Dad made me apologize and Melva told him to stop interfering in our relationship because she could handle—"

"Okay, let's get back to last night," Nathan said. "You told us you'd heard whispers."

"Yeah, but I couldn't tell what was said. Later, after I woke up in the cave, I could hear more clearly, and the whisperer called my name and then got all freaked that I was gone." Carissa hesitated, looked at Noelle. "I still think there was something familiar about that person."

"Can you remember any more?" Nathan asked.

Carissa squeezed her eyes shut, as if attempting to jump-start her brain. Then she opened her eyes and shook her head. "Nothing."

"No idea about why the familiarity?" he asked.

"Well, in the first place, whoever it was knew my name. But I think it could've been the sound of the voice. Or maybe it was the accent, or . . . I don't know. It's like a dream, you know?"

Someone knocked at the door, and Carissa reached for Noelle's hand.

"It's okay, sweetie," Karah Lee said as she opened the door. "It's food."

Fawn Morrison walked in carrying a covered tray. "Hey, squirt! You sure go to a lot of trouble to play hooky from school." The slender, cheeky seventeen-year-old, with her super-short brown hair and gamine

170

grin, seemed to take over the room when she crossed to the bed and set the food on the hospital bed tray table. "Time to eat."

While Fawn and Karah Lee kept Carissa company, Noelle ushered Nathan from the room. "We need a brief powwow," she explained to Carissa. "One of us will be right back."

Noelle felt Nathan's intense interest as she gestured for him to follow her into the hallway. She closed the door behind them, then turned to him. "Can I borrow your truck for a while?"

He reached into his right front pocket for the keys. "What's up?"

She glanced down the temporarily deserted hallway. She could hear the muffled voices of the sheriff, talking with Pearl in Cheyenne's office, and Cecil's voice, coming from down the hallway through the reception window, which meant the rest of the family was close by.

Keys in hand, she said, "I'm going back out to the hollow before it gets dark."

"Oh, no, you don't." Quick as a snake, he grabbed at the keys.

She jerked away and stepped back. "Keep your voice down. And don't cause a scene, or they'll wonder what's up."

He glared, leaning close to her ear. "We were just out there," he whispered. "We searched the mill and found nothing."

"I know, but Carissa's given me some ideas," Noelle said. "I want to check the attic at my old home place. I forgot all about it. The attic's as big as the living quarters. And Carissa found that poem up there. And the box from Harvey's office. What else could she have found? Something someone felt she shouldn't have?"

"She didn't say anything about—"

"She might not realize what she's found. Or maybe someone thought she found something that she didn't when she was researching that family history for school. Now's the perfect time to do some checking around, while everyone else is here in Hideaway. Nathan, until we find out differently, I don't want to imagine that anyone in my family would hurt Carissa, but it's obvious she thinks she knows her abductor. Or at least, her abductor knows her. The sheriff needs to get Cecil to release the personnel files for the sawmill employees, and someone needs to check on my ex-husband and find out if he has an alibi for last night at eight o'clock."

"We can tell Greg to do that as soon as he finishes with Pearl, but let *him* do it. You don't need to go back to Cedar Hollow tonight."

"Yes, I do, and would you lighten up a little? Taylor Jackson's there." She glanced down the hallway toward the waiting room, then decided to use the rear exit. She wasn't up to facing family right now.

Nathan followed her. "I'm not going to stay here while you traipse off to the hollow alone."

"Don't be so overcautious." She suppressed a smile at

his glare of outrage. She reached up to touch his shoulder. "Nathan, nobody's going to attack me, not with Taylor Jackson on duty. I'll be okay." Still, she couldn't deny the warmth that spread through her at his protest. "Look, if you and I both take off, Carissa will think we've abandoned her. You heard her in there. She's still terrified, and she's not covering it that well. What happens if she feels we've left her alone?"

"You stay with her and let me go. Just tell me where to search," he suggested.

"I'm the best candidate for the job, since I know the house so well." She could read his inner conflict by the worry in his eyes, and she clasped his right hand in both of hers. "Thanks for caring. It'll be dark before too long, so I've got to get going now if I want time to search."

He held her gaze for a long moment. "I'm not going to talk you out of this, am I?"

"No. If you don't let me use your truck, I'll find some other way to get out there."

He pulled his hand from hers and touched her cheek. "Be careful, Noelle."

Impulsively, she stood on tiptoe and kissed his chin, scratchy with two days' growth of beard. "I'll be back, don't worry."

Chapter Sixteen

The rain had ended by the time Noelle drove through the gate onto Cooper land and splashed through the rising level of water that gurgled over the low-water bridge. A noisy duet of crickets serenaded her from the woods with a high-pitched *cree-cree,* a sound that always accompanied autumn dusk in the Ozarks. It created a minor-key harmony with the song of tires on damp pavement and reminded Noelle of gentle autumn evenings when she was a kid, walking with Nathan along this lane, talking late into the night—or until someone called to them across the hollow to get their homework done or to go to bed.

The breeze felt good, filtering through the window. The scent of freshly washed earth and the living green forest drifted through the cab of the truck. If not for the sense of loss that Noelle associated with this place, she could almost miss it. One could be seduced into believing this was a place of peace and rest; one could be fooled.

She crested the final rise before the descent into the small valley and caught the outline of the sawmill roof against the gray sky, surrounded by the forest. The last of the daylight faded and gloom deepened around her. The breeze grew cooler, and Noelle closed the window.

She allowed her foot to slide from the accelerator. The truck hesitated before coasting down the incline, as if drawn by some invisible force more deeply into the hollow. The closer Noelle came to the mill, the more alone she felt, and the more she wished she'd let Nathan come with her.

Cedar Hollow covered a lot of territory, after all, and even as she caught sight of Taylor Jackson's light-green, mud-spackled Jeep parked in front of the sawmill, Noelle knew the ranger might be almost any-where.

Perhaps she and Nathan should have told Cecil every-thing. Couldn't *he,* at least, be trusted? Hadn't she grown up with him? Hadn't she known Melva since they were kids? Perhaps Carissa's sense of familiarity with her attacker could be explained by a scent—a cologne, or shampoo, maybe, the same brand used by someone in the family, or a friend.

The truck drifted to a stop at the bottom of the hill, and Noelle stepped on the gas and continued. She had come here to search.

But for what?

Did the past hold some clues? Was there a connection between the deaths ten years ago and her young cousin's abduction last night? Carissa had been doing research on that past when she was taken.

A hoot owl called an invocation over the shadowed evening as Noelle drove past the mill and entered a tunnel of green where the pavement ended and muddy gravel began. This lane led to Cecil and Melva's house. She hadn't gone far when a loud honk startled her so badly she slammed on the brake and cried out. Glancing out her window, she saw two geese stalking out of the woods toward her, flapping their wings in a show of bravado.

Noelle slumped against the headrest, adrenaline surging through her body. The blare of the noisy geese underlined the tension that sang through her like tight dulcimer strings.

"Back off," she told the glaring geese, waiting for the dogs to enter the fray. They didn't.

She drove past the white picket fence, then around to the backyard. Anyone arriving in the hollow wouldn't see the truck unless he or she drove to the back. And the geese down on the driveway might alert Noelle to any approach. She wouldn't count on it, but she'd listen for it, just in case.

Cecil's house was unlocked, like all the houses and buildings on Cooper land, and she glanced over her shoulder with guilty nervousness as she opened the front door on silent hinges. She knew the disarray in the living room was unusual for this household. Cecil's insistence on tidiness had been a family joke since he'd inherited this place in his twenties—when his parents, Aunt Harriet and Uncle Todd, ripped a branch from the family tree and moved to Texas to follow Todd's dream of owning a dude ranch. In fact, they had left only a few months before the accident that left Cecil in charge of the property and sawmill.

Noelle went to Carissa's bedroom and pulled open the same dresser drawer that Melva had opened this morning. Shuffling through Carissa's papers, she realized her young cousin's creative writing had improved over the past months. There were several school test papers marked with big red *A*'s, and a five-page story about her relationship with her horse. Noelle skimmed the story, then folded it and set it aside.

She still felt Carissa could have stumbled across some incriminating information during her research for her report. She certainly hadn't kept her investigation quiet. Maybe she'd spoken to others besides family—such as employees, past and present? Hideaway locals? Friends of the family?

Could the tragedies in their history have been something more than accidents?

Noelle found the poem Melva had shown her earlier and pocketed it. Leaving the room, she glanced out the kitchen window. The sky, low with clouds, had darkened to gunmetal. She quickened her steps up the staircase to the master bedroom.

Noelle's grandfather had built this house with his own hands. He had lovingly carved the oak handrail for the stairs and fitted the molding to the door casings. When Uncle Todd married Harriet, Grandpa and Grandma graciously gave them the house and moved to town, where they purchased the Victorian-style house in which Jill now lived. Although it had been Pearl's right to move into the house in town after the deaths of her brother Joseph and his wife, she'd opted to remain in her house on Cooper land, where she'd lived all her life. "It's where I belong," she'd told the rest of the family.

Noelle felt a swell of empathy for her great-aunt.

The shock of loss must have affected her even more deeply than it had the rest of the family, secluded as she had been in this hollow for most of her sixty-seven years. Jill had always contended that Pearl stayed so she could keep watch over the operations, make sure the ranch and the sawmill were running smoothly.

The last of the day's dreary illumination crept through the wall of windows in the master bedroom, the apricot sheers at the window lending their color to the light. The bedspread, too, was apricot. The delicate ornaments that decorated the elaborately carved dresser and chest of drawers showed no sign of male influence.

Noelle felt like a voyeur as she took in her surroundings. Melva had a taste for ultrafeminine decor.

She opened the dresser drawers and methodically worked her way through feminine underclothing, winter sweaters, scarves. No papers, no clues. Next she searched the bureau, glancing warily out the window, listening for any sounds of approach. She could imagine Melva's hurt reaction if she suddenly arrived home and found Noelle snooping through her private things.

The problem was, sound didn't carry well up here, not through closed windows to an upstairs bedroom. Aunt Harriet used to brag about how well the triple-paned windows blocked the sound of the whippoorwills in the wee hours of the morning.

Noelle was reaching for the headboard of the queen-size bed when a sound stopped her. Had one of the geese honked? She held her breath, listening, and heard another honk. Definitely a goose.

She opened the sliding door in the headboard, revealing a shelf that contained a stack of papers, old envelopes and a dog-eared paperback romance novel crowded into the corner. She reached for the stack of papers, only to stop, listening. The lone goose honked again.

Noelle took the papers with her to the window and peered out, praying Cecil and Melva had not decided to return home for the night.

Only silence greeted her. She could see no sign of an automobile on the muddy lane and heard no splash of tires in the slick mess. She couldn't let fear stop her now—she had to finish her search tonight, for there might not be another chance.

Remaining at the window for better light meant no need to turn on a lamp and announce her presence to anyone who might be in the hollow. She shuffled through the papers in her hand.

She stopped at Harvey Sand's return address on one of the envelopes. It was addressed simply to "Mrs. Cooper." No street address, so it obviously had been hand-delivered. The envelope was empty. Noelle shuffled through the rest of the papers and found nothing more of interest. After returning the stack to the headboard, she made a brief check of the remaining papers. Picking up the romance novel to put it back, she noted the corner of a folded sheet of paper tucked into the middle of the book. Probably just a marker. But Noelle pulled the sheet out.

It was a photocopy of a ten-year-old cashier's check in the amount of $100,000, made out to Frazier Logging Company, signed by Cecil Cooper. Across the top, someone had neatly printed: This is just the appetizer. You'll get the full course when you pay for it.

"What on earth . . . ?"

The sound of a muffled clunk startled Noelle. The paper slipped from her fingers to the bed as she jerked toward the window. A car door? She shoved the photocopy back into the book and put the papers back where she'd found them.

She raced silently out of the bedroom and down the stairs, expecting at any second to encounter her cousin and his wife walking through the front door. But no one came. And no cars were parked outside. So what had she heard?

Brush rustled beneath the trees at the edge of the backyard, and Noelle froze. She turned toward the sound and spotted a cow rubbing against the fence to get at the edges of grass that extended from the yard.

Impatient with herself, Noelle returned to the truck. She had another house to search; she couldn't afford to panic now and go speeding back to town.

The track to the old house was crowded with blackberry brambles and weeds that scraped along the muddy sides of the truck like fingernails on a chalkboard. Noelle parked, opened Nathan's glove compartment and found a hefty battery lantern. She flicked it on and blinked at the brightness, then glanced out the window at the sky. A sunset of pink and mauve cirrus clouds drifted across a section of horizon. Good. That meant the cloud cover was lifting, and the weather would clear.

The family cemetery between the old house and Noelle's parking spot was well-tended. Fifteen gravestones, dating back to the late 1800s, were clean and free of grass. Pearl had taken care of the cemetery for the past ten years, inheriting the job from her brother, just as she had inherited control of the property from him.

Noelle stepped over to the waist-high black marble monument her father had selected when her mother died. Now he lay beside her. Noelle put her hand on the smooth corner of the stone. She'd been so young when her mom had died—far too young to have the presence of mind to consider how her daddy had been affected by the loss of his wife.

Now she realized that he'd dealt with his pain by burying himself in work. Typically male. Typically Cooper. It had become a habit he'd never broken. Until his death, he spent most of his time at the mill, leaving Jill to tend to Noelle. It had been a mistake for all of them.

When Jill's classmates left for college, she had stayed home to care for Noelle, and her firm hand remained planted on her younger sister for the next three years. Even after she'd enrolled in nursing school in Springfield, Jill insisted on coming home every weekend, denying herself any extracurricular activities. In fact, Jill's rock-hard determination to oversee the nurturing, education and discipline of her little sister had led to more than one failed romance . . . and a broken engagement. In spite of all Jill's efforts—or because of them—Noelle had rebelled with a vengeance. And she was still paying the price for that rebellion, suffering the ongoing fallout from a broken marriage and a failed career.

Before going on to the old house, Noelle glanced at the inscriptions on some of the other monuments. Grandma's read: She gave all she had to the family. Grandpa's: The gifted die young.

That was a chilling thought, considering Nathan felt Noelle was gifted.

Pearl had not always seen eye-to-eye with her brother, but the epitaph obviously bore testament to the esteem in which she'd held him.

The well-worn footpath to the cemetery twisted between two tall towers of cliff, extensions of a mother cliff behind the cemetery. In the deepening dusk, shadows as dark as blackberries stained the imposing walls of dirt and rock. A knobby boulder at the edge of the left cliff seemed to stand as a sentinel over the gravestones.

As a little girl, Noelle had once been nervous about this stretch of pathway, her imagination peopling it with all kinds of monsters despite how much she and Nathan loved playing here, precisely *because* it inspired imagination. For Noelle, at times, it inspired too much. For some reason, this evening she was walking beneath the shadows of the cliffs with the same quickened heartbeat she'd felt all those years ago.

Her heart rate refused to slow down, even as she approached the old home place. She stepped up onto the wooden-planked front porch that encircled three sides of the wood-frame house. The back nestled into the face of the cliff, with barely enough room to walk.

She pushed open the front door, resisting the urge to switch on the battery lantern as she stepped inside. This had been her home for almost eighteen years; she had nothing to fear.

She needed to keep reminding herself of that. This roomy, three-bedroom house had withstood many storms in the shelter of the sturdy, clefted mountain-side that abutted it. Built nearly a century ago, it had housed generations of Coopers, as had Pearl's house a few hundred feet to the east. The hardwood floor, now buckled with age, creaked and rocked as Noelle stepped through the front room toward the bedroom. As she had expected, memories assaulted her. She remembered how empty the house had felt when Jill left for college.

The house darkened with night, and she switched on the lantern. The electricity had been disconnected after her father's death.

Carissa had found that strange poem up in the attic, and Harvey's box of records was up there as well. What else would Noelle find? For generations, Coopers had stored their surplus clothing, furniture and every other kind of junk in this attic. Could someone have stashed something that Carissa should never have discovered?

But why would anyone do that? Why not just destroy any evidence?

Noelle pulled the rope that released the sturdy attic steps, each one unfolding and falling into place with a creak-thunk-creak-thunk. Holding her lantern high to penetrate the black depths, she climbed up to the attic floor and peered around the familiar, cavernous room, with its shadowy corners and dormer windows. Wax-coated storage boxes lined the low walls. An old bed-side stand, top drawer half open, beckoned from beneath a window that shimmered in the purple-black hues of a dying sunset.

The floor creaked as she crossed to the stand and peered into the drawer. It held papers, scattered in an untidy mix, as if someone had quickly and carelessly shuffled through them. She sifted through old checks, deposit slips and two paperback novels before she found a folded bundle of ledger sheets, familiar because the sheets matched the ledger that she and Nathan had studied in the sawmill this morning. Noelle unfolded the papers and studied the neat, small printing. The dates were last year's, and the bottom line showed a good profit.

In the middle of the stack, Noelle found an envelope from the Hideaway Bank, postmarked three months after the last entry in the ledger sheets. It contained a copy of a cashier's check, signed by Melva, made out to Frazier Logging for fifteen thousand dollars. Why did Frazier Logging receive cashier's checks when the other outfits received their fees in company checks?

The trail ended, so Noelle stuffed the folded papers into the pocket of her jeans and burrowed through a storage box filled with assorted personal effects. She found one small, cloth-bound journal, containing pages of dated entries written in a familiar, barely readable script. Then Noelle spied the file box from Harvey's office. Someone must have moved it, since Carissa had recalled tripping over it, and it was well out of the way now.

Had someone checked out the contents of the box since Carissa had been here?

A downstairs floorboard creaked. Noelle stiffened, freezing in place. Someone was in the house.

Chapter Seventeen

Nathan stood in a shadowed corner of the clinic ward absently staring out the window. Lights along the shore shimmered on the surface of the lake. This large room had previously been a clothing shop next to the clinic, but earlier this summer, the building was donated to the city to be used as a medical facility.

When Cheyenne Gideon announced her intention to extend the hours, services and space of Hideaway Clinic, the town had discovered the resources to make her wishes come true, completing the expansion and new construction in a very short time. Although the clinic was not a designated hospital, that didn't prevent the citizens from treating it as such.

Carissa's deep even breathing provided a gentle harmony to the soft snores of her elderly roommate on the other side of the drawn curtain.

Eyeing the fold-out cot Blaze had provided, Nathan swung away from the window. No way could he sleep while Noelle was in the hollow, but he desperately needed rest. What was taking her so long? She'd been gone two hours, and he felt torn between being offended because she had insisted on going without him and berating himself for allowing her to browbeat him. But he couldn't leave Carissa now, and he couldn't drag the girl out of bed and take her with him.

Carissa shifted, turning on her side toward him. Just when it seemed she'd settled back into sleep, she raised her head, the delicate lines of her face—and her wide-open eyes—visible in the glow of a night-light.

"Nathan?" Her sleepy voice held an edge of panic.

"Yes, it's me." He crossed to her side. "You're safe."

"Where's Noelle?"

"Probably on her way here right now. She went out to the hollow to check on some things."

Carissa tried to sit up. "She went back there? But—"

"Why don't you lie back down and close your eyes? We'll wake your roommate if we keep talking."

The girl lay back, but her eyes remained open. She shifted to her side and kicked off her top sheet, then sighed with impatience. "How long has it been dark?

Shouldn't she already be back?"

"Any time. It hasn't been dark long."

Carissa raised her head again. "Really, I mean it. Something might be wrong. Can't you check? What about her cell phone?"

"Not a good idea, especially if she's trying to keep a low profile."

Carissa grimaced and nodded. "Okay, but can't you go find her?"

"She took my truck," he said dryly.

"Take Karah Lee's car. She lives down the street."

He sighed. This kid argues as well as Noelle ever could. "I can't leave you alone, Cis, you know that. And you know why. We'll wait a little while before we call out the backup forces, okay? Besides, Karah Lee's car probably wouldn't make it over the low-water bridge by now." Still, he might reconsider if Noelle didn't come back in the next fifteen minutes.

Carissa took his hand. "Nathan, I'm scared."

The steady snoring softened in the next bed. Nathan and Carissa stared at each other in waiting silence. The snores deepened once more.

"I've remembered something else that happened," she whispered.

"What's that?"

She crooked her finger at him and he leaned close. "You know that report I'm doing on the family history?"

"Of course. You grilled me about it like a seasoned newspaper reporter."

"I saw Harvey Sand drive up to the sawmill a couple of Sundays ago, when Melva was down there catching up on some office work? I decided to talk to Harvey about the history, because he'd been the accountant for the business for so long? But when I reached the building, I heard shouting and decided not to go in."

"Someone was actually shouting?"

"Well, okay, maybe not shouting, but I could sure tell Melva was mad."

"Melva?"

Carissa nodded. "Yeah. I heard her say, 'We can't afford that! Are you crazy? You wouldn't take that kind of chance, or you'd end up in prison, right beside my husband!'"

"You remember those words?"

Carissa nodded. "I wrote it down so I would."

Nathan digested this in silence. What was going on here? "Could you hear Harvey, too?"

"Not as well. He kept shushing Melva, but I did hear him say, 'I'm not the one who'll rot in prison.' Or something like that. I couldn't write fast enough to get it all down. But then I heard a crash, glass breaking, I think, and Harvey came running out of the office and almost tripped over me. He didn't even stop. I thought maybe he'd hurt Melva, so I ran inside to see if she was okay, and there she was, standing by the desk, crying. Then Justin sneaked up behind me and scared me so bad I practically had a heart attack. He took me by the shoulders and shushed me and pushed me out

188

the door before I could even say anything to Melva. Like I was a little kid."

"Did you hear what happened then, between Justin and Melva?"

"Nope. I ran to the house."

"Did you talk to either of them about it later?" Nathan asked.

Carissa shook her head. "I don't think Melva even saw me, and Justin's been all quiet and weirder than ever."

"Did you talk to anyone else about it?"

"Nope. Melva was all crying and everything after that, and I decided I'd better give her a break, especially since she and Dad've been arguing a lot lately."

A soft movement at the doorway interrupted them. A band of light widened as the door opened slowly.

Nathan stood up, placing himself between Carissa's bed and the entryway. The door opened farther and more light spilled inside to silhouette a tall, broad-shouldered figure.

"Carissa?" the man's whisper sounded like a growl.

Nathan relaxed slightly. "Cecil."

There was a long, taut pause, then a heavy exhalation of breath. "Nathan, what are you doing here?"

"I felt like keeping Carissa company for a while."

Cecil stepped through the threshold, the shadows of the room contrasting against the light from the hallway to throw the outline of his brooding gaze in sharp relief. The bulk of his shoulders seemed to block the light. He glanced at the curtain that provided visual privacy but no sound barrier from the next bed. He frowned at his daughter. "You insisted you didn't want anybody to stay with you."

"I couldn't bring myself to leave her alone in case she woke up tonight," Nathan said, before the girl could respond. "After what she went through . . ." He shrugged.

There was a short pause. Then: "Good thinking." Cecil did not disguise the edge in his tone. "Comes with the pastoral training, I suppose?"

"Of course." Though Cecil was two years older than Nathan and Noelle, he had often been a part of their childhood adventures in the hollow. Cecil had a fun, social side when he made an effort—which he clearly wasn't doing now. He obviously had a lot on his mind lately.

He strolled over to his daughter's bedside and placed a hand on her forehead. "How're you feeling, punkin?"

"I'm fine, Dad. Just tired and sore."

"No more breathing problems?"

"Nope. Karah Lee says I just inhaled too much water. They gave me a treatment, and I'm feeling better."

"Why don't we let Nathan go home and I'll stay here with you? I know he's as tired as I am."

"I told you I was fine."

Carissa did whiney really well when she wanted to, Nathan noted, suppressing a grin.

"Nathan's just waiting for Noelle to bring his truck back, and you're tired, too, Dad."

Cecil turned his frowning attention back to Nathan.

"Noelle's got your truck? I told her she could use our car if she needed it. Where'd she go?"

"Errands."

"Jill said Joel was back in Springfield. Tell me Noelle didn't go traipsing back up to Springfield to confront him."

"Why would she do that?" Nathan asked softly.

Cecil shrugged. "Sounds like something she'd do. The sheriff sent someone up to have a little visit with Joel and see if he has a decent alibi for last night."

"Any report on that?"

Cecil snorted. "Said he was in church. That's unlikely, though, on a Thursday night, so they're still checking out his story. I wouldn't put anything past that picklehead. Noelle staying at your house tonight?" Typical Cecil. He had a habit of setting up his listener with distracting conversation, then slipping in a pointed question. Jill and Nathan weren't the only ones, apparently, who were protective of Noelle. No wonder she was hesitant about coming back to Hideaway.

"You know better," Nathan said calmly.

Eleven years ago, when Nathan had returned to Hideaway as a pastor, Cecil had made it obvious he did not approve of his childhood friend's profession, though he remained friendly. Something in Cecil had turned bitter, as if he blamed God for the breakup of his first marriage, and possibly even for the sawmill tragedy. The change of heart had distressed Nathan, because it appeared Cecil had abandoned the Christian faith of his childhood.

But lately Nathan didn't think that abandonment was going to last forever. In recent weeks, he'd noticed less antagonism toward God in Cecil, and more questioning. A good sign, though not always comforting, since Nathan was most often expected to answer those questions. Cecil had a habit of trying to catch Nathan at a disadvantage, as if playing a game of spiritual sparring, testing him to make sure he practiced what he preached. Or, at least, what he used to preach.

"How did it go with the sheriff today?" Nathan asked.

"Nothing new." Cecil's voice had always been deep, but fatigue and anxiety about his daughter had roughened it until it seemed to vibrate the rafters.

Carissa sat up in bed. "What did he ask you, Dad?"

"Just if we'd noticed you talking to any of the workers at the mill, or to the ranch hands or any new friends, maybe some older kid at school."

"I don't talk to any of the sawmill employees," Carissa said. "You don't like me at the sawmill when it's running. And the ranch hands have been too busy to talk lately."

"That's what I told the sheriff," Cecil said. "What about kids at school? Anyone seem strange to you? Anybody scare you?"

Carissa shook her head.

"They asked about Justin's friends." Cecil glanced at Nathan, clearing his throat, and Nathan understood the message. He hated that he understood. Was Justin a suspect simply because he had an overt quirk in his personality?

"Why would he ask you about Justin's friends?" Carissa asked.

"You know Greg. He's got a suspicious nature. That's what makes him a good sheriff." Cecil focused more closely on his daughter's face. "He seems to be working under the assumption that you were abducted, Cis."

Carissa blinked up at her father innocently. "I haven't remembered anything else since the last time you asked me about last night, Dad."

The girl could act. Nathan made a note to remember that in the future.

"You'll tell me if you think of anything, won't you?" Cecil asked her.

She nodded.

"Okay." He paused, shooting another quick glance at Nathan. "Well, I guess I could use a few winks. You sure you're gonna be okay, Cis?"

"Yes, Daddy. See you in the morning."

Noelle waited in complete darkness, listening for another squeak of the floorboards below. She strained to hear a clue that the intruder knew she was there. But a Black Angus bull could be running through the house and she wouldn't hear it over the beating of her heart.

The floorboards squeaked once more, and her whole body stiffened. Surely it was Taylor Jackson patrolling? She should call out and let him know she was up here.

But something kept her from it.

Footsteps creaked with painful slowness through the

front room, toward the kitchen in back, closer to the steps hanging down from the attic entry. Noelle held her breath. *Oh, Lord. What have I done? Why didn't I check with You before making this crazy trip out to the hollow alone?* When the footsteps stopped just below the attic entrance, the silence lengthened. She knew she couldn't pretend not to be here.

Before whoever it was started up those steps, she would have to bluff, somehow. She couldn't let on how frightened she felt.

Noelle picked up the heavy battery lantern from the floor and straightened. Taking a deep breath, she stepped forward briskly.

"Nathan, I'm up here," she called, striving to sound casual. "You're late. I found that poem we talked about. I think I'll take it to Carissa and let her have it, since she seemed to like it so much." She switched on the lantern. "You should have been up here to watch the sunset, it was beautiful." She aimed the beam down the attic entrance. It reflected off the steps and spotlighted the empty floor below. "Nathan? Come on up here for a minute. I saw some old pictures I'd like to have framed."

Thrusting the light down through the entry, she illuminated the kitchen. The room was empty. She waited, then heard a sound that her chatter had been covering—light footfalls rushing out the front door, across the porch and down the wooden steps.

So it wasn't Taylor. He would have answered immediately. Someone else was getting away. She needed to know who'd been here.

Praying for courage, Noelle dived down the attic steps, skipped the last riser, jumped to the floor and dashed to the open front door. She stopped on the threshold, holding her breath, listening.

Brush crackled near the old path that led to Pearl's house. Noelle aimed the lantern in that direction and ran toward the sound, holding her light high. All she needed was a glimpse. Then she would know who'd abducted Carissa.

Wouldn't she? Who else but Carissa's attacker would be running away from her?

She paused at the spot where the path entered the woods, no longer hearing any rustling in the brush ahead.

She peered into the thick blackness, lightened only a little by the thin crescent moon peeking through the trees. The darkness was so thick, it seemed to swallow the light from the lantern. She hoped Nathan kept these batteries charged.

Someone waited in those woods.

Chapter Eighteen

Carissa didn't like spending the night in the clinic. Sure, it was going to be cool to tell all her friends about it—as one of the first overnight patients in the new section, she'd milk some good attention. Maybe even write about it in the school paper. Even better, now she could make herself a part of the history paper she was writing.

But there was too much going on for her to be lying here in bed trying to get well, especially since both of the doctors said she was in "surprisingly good shape, considering . . ." They only wanted to watch her for any signs of developing pneumonia.

The patient in the bed on the other side of the curtain sounded like a high-speed wood saw, making it hard for her to sleep. And Noelle still wasn't back. Nathan sat staring out the window, trying hard to act like he wasn't worried, but Carissa could tell by the stiffness of his shoulders and his silence that he wasn't relaxed.

"Nathan?"

He glanced over his shoulder at her. "Aren't you asleep yet?"

"Nope. Do you think maybe I could go up and stay with Noelle for a few days when she goes back home to Springfield, after I get out of this place? Then I'll be safe."

"You don't know that."

"I think I would."

"Others might not agree."

Carissa sighed. "Melva wouldn't let me go, anyway. She wants me in school if I have a pulse and am breathing."

"Sounds like the best place for you."

"She won't let me go see my own mom, so why let me go to Springfield with Noelle?"

"It isn't the same thing at all," Nathan said gently.

"But if I could just stay at Noelle's a couple of days, maybe. To recover, you know? She's a nurse. She could take care of me. I mean, if it hadn't been for you and Noelle, I wouldn't've been found for another couple hundred years, probably, and by then my white skeleton would've become one with the rocks, or would—"

"Carissa, where did you get that morbid imagination?"

"Noelle. Dad says I take after her. I've heard him and Melva arguing about that. Melva doesn't think a personality can be inherited. Dad says she's wrong."

"I think personality can be inherited."

"Me, too. I am a lot like Noelle, aren't I?"

"Yes."

"So you think I'll be a nurse someday?"

He hesitated. "Not necessarily."

"Why isn't Noelle a nurse anymore?"

He glanced over his shoulder at her, flexing his shoulders as if they were stiff. "Why are you suddenly so talkative?"

"Because I can't sleep, and I'm tired of thinking so much."

He returned to his study of the moonlight. "Noelle's a nurse. She always will be."

"You know what I mean. She doesn't *work* as a nurse anymore. Jill wants her to come back down to Hideaway and work at the clinic, but one of my friends at school—you know, Lacey, she's Junior Short's cousin who moved here from Arkansas last year?—she said Jill shouldn't try to convince Noelle to come work here because Noelle had already blown it and proved she couldn't be trusted. How did she blow it?"

Nathan turned away, but not before she saw his flash of annoyance in the dim glow of the streetlight. Nathan hated small-town gossip. So did Carissa . . . to a point. But it sure did help her fill in the blanks in her report, especially when she talked to the old locals, like Bertie Meyer.

"Never mind," she said. "I'll ask Noelle."

"No, you won't, and stop trying to manipulate me. It isn't an attractive trait, and Noelle's job circumstances are no one's business but her own."

She blinked at the sharpness of his tone. "Yeah, but a good researcher makes everything her business."

He turned away from the window with obvious reluctance and stepped to Carissa's bedside. "Noelle would be hurt to know you've been talking about her behind her back."

"But I'm not saying anything bad about her."

"You're repeating hurtful comments made by someone else in order to dig up more information. That's called gossip."

Boy, he was cranky tonight. "Okay, fine. Besides, I know why she lost her last job—because her stupid ex-husband made crank calls and told lies about her. But Lacey Short says Junior says Noelle was fired from her first job because she was arrested for possession of—"

"Junior Short needs to put a plug in that mouth of his," Nathan snapped, loudly.

There was sudden silence in the other bed, and for several long seconds there was no other sound.

When the snoring filled the room again, Nathan sighed. "I'm sorry, Carissa, but no one has a right to dredge up dirt about something that happened years ago, and that includes you."

Carissa swallowed hard and stared up at the dark ceiling. "So it's true?"

Silence.

Carissa closed her eyes. *Oh, Jesus, please, no. My cousin Noelle wouldn't do drugs like that, would she? Please let this not be true. I'm sorry for listening to gossip.*

"I know Junior and Lacey probably don't mean to make trouble," Nathan said at last, "but there's never a good reason to smear someone's name with details about their past mistakes."

"Okay."

"Why don't you give the research a rest for a few days?"

Carissa grimaced. She wasn't really interested in what Lacey Short, the school bigmouth, had to say about anything.

There was a silence, then Nathan sighed. "Carissa, as you get older you're going to discover that pretty much everyone you meet—and everyone you love—has something in their past they're ashamed of, that causes them pain. Don't multiply that pain by reminding them of something they're trying to overcome."

Carissa swallowed and closed her eyes. Last night, she'd nearly died because of some crazy person— someone she probably knew. Dad and Melva were fighting a lot lately, and now she'd discovered Noelle had once been arrested for possession of drugs. Oh, yeah, and Justin was just plain wacked lately, which was no big deal even though everybody seemed to think it was.

What next?

Noelle swallowed hard. Why was she even out here? Why hadn't she let Nathan come instead? She could have stayed with Carissa at the clinic, where there were people around, and help was just a shout away. Sure, Nathan wouldn't have known where to search, but he was bigger, stronger and he had more common sense. Most of the time . . .

Someone had run from the house and was crouching in the woods.

Why?

Impatience and curiosity overcame some of her fear. "This is silly," she said aloud, speaking to the trees that towered over her. "This is Noelle, you know, not some stranger. Come on out."

For a moment, there was no response. Then some brush rustled to the left of the path. Noelle resisted the urge to shine her light directly at the figure that stepped from between two low-hanging branches.

"I've got to admit, you gave me a good scare, kiddo," came Pearl's gruff voice.

Noelle felt her legs go weak with relief and surprise. "Aunt Pearl!"

"Everyone else is in town. I thought I was the only one who came back." Pearl walked into the path of the light and strolled toward Noelle, her hand straying toward her chest out of habit.

Noelle aimed the light low. "Why didn't you just come on up to the attic when you recognized my voice? Why did you run away?"

Pearl stopped several yards away, arms crossed over her chest, slightly turned away, as if she might bolt. She shrugged, her movements stiff. "Guess I wasn't expecting it to be you. All I saw was that ranger's Jeep up by the sawmill."

"So I startled you?"

"That's right."

Noelle heard an unusual tremor in the older woman's voice. Tough, blunt-spoken Pearl Cooper was afraid of her great-niece. Noelle didn't have to read body language to recognize the fear in Pearl's blue eyes.

A sudden thought sent a wave of disbelief up Noelle's spine. "You can't think *I* had anything to do with Carissa's disappearance last night?"

No reply.

"Aunt Pearl, how *could* you suspect me of hurting Carissa?"

Pearl snorted. "Didn't say that, did I? I'm just curious about how you found her so fast, is all. That fact makes me nervous, and don't try to give me the God talk the way Nathan did Cecil today."

"I don't know any other way to explain what happened," Noelle said softly, holding Pearl's gaze across the lantern light. "I'm not a kidnapper. I was at work around the time Carissa was abducted."

201

"Like I said, Noelle, I didn't say I thought you'd abducted Carissa."

"So what *did* you think?"

Pearl studied the ground for a moment, then, "Come with me. I want to show you something." She brushed past Noelle and plunged through a stand of under-growth, heading toward the cemetery.

Noelle hesitated. Pearl turned back, hands on hips. "Well? You coming?"

"Yeah, coming." Noelle followed her great-aunt through the darkness past the house, between the looming cliffs to the cemetery.

Pearl took the lantern from Noelle and aimed it at some of the weathered tombstones. "Ever read these inscriptions when you were growing up, Noelle?"

"Sure. I even stopped here on my way to the old house tonight."

Pearl stepped to her brother's stone. "Ever wonder about this one? 'The gifted die young.'"

"Of course."

Pearl grunted. "Your grandfather had gifts of all kinds. He could run the sawmill with his eyes closed, and he could pick the right employee for the right job. Most of all, though, were the things he knew that he shouldn't have known."

Noelle waited for her to explain.

"Thought I was just an overly emotional old lady for having that inscribed, didn't you?"

"You're only sixty-seven, Aunt Pearl, and you're in better shape than some of the men at the sawmill. I've never thought of you as overly emotional. What was it Grandpa knew? What are you talking about?"

"Like I said, my brother was one of those people gifted to know things others miss." Pearl reached down to pull up a stalk of grass beside the stone. "I had that inscribed because those were the words I always used to tell him, and he always laughed. It got to be a joke with us."

"What got to be a joke?" Noelle asked. "What gift are you talking about? What kinds of things did he know?"

"He called it a spiritual gift. I called it nonsense, but I couldn't ignore that it happened."

"You mean this knowledge?"

Again, Pearl fixed Noelle with a stare. "Most folks don't believe that, but it's true, and don't look at me like I'm talkin' crazy. Joseph didn't know to keep quiet about what he knew, and I guess somebody didn't want him telling."

Pearl was talking in riddles, a habit that had always driven Noelle nuts. For a moment, her aunt's words didn't make sense. And then they struck Noelle with the impact of truth. "Aunt Pearl, you can't be saying that the accident ten years ago—"

"There wasn't any accident . . . even though I might've said so in the past."

Noelle felt as if she'd been kicked in the stomach. She leaned against the gravestone and stared toward the cliffs. "That . . . special talent Grandpa had, do you know of anyone else in the family who has it?"

"Maybe. I wouldn't go tellin' it around if I did. People'd think I wasn't all there. Folks don't believe in stuff like that. Us Coopers've had enough gossip about us as it is, what with the curse and all."

"The curse?"

"They've got a new name for it these days. It's called that Obsessive-Compulsive Disorder."

Noelle had never heard her great-aunt talk this way before. Pearl had always talked about the best way to run the sawmill business, how to handle an ailing cow, what kind of herbal brew to fix for a bad cough. She'd never talked about curses or gifts. So why was she talking about them now?

"Someone with the gift can identify the curse in someone else," Pearl said.

"OCD isn't a curse, Aunt Pearl, it's just a benign psychological disorder."

"Benign?" Pearl peered at her through narrowed eyes. "You know that for a fact? It twists the mind, makes people think frightening thoughts. You don't know how Justin suffers, and how others in the family have suffered before him. You don't know the prejudice involved." She shook her head and gazed around at the tombstones. "Some of our own kin didn't even try to understand."

"So you're saying OCD runs in the family as well," Noelle said. That was no surprise.

"That's right. It destroys normal life. The poor sufferers get stuck with such overwhelming habits and fears, they spend hours a day doing silly things like washing their hands or checking fifty times to make sure all the doors are locked. In our family, when the sufferers tried to cover up their problem, there always seemed to be someone around pointing it out, making them feel even worse, calling attention to the problem."

"Someone with the gift?" Noelle asked.

Pearl nodded.

"Grandpa had the gift?"

Pearl nodded again. She reached out with both hands and grasped Noelle's shoulders, leaning close enough that Noelle caught the scent of rosemary that always clung to the older woman from her herb garden. "So do you, but don't you tell. You've probably already given yourself away, finding Carissa like you did." Her fingers tightened on Noelle's flesh. Her voice lowered to a whisper. "You watch that sister of yours, hear?"

Okay, this was too much input. Noelle wished she could shut down.

"She's wily, that one is," Pearl said. "She's got a temper, too, quick and hard while it lasts, though it burns itself out fast enough. She pushed me down the sawmill steps one day when she caught me down there showing you around. Knocked me out colder than spring water. Remember?"

Noelle hesitated, then nodded. "I was there." It was the first time she remembered being frightened of Jill's intensity.

"You've got a good memory, then, because you were just a little thing, about five years old. Jill was always way too possessive of you, didn't want anyone else near you. Lately she's taken a special interest in Carissa. I know she's your closest kin, and you love her an' all, but you just keep an eye on her."

Noelle suddenly felt overwhelmed. She didn't want to hear more.

"You goin' back to town tonight?" Pearl asked.

"Yes, I don't want to leave Carissa alone."

"I'm stayin' right here in the holler. You be sure and call me if anything comes up, you hear?"

"I will, Aunt Pearl."

As Noelle made her way back to Hideaway, she felt as if all sense of security had been knocked from under her. It was a feeling she'd experienced before in her life, and had hoped never to face again.

How must Carissa be feeling?

Noelle had been aware of some deep-seated jealousy between Jill and Pearl for many years after Mom died, and she knew that, from time to time, Pearl had attempted to take responsibility for helping raise Noelle. Jill had pitched a fit about it until Dad gave in and told Pearl to back off.

Was the rivalry still rearing its ugly head after all these years?

What other explanation could there be?

Chapter Nineteen

Noelle crept along the clinic corridor and entered the darkened room. She hesitated in the open doorway while her eyes adjusted to the glow of the night-light, and she saw movement of ghost-white drift from the bed nearest the window.

"Noelle!" came an eager whisper. The ghost emerged from the gloom, arms outstretched, dark, curly hair falling into her face as Carissa flung herself into Noelle's arms. The enthusiastic embrace nearly knocked her sideways.

"Hey! I thought you were sick," Noelle exclaimed as she caught her young cousin in a loving hug.

"Headache's all I've got. Where've you been?" Carissa's arm snaked around Noelle's waist, clinging like a sprung steel trap.

"That's what I'd like to know." A darker shadow rose from the chair beside the window. Nathan. "You said you wouldn't stay after dark." He, too, kept his voice low so he wouldn't disturb the elderly patient who slept loudly in the other bed.

"Sorry," Noelle whispered. "I didn't mean to be gone so long, but I got sidetracked." With her arm around Carissa's shoulders, she walked the girl back to her bed and pulled down the covers. "Hop in," she whispered. "If Karah Lee finds you running around like this, she'll have our hides, and we've already got enough problems." She glanced at Nathan. "We can't afford more."

"What did you do in the hollow?" Carissa asked.

"I . . . visited the old house tonight, and Pearl came in and startled me."

"Pearl?" Nathan asked. "She didn't stay in town with the others?"

"She doesn't feel safe sleeping anywhere but the hollow," Carissa explained as she climbed beneath the covers. "She never spends the night anywhere. Once she had to drive to Omaha to help a sick aunt, and she told me she didn't sleep the whole time she was gone. Noelle, did you find anything?"

"A few items, though I'm not sure if they have any significance."

Nathan placed his hand on Noelle's shoulder, and she met his gaze. She needed to talk with him.

"Carissa, it's time you tried to get some sleep. I'm here and I'm fine, so settle down. Karah Lee's on her way in to check your vitals, so Nathan and I will be out in the waiting room for a few minutes." She eyed the folded cot. "Then one of us will sleep in here."

She kissed Carissa's forehead, then preceded Nathan from the room. The force of his curiosity was almost palpable, and in spite of everything she couldn't hold back a grin. Nathan the curious. Some things never changed.

They passed a tired-looking Karah Lee in the hallway.

"Everything go okay?" she asked.

"I'm not sure yet," Noelle replied. "I've been digging up some unappealing family history."

"But no definitive answers?"

"Not yet. We still need to keep a close eye on Carissa."

"Gotcha." Karah Lee gave a half salute and continued on her nighttime rounds.

Two night-lights glowed in the empty waiting room, which promised privacy—a place where Noelle could sit in silence, in safety, with Nathan, and sort out the events of the night. Maybe she could make some sense of it. Maybe Nathan could.

He took her hand. "You want to let me in on what happened?"

She grasped his hands in both of hers and allowed his strength and warmth to bolster her.

"Noelle?"

She pressed her forehead against his chest and sighed. No place in the world had ever felt so safe. For a moment, she just stood there, glad for his silence, allowing his strength to calm her. Her dear friend, whom she held in her earliest memories.

As she pressed her cheek against his shoulder and felt his arms wrapping around her, for a moment, she sensed an undercurrent of new emotions entering their relationship.

Her fingers tingled where they touched him. With surprise and wonder, she looked up to find her feelings mirrored in his eyes. "Nathan," she whispered.

She put her arms around his neck and drew his head down until she could press her lips against his. For a moment, he tensed with surprise, then his arms tightened around her. His kiss deepened. All her carefully guarded feelings escaped their boundaries, and her heart filled with the comfort that came from the exquisite presence of her beloved friend.

How she had missed the special bond they'd once shared . . . and yet, this was different. This wasn't the innocent friendship of children, but something that eclipsed that treasured bond.

Threatened and challenged it, maybe? Did she really want to breach the boundaries of that sturdy companionship?

How could she know Nathan returned those feelings as deeply? Was she so caught up in her own emotions that she mistook his? What kind of friendship . . . what kind of love . . . did they share?

Nathan drew back, loosening his tight hold on her. She could see that he was trying to keep his face free of expression. Nathan had never been good at that.

Was that his heart she felt beating so forcefully, or was it hers? Or were their hearts so attuned that they actually felt the same emotions?

She withdrew from his embrace, breaking contact, fear extinguishing her inner fire like a spray of icy creek water. This was no time to break new ground in their relationship, not when she needed the comfort of familiarity to anchor her. Not when they both needed to keep their heads and think this whole nightmare through to a logical ending.

"Noelle?" His green eyes betrayed his confusion.

"I'm sorry. I'm . . . upset."

He took her hands and led her to a couch. "Sit down." He pulled up a chair and sat facing her. "How did Pearl upset you?"

"I think she may guess that a family member might be involved. Nathan, she mentioned a special gift that runs in our family. She told me Grandpa had it and she implied that it could be dangerous to tell anyone about it."

"The kind of gift you have isn't specifically heredi-tary."

"But if Grandpa had it, too—"

"I'm not saying our Creator can't use the genetic code in any way He sees fit, but God doesn't need it in order to work. Your grandfather could have prayed for you to receive his gift."

"I'm not *saying* anything, I just feel so confused. Pearl mentioned a curse, just as your grandmother did. Except Pearl says it's OCD. Others in the family must have suffered from it."

"And still are," Nathan said.

"Pearl warned me not to trust Jill."

"Did she say why?"

"She mentioned something about Jill pushing her down years ago." Noelle shrugged. "Jill's always been possessive of me, the same way Melva's possessive of Carissa. My big sister didn't take kindly to Pearl's attempts to mother me after Mom's death. It's an old feud that I thought was forgotten long ago. I'm not sure why Pearl brought it up tonight."

"It doesn't sound like she had any real reason to warn you not to trust your own sister," Nathan said.

Noelle slumped in her chair. "Nathan, if you knew about this gift of mine when we were growing up, doesn't it stand to reason that Jill knew about it, too? She lived with me. She knew me."

"Has she ever said anything about it?"

Noelle rubbed her eyes wearily, trying to recall. "I don't remember ever talking about it with her . . . I don't think. If she did know about it, why didn't she call me when Carissa disappeared?"

"You heard her explanation."

"That isn't good enough." Noelle touched his hand. "Nathan, Pearl may think that someone with this gift could tell if someone close to them was suffering from OCD."

"Can you tell?"

"It doesn't work that way."

"But what if someone thought it did?" Nathan asked. "For instance Carissa was the first to pick up on Justin's disorder. She complained about his need to constantly check everything over and over again. If someone believes she does share your gift—"

"Then someone may feel that Carissa's a threat," Noelle said.

"It's a possibility."

Noelle stared down at her clasped hands. "You still don't think it's possible that there's a strain of the OCD that leads the sufferer to violence? I know some sufferers worry that they've committed a violent act and can't remember it."

"No way," Nathan said. "OCD is a neurosis, not a psychosis," Nathan said. "The obsession or compulsion takes place in the mind. Come on, you know this."

"But it's also carried out with overt actions, such as obsessive washing, checking, counting or the excessive saving of all sorts of things. Those are actions."

"Repeatedly washing your hands is a far cry from murder."

"But I'm only asking what if the obsession is powerful enough to lead to violence? Or what if the compulsion is murder?"

"It's murder only if an overload of words can kill. You've seen Justin when he's wound up. Sometimes he gets to talking about something he's obsessing about, and he can't seem to shut up about it."

Noelle scowled at him. "You're joking now, but I'm serious."

"I've done quite a bit of research online with my medical links since we discovered Justin's problem. The only record I ever found of an OCD patient committing a violent crime contained an indication that the individual had other neurological damage. In other words, no. Absolutely not. OCD is not dangerous."

"Then maybe there's also an inherited brain disorder in the Cooper family." Noelle caught his look, shrugged, stood up, impatient with herself, with Nathan, with the whole situation. "I know, I know, I'm getting into science fiction, but a couple of days ago I'd have told you everything that's happened today could never happen." She picked up a magazine, glanced at the country living scene on the cover, then tossed it back onto the table. "Pearl told me something else tonight."

"What?"

"That the sawmill accident ten years ago was actually murder."

Nathan blinked at her. "Whoa! Where did she come up with *that?*"

"It could be true. You questioned the accident your-self. My family worked with heavy logs for many years. An accident with all three of the principle man-agers in the line of fire, with no malfunctioning equip-ment? Not likely. I know the sheriff checked everything out, but we didn't have Greg then. The former sheriff wasn't much of an investigator."

"Did you find anything useful on your search?"

"Nothing concrete, but enough to rouse my curiosity. Have you heard if Greg's come to any conclusions about evidence of foul play in Harvey's death?"

"Nothing. But Cecil told me that someone was sent to see if your ex-husband has an alibi for last night."

"And?"

"He gave one, but they were still checking it out. Here's another interesting development. Carissa over-heard an argument between Melva and Harvey Sand not too long ago."

"What kind of an argument?"

Nathan stretched and combed his fingers through his hair. He was obviously suffering from sleep depriva-tion, and Noelle decided she would be the one to keep first watch on Carissa tonight. Nathan desperately needed some snooze time.

"Harvey apparently wanted money to keep someone from going to prison, probably Cecil."

"*Cecil?* For what? You mean Harvey was black-mailing them?"

"That's what it sounds like to me," he said. "But what would Harvey have on Cecil that he could use to blackmail him? Did you find anything in the attic?"

Noelle reached in her jacket pocket and pulled out the papers she had gathered on her foray. "Look at these ledger sheets. They show a good profit, don't they? Nothing for Jill and Cecil to be worried about. But look, I found this, too." She pulled out the copy of the cashier's check for fifteen thousand dollars made out to Frazier Logging, signed by Melva. "Do you recognize this company?"

Nathan took the copy and studied it. "Frazier was Melva's mother's maiden name."

"How do you know that?"

"I filled a prescription for her grandmother when they came down to visit a few weeks ago."

Noelle tapped her finger against the copy. "So Melva's definitely mixed up in this somehow. But she and Harvey were talking about Cecil going to prison. What could Cecil have done to get himself into so much trouble?"

"It's hard to believe Cecil would do anything criminal."

"I saw another photocopy of a check in the bedroom at the house," Noelle said. "It was made out to the same company, but it was for a hundred thousand and signed by Cecil. It was ten years old."

Nathan whistled softly. "Ten years ago? But there's a statute of limitations. . . . Except for murder."

"No way," Noelle said. "I don't believe it. Not Cecil."

"I don't believe it, either, but what if Harvey was convinced it was the truth? If he had no proof, how would he be able to blackmail Melva?"

Noelle jumped to her feet, shoving her hands in her pockets as she stalked across the room. "I can't believe you're even thinking like that, Nathan." She turned back. "You know Cecil better."

"Yes, I do. I wonder what Greg's found. You told me earlier about some undercurrent of tension within the family after the mill accident. Any idea what that was all about?"

"I was in a rotten marriage and busy messing up my own life at the time, Nathan. I could have imagined it. We're jumping to conclusions here. We don't have all the facts yet."

"What else did you find tonight?"

Noelle switched on another table lamp. Its soft glow lit the poem that she pulled from her pocket, the verse she had taken from Carissa's room. "You heard me ask Carissa about this." She handed it to him. "Do your stuff, counselor, and tell me what this means to you."

Nathan read the poem twice while the clock ticked from the wall in the reception office and a car passed by slowly on the street outside. Noelle watched the play of emotions across his face as he read. She returned to her chair.

He looked up, shaking his head. "Looks like the typical morbid teenage poem. Who wrote it?"

Noelle reached into her jacket pocket for the diary she had found. "This was Jill's. I noticed the writing earlier, but didn't put the two together until just now." She opened it randomly. "Good match, wouldn't you say?"

"I didn't realize your sister was given to literary endeavors."

"Especially such morbid ones. She apparently liked to put her thoughts down on paper." Jill had always been outspoken, honest to the point of bluntness, leaving no one in doubt about the direction of her thoughts. This new dimension of Jill Cooper made Noelle wonder how well she'd actually known her sister.

Thumbing through the pages of the journal, Noelle read snatches of words but found little of relevance to their present problem. Until she reached the last few pages.

"Listen to this, Nathan. It says, 'I don't feel I can trust anyone anymore, sometimes not even myself. Dad's withdrawn when he comes home from the sawmill late at night.' "

"What kind of trust is she talking about?" Nathan asked.

Noelle turned another page. "I don't know. Listen to this. 'Noelle has started it again. She doesn't realize what she's saying, but if anyone listens to her and guesses about her, that could be the end of it. I've told her so many times to be careful, and last night I slapped her, hard, when she asked what was wrong. This morning, there was a bruise on the side of her face. I've got to be more careful with her.' "

Noelle's voice caught. She reread the words, and her fingers, gripping the book, turned white.

Nathan took the diary out of her hands and continued

reading softly. " 'It shut her up. She didn't even cry. But she wouldn't look at me the rest of the evening. I hated that, but I'll do it again if I have to.' " He glanced at Noelle, then back at the page. " 'I don't have a choice.' "

Noelle looked down for a long moment. "I'm going to have a talk with Jill."

"Why didn't you ever tell me about it?"

"I honestly don't remember the incident. But I'd sure like to know why she wanted to shut me up so badly, because that wasn't a normal thing for her to do."

"You don't remember? She bruised you and you *don't remember?*"

"Why should I? I was very small and she was a kid trying to do an adult's job. What's so bad about that? Don't forget she'd just lost her mother, too. It was hard on all of us."

"Okay, but what were you doing—or rather, saying— that was so bad? Can you remember that?"

"All I remember is how I kept picking up on strong emotions coming from many different people. It was a horrible time of grief, and I thought I was going crazy. Then, when I told Jill about it, she got mad."

"Okay, but I'd like to know why Jill was so interested in keeping you quiet." He glanced through the last few pages of the diary, closed it, then laid it beside the poem.

"I'm going back to that attic in the morning," Noelle said. "I found the accounting records. Someone must have put them up there to get them out of the way. I know there must be identical copies in company files, but Harvey's would be consolidated." She stuffed the poem and diary back into her pocket and stood. "I'm going to Jill's first thing in the morning and confront the family about what happened. I'll let them all know that we suspect Carissa's abductor could have been someone close."

"You think that's wise? Won't we just be warning Carissa's attacker that we're getting close?"

"Yes, but we'll also be warning the others to watch out for Carissa. She'll be safer that way."

"I'd like to be with you when you tell them. I'm not going through another night like tonight, afraid for your safety and not able to get to you."

She smiled at him, feeling a rush of affection. "Nathan." It felt good to have him worry about her. The more time she spent with him, the less alone she felt.

"Do you remember when we were kids," he said, glancing at her hesitantly, "and we went walking up our favorite trail in the national forest after a heavy rain?"

"I remember lots of times like that."

"Right now I'm recalling one special time. Remember that pink crystal we found? The one you carried with you for so long?"

"I still have it."

"We overlooked it for such a long time, thinking it was just another rock because it was covered with dirt, before the rain washed the dirt away."

"Rain does that."

"I know. Things work that way in life, too. We've

been through a lot of trouble in our lives, and I can see that, for you, anyway, the struggle has brought changes. There's something more solid about you, now. You've grown so much."

Noelle couldn't prevent the wry twist of her lips. "It's called cynicism. I've seen too many failed lives, including my own."

"I know better, Noelle. How can your life be failed when it isn't over yet?"

She bit back a grin. "Okay, sorry, I didn't mean to start an argument. What were you saying about that little rock we found?"

"Not a rock, a gem. I don't want anything to happen to this new gem we've uncovered. I don't want anything to happen to you."

"Have we uncovered a new gem?"

His mouth quirked, and he eyed her with bemusement. "I think so. A beautiful crystal, very rare."

Noelle felt a sudden happiness that eclipsed all the horror of the day. She placed the palm of her hand against Nathan's cheek, her eyes searching his. "Thank you for caring about me."

He held her gaze, covering her hand with his. "I do much more than that, Noelle Cooper." He raised her hand to his lips and kissed it, then released her.

"Time for you to get some sleep," she said. "I'm taking first watch."

Chapter Twenty

They know something, but how much of the past do they know? I can remember it like it had happened last week. Can they?

I should have known Nathan and Noelle wouldn't leave Carissa's side after yesterday. Why didn't they say anything about the rope? What are they up to?

Their silence won't last long. That's the only thing I can depend on. I have to keep the secret safe.

The gray fog of early morning hovered like a protective shield as Noelle crept through the woods toward the creek. She'd better wash off and get back to the house before anyone noticed she was gone.

She squatted at the creek bank and splashed her hands in the water. In the dim light, she imagined she could see the red spreading, dissolving. There wasn't really any blood on her hands. She knew that . . . didn't she? And yet, when she looked at her hands, she could almost see the crimson stains.

No one would catch her. No one knew her secret.

But she knew. She lived with it always, along with the weight of guilt and her helplessness to control herself. The secret dragged at her as she stood to walk back home. How much longer could she live with it?

"Noelle, you awake? Noelle?"

Carissa's whisper reached Noelle at the moment a muscle cramped in her calf. She sat up with a jerk, grabbed her leg and massaged it, blinking into the darkness. Vestiges of her dream pressed at her. She could not shake it.

"Noelle?" Carissa whispered again.

"Yes, I'm here." Noelle took a deep breath and pushed back the lingering impressions of the dream. Outside, dawn touched the sky with bare traces of light.

Sheets rustled, and Carissa peered over the edge of her bed, her curly brown hair tousled around her face. "Think they'll send me home today?"

"I don't know. How's your head?"

"Sore, and I'm not feeling too good."

"You're hoping to stay here another day, right?"

"Uh-huh."

"I don't know, but we'd better plan on it, just in case." Noelle rubbed her leg again, then swung her feet around and stood. "It'll be a while before the doctor comes," she said dryly. "I don't think Cheyenne or Karah Lee get up before daylight to check patients."

Nathan stirred from his cramped position in the recliner beside the window, opened his eyes and stretched. "What's the deal? Can't a guy get a little sleep around this place?" He saw Noelle standing beside the bed. He sat up. "What's wrong?"

"Relax, Carissa's just restless."

"Why, Cis? Didn't you sleep well?"

Carissa shook her head. "What's going to happen today? What will happen when I go home? You are staying with me, aren't you? You're not going—"

"Of course we're staying with you." Noelle reached

out and hugged her cousin. "Nathan and I know it's not over." She glanced at Nathan over the top of Carissa's curls. She found warmth there and strength. She knew that she could depend on him.

"What'll you tell the others?" Carissa asked.

"The truth," Nathan said.

Carissa stiffened. "You can't."

"It's the only way, Cis," Noelle said. "I know it'll be hard for you, but you're going to have to back us up. You're going to have to tell them that you think it was someone you know who abducted you. And we'll have to tell them about the missing rope."

"But if we tell everyone about what happened, then—"

"Then your attacker will know we're catching on," Noelle said.

Carissa frowned, then nodded.

Noelle took her cousin's hands and squeezed gently. "Carissa, no more recall yet? No idea what was familiar about your attacker? Was it the voice?"

"All I can remember are the whispers in the cave from a crazy person, and no one I know talks like that. It was like . . . well . . . I just felt something."

"The way you felt Justin's problem?" Nathan asked.

Carissa frowned at him. "What do you mean? Jill asked me the same thing. How could I feel something like that? Justin just kept making us late for everything all the time, because he'd do weird stuff like wiping the bathroom counter over and over again, and making his bed about fifty million times and checking and rechecking his face in the mirror. I mean, my brother stares at himself in the mirror like he's in love with himself or something. It's gross."

"Jill said something to you about Justin?" Noelle asked.

"Yeah, she kept asking me how I knew about Justin's problem. I mean, duh, was everybody else blind?"

"Okay, good," Noelle said. "I'm sorry for pushing you, but if we tell everyone about what happened yesterday, more people will be able to help protect you."

"Melva's going to make a big deal out of it," Carissa said.

"Only because she loves you," Noelle said.

"Yeah, but she'll worry, and you know when something's bugging her, she has to talk about it or she'll explode."

Noelle chuckled. "That's our Melva."

"But if we tell them what's going on, then it'll hurt everybody's feelings," Carissa said.

"We're going to take care of you," Noelle said. "We can't take chances with your life, and they'll understand that."

"Maybe," Carissa muttered.

Noelle nodded. "Eventually. It's okay, honey. We'll get through this together." She turned to Nathan. "You'll stay here while I go to Jill's?"

"Now?"

"Jill gets up early. We have some talking to do."

Nathan jerked his head toward the door. "This time I'm going with you. Taylor came on duty at four. I'll call him to sit with Carissa until we get back."

● ● ●

The abundant plant life in Hideaway revealed one of God's perfect backdrops this autumn morning, displaying a rich beauty of which Nathan never tired. Mockingbirds filled the air with music, and sunshine turned the tiny dewdrops on the grass and thick foliage into diamonds. The rising sun illuminated the brightly colored Victorian-style houses that Nathan and Noelle passed, walking through town.

The serenity that surrounded them obviously did nothing to lighten Noelle's mood. Nathan didn't have to look in her eyes to know she was distressed.

"Want to tell me about it?" he asked at last.

She glanced at him. "About what?"

"Something's bothering you."

"Big surprise," she said dryly.

"You might as well tell me what's wrong."

She kicked at a walnut on the uneven sidewalk and sent it shooting out into the narrow street. "I was having a dream just before Carissa woke me this morning."

"What kind of dream?"

"Nightmare. I'd just killed someone."

He winced. He'd forgotten how she'd often had terrifying dreams as a child. "You've had those nightmares before."

She walked beside him in silence for a moment, kicked another walnut into the street, arms held tightly to her sides, hands stuffed into the pockets of her jacket. "The guilt is debilitating."

"Guilt? From the dream?"

She nodded. "I couldn't help feeling that I was eavesdropping on someone else's emotions, someone close to me."

"Do you remember any more about it?"

"Just that I was washing my hands in cold creek water and I kept imagining there was blood on my hands, even though I couldn't see any. I can't help wondering if this was what Carissa's attacker was feeling." She glanced up at Nathan, then returned to her study of the sidewalk. "It was horrible."

"I'm sorry. I can't imagine how that must feel."

"Last night, when Pearl came to the old house and scared me, I didn't know who it was, but I knew it was family, just like I sense the presence of family at other times, even though I'm not always conscious of the knowledge. Could that be the kind of thing Carissa sensed?"

"I can sense my mother's presence by the scent of her shampoo," Nathan said. "I can tell my father's presence by his footsteps."

For a moment, Noelle didn't reply. "For me, this gift, when it comes, is just like another sense, like sight and hearing. You know how sometimes you'll hear something without paying any attention to it, without even realizing you can hear it?"

He nodded.

"I want to just tune it out."

"Of course, I understand. I try to tune out things I don't want to know, but are you sure you want to tune out God's voice?"

She fell silent.

"Don't avoid something if it's the right thing to do," he said softly. "You've avoided a particular connection with me, maybe because I'm a link to your past, and you don't want to remember that."

"I'm not avoiding you. How can you say that?"

"That isn't what I said. You're resisting a deeper relationship because of the past."

She walked several yards before replying. "I couldn't do without you right now, Nathan. I cherish our friendship, and I don't want to do anything to jeopardize that at this point."

"What do you mean, 'at this point'?"

Another long silence. "I mean I haven't exactly been at my best lately, and I don't want to take advantage of you just to have someone in my life."

"Someone in your life?"

"You know. Someone to depend on. Someone to . . . care about."

"So what I hear you saying is that you don't want to consider a more meaningful relationship with me because you feel you'd be exploiting me somehow?"

Her steps slowed. She looked up at him. "That isn't what I meant. It's just that I don't have the most sterling reputation in Hideaway, and I earned my bad name fairly. You could meet someone—"

"Oh, what a load of hogwash!"

She frowned and looked away. "Okay, maybe I *am* getting a little carried away with remorse, but that truly is one of the reasons that I've been reluctant to come back to work at the Hideaway Clinic. I can't help wondering why anyone would want to take a chance on me."

"We don't have time for me to list all the reasons I think the clinic would jump at the chance to have you," Nathan said.

He was rewarded by a slight upturn of her lips.

He watched as her smile was replaced, once more, by quiet brooding. "Do you think the guilt you experienced in the dream might be a remnant of the exaggerated shame you insist on carrying because of your past?"

Her steps slowed. "*Exaggerated* shame?"

Oops. He heard the challenge in her voice and immediately regretted his choice of words.

"The things I did were more than just little mistakes, Nathan. I don't think I'm exaggerating the consequences of my actions."

"Okay, so you blew it completely. You crossed the line in a few parts of your life, and now you regret it so much you believe that you deserve to pay for the rest of your life."

"And you don't agree," she said dryly.

"Absolutely not. You've learned and grown from your experience, and now you need to give yourself a break. Don't you think you've been punished enough, losing your position and enduring all the abuse and manipulation Joel dished out?"

"I was willful enough to marry him in the first place,

without considering the impact on myself or my family."

"So one bad choice negates your chance for a future relationship? A good one this time?"

He barely heard her sigh. He studied her profile as she walked beside him. Noelle Cooper had always been beautiful, the image of her mother, with delicate features, eyes that seemed to see into a person's soul, and a wide smile that could rival a sunrise. At least, so it always seemed to him.

"How do you know so much about my marriage to Joel?" Noelle asked.

"This is Hideaway, not Springfield. However I try to avoid the grapevine here, it hits me right between the eyes with dependable frequency. I know Joel was under surveillance for illegal drug activity when you married him, and that your family heartily disapproved of the marriage, so you moved to Springfield."

"After which he continued his illegal methamphetamine manufacturing, became victim to his own poison and took me right down with him," she finished.

"That was your choice *then*. But God doesn't hold past mistakes against anyone for life. He doesn't work like that."

"I don't know everything about how God works."

"You don't have to know or understand everything about God before you let Him work through you," Nathan said.

She raised a hand to silence him. "I'm not at my best

right now. I can only focus on one thing at a time, and this morning I'm desperately trying to figure out how to confront the people I love with the possibility of family involvement in Carissa's abduction."

"Okay. I have one more question about Cecil. What happened to change him from the outgoing, friendly guy I knew in high school?"

"As you pointed out, this is Hideaway, not Springfield," she said, dabbing at her eyes with her fingers. "Haven't the local gossips filled you in? Or is *my* past the only subject of conversation around here?"

"Let's just say that you're a more likely subject for the church ladies. You and I are both single, and there are some hopeless romantics in this town."

She let out a give-me-a-break sigh. "Well," she said, "Cecil's story is pretty simple. When Uncle Todd and Aunt Harriet moved to Texas ten years ago, just before the accident at the sawmill, Cecil, who was married with two children then, wanted to take an engineering job in St. Louis. But Uncle Todd laid huge responsibilities on him, convincing Cecil that if he took the job, the sawmill would go under and the family business would be destroyed. He claimed that Cecil would be failing in his Christian duty to the Cooper family."

Nathan shook his head as they strolled up the sidewalk to Jill's house. "Spiritual blackmail."

"You call it blackmail, I call it manipulation. When Gladys divorced Cecil, she accused him of not standing up to his parents, and I think he agreed and blamed himself for the failure of their marriage."

"Sounds like guilt complexes run in the Cooper family."

"We all have our issues. I think Cecil's allowed bitterness and regret to change his personality, and I know it worries Melva. But, please, don't preach him a sermon about it today, okay? Right now, we've got other subjects to pursue."

Chapter Twenty-One

Jill's seventy-five-year-old Victorian-style house, sky-blue with navy-and-pink trim, looked clean, crisp and inviting as Noelle preceded Nathan up a flagstone walk to the porch. She knocked gently at the door, unwilling to use the bell in case someone was still sleeping. Since Jill seldom locked up when she was home, the delicately carved door opened with ease when Noelle tried it.

As she led the way through the foyer, Noelle inhaled the aromas of bacon, fried potatoes and maple syrup. "I just remembered I haven't eaten in forever."

Nathan closed the door behind them. "I'm starved, too."

"I doubt Jill's cooking my typical breakfast fare, though."

"Don't tell me. Yogurt and bananas and some kind of dried seaweed?"

Noelle shot him a grin over her shoulder. "Specifically, goat's milk yogurt or salmon—highly nourishing and delicious, but I'll make an exception today." If she could swallow anything, since for her, stress had never been an appetite stimulant. "I don't suppose we could grab a bite before we drop the bomb?"

"What bomb?" came a sleepy-gruff voice from the staircase above them.

For a moment, Noelle couldn't tell who was speaking, Cecil or Justin. Then big, bare feet and jeans-clad legs descended the steps. Justin emerged down from the shadows, shirtless, dark hair sticking up in all directions. He was the image of his father at the same age, down to the cowlick on his crown that never behaved.

Justin had just turned seventeen, and Noelle couldn't help the wonder she felt at the new depth in his voice, and the recent dark shadow of beard on his chin and jaw. Hadn't it been just a few moons ago that she'd been racing bicycles with him down the lane and playing catch in the hollow? How time had flown. She missed those days.

"You're dropping a bomb?" he asked.

"After breakfast," Noelle said.

He pulled a shirt down over his head as he descended the final step and joined them in the foyer. "Carissa okay?"

"She's fine, and we want to make sure she stays that way." Noelle once again sniffed the delicious aromas emanating from the back of the house. "Is everyone in the kitchen?"

He shrugged a lanky shoulder. "Pearl's not. She went home last night."

"I know, I saw her."

He frowned at her. "You went out there?"

"Yes. I needed to check out a few things."

"Like what?"

"Some records, some memories." She headed down the hall.

"You might not want to go to the kitchen right now," Justin said. "I could hear arguing all the way upstairs. Voices carry through the heat vents."

"Arguing about what?" Nathan asked.

Justin gave an impatient snort. "What else? It's always about the business. A real cozy family get-together in there. I wish Dad and Jill had never formed that partnership. Jill keeps insisting on helping with data entry, and now it's all one big mess. They can't get anything to balance."

Noelle motioned for Justin to join them, and led the way to the back of the house, where the kitchen, dining room and family room were located. She heard the sharp clip of Jill's voice in counterpoint to Melva's dulcet tones—a sure sign Melva was attempting to placate Jill about something.

"We'll get it all worked out, Jill, I promise." Melva's Ozark accent was heavy, betraying her tension. "If Harvey were alive, I know he'd be able to find the problem in two shakes, but—"

"Well, we can't turn to Harvey," Jill said. "You've been keeping the books for how long? Years before you and Cecil got married. You should know where the money went."

"Jill, slow down a minute," came the rumble of Cecil's voice, sounding irritated. "We've got a little more on our plates than usual, and money isn't so tight we can't wait a few hours to see how Carissa's doing."

"Carissa's fine." Jill's tone held a note of weariness that Noelle hadn't heard in years. "I just talked to Taylor on the telephone."

"If you don't mind, I'd like a final verdict from a doctor," Cecil drawled.

Noelle rounded the corner of the hallway that opened up into the kitchen and dining area. Cecil stood at the breakfast bar holding a coffee mug. Melva sat perched at the bar, her arms over her chest, shoulders squared. Jill stood at the stove, flipping pancakes with quick, sharp movements that revealed her anxiety.

They all looked around when Noelle entered with Nathan and Justin.

"So the prodigal cousin shows her face at last." Cecil's deep voice, so like his son's, held an undercurrent of relief—no doubt at the sudden opportunity to change the subject. His blue eyes took in her appearance at a glance.

He gave her a brief smile and pulled a chair back from the table. "Have a seat. You look tired."

"Thanks," she said, not moving from the doorway.

His eyebrows arched as he glanced past her shoulder toward his son. "Up so early, Justin?"

"Couldn't sleep with you three harping on each other down here."

Jill turned from the stove and gave an unamused

snicker. Her gaze passed over Noelle, then returned to her face for a closer examination. "Where were you last night? I thought you'd stay here."

"I was at the clinic," Noelle said. "I spent the night with Carissa."

"All night?" Jill turned off the burner and slid the skillet of bacon to a hot pad.

"You weren't there when I left," Cecil said. "Funny thing was, Nathan couldn't seem to tell me where you'd gone." He flicked a gaze at Nathan, who stood beside Noelle with a hand on her elbow.

"I'll tell you all about it," Noelle said, taking the chair her cousin had pulled out for her, "*after* breakfast."

As Jill and Melva placed the food on the table, Cecil poured coffee. Noelle waited. This was her family. She loved them. But she didn't need a special gift—natural or supernatural—to feel the tension in this room. The bits of argument she'd overheard disturbed her.

Nathan sat beside her, and she drew strength from his calm presence. She must have lost her senses in high school, when she let other guys and popularity lure her away from the best friendship she'd ever had.

While grace was being offered, Noelle felt tears stinging behind her closed lids. She'd been on the edge of tears since yesterday morning. What had gone wrong with her family? With her whole life?

When the others began to eat, Noelle realized she couldn't swallow a bite. She placed pancakes and bacon on her plate and picked up her fork, but she could only mangle the food. She finally put down her fork and sipped her coffee, while Melva tried to make conversation with Nathan about the project to beautify the town square.

Noelle began to notice the way Justin consumed his food—slowly, passing his fork from his left hand to his right hand before placing each bite in his mouth, then replacing the fork precisely between his plate and his milk glass before picking it up again and repeating the ritual.

No one else seemed to notice. Noelle looked up to find her sister watching her closely, blue eyes dark with worry.

Melva finished her plate first, then delicately patted her lips and pushed her chair a few inches from the table. "Noelle, no wonder you're so skinny. You said you wanted to wait until after breakfast to talk, but you didn't eat a thing. Don't you ever have breakfast?"

"Goat milk yogurt," Nathan answered for her.

Melva wrinkled her nose. "You and your health food."

"Actually, it's delicious," Noelle said. "And I didn't start eating goat's milk yogurt to be healthy. Bertie Meyer introduced me to it years ago, and I've loved it ever since."

"So when are you going to tell us about what you were doing at the clinic all night?" Cecil asked, pushing his half-empty plate away. "Especially after Karah Lee told us Carissa would be fine without us."

"Karah Lee knew you were all tired, since none of you slept the night before. I did. You needed the rest."

Nathan placed a hand over one of hers, and she looked down to find that she had been shredding her paper napkin. She could feel the attention of the others.

"What's going on?" Jill asked.

"We needed to talk to you all this morning," Nathan said quietly, squeezing Noelle's hand with gentle firmness. "We've got a problem, and we were reluctant to say anything until we'd had time to think about—"

"What's this 'we' bit?" Cecil asked. "Don't tell me *you* stayed with Carissa, too."

Noelle put her other hand over Nathan's and squeezed. Everyone at the table was focused on their clasped hands. "Carissa didn't just have an accident Thursday night," she said. "Someone chased her into the sawmill. She fell and hit her head, and then her pursuer carried her to Bobcat Cave."

For a moment, no one seemed to breathe. The color drained from Melva's face, while Cecil's expression darkened. Jill froze, holding her coffee mug in midair.

"I'm surprised at you, Cousin," Cecil drawled. "Carissa has an active imagination. You know that."

"She didn't make it up, and she didn't imagine it," Noelle said. "Someone pulled the rope from the sinkhole after Nathan and I climbed into the cave."

Jill caught her breath. "And you're just now telling us? What about the sheriff? Did you call Greg and let him know what happened?"

"The sheriff's office knows about it," Nathan said. "That's why Greg spent so much time questioning everyone yesterday after we found Carissa."

"How *did* you get out of the cave?" Melva asked.

"Nathan had to swim out through a cavern pool," Noelle said. "Cecil, you remember that whirlpool. We went in there a few times—"

"I remember," he growled, his temper obviously growing sharper as he realized the danger of the situation.

Melva swallowed audibly. "Somebody really tried to kill Carissa?"

"Not exactly," Nathan said. "Granted, we could all have died if we hadn't found another way out of the cave, and if no one had found us, but Carissa wasn't injured except for the blow to the back of her head, and she admits that's probably from a fall."

"But who would take her like that?" Melva asked.

Cecil set his coffee mug on the table with slow deliberation. "Why didn't Carissa tell me about this?" Again, his voice rumbled with anger, his dark gaze trained on Noelle.

"Because she thought somebody in her own family did it." Justin didn't look up from the table. His hands remained busy as he positioned and repositioned his plate, glass and silverware, meticulously measuring the rim of the plate from the edge of the table with his fingers.

Silence filled the room. Noelle watched Justin's movements, fascinated. She glanced across the table at Jill, who was staring fixedly back at her.

"So who did it?" Justin carefully wiped the moisture from his glass with his napkin.

"We don't know," Nathan said. "She didn't see who it was, but she heard a whispering voice and—" he paused, then went on "—the voice whispered her name. She picked up on something else . . . some impression or sense of familiarity that she can't recall. But she suspects the stalker was someone in the family, or a friend or neighbor. She was afraid to tell anyone."

"Family." Cecil's deep voice deepened further with outrage.

Nathan caught and held his gaze. "Yes, someone who knew her."

"So she didn't see who it was?" Jill asked.

"If she did, she doesn't remember it," Noelle said. "The blow to her head may have caused some short-term memory loss, so even if she did see someone, she's forgotten."

"So you two knew all this, and you manipulated our movements at the clinic to keep us from being alone with her?" Deep color was creeping up Cecil's neck.

"Yes, exactly," Nathan said. "I'm sorry, but we couldn't take any chances."

"No," Melva said. "You're wrong. Carissa's imagining it. She's got to be." She turned to Cecil. "Tell her about Justin. Tell her Carissa may have the same—"

"Melva, we know she didn't imagine it," Noelle said. "Don't forget about the rope being taken from the sinkhole. Someone left us there."

"But maybe that was a mistake," Melva said. "You know, one of the searchers took the rope. I know that'd be a stupid thing to do, but there were a lot of people in

Cedar Hollow, and not all of them understand about hiking around the caves."

"None of us can afford to go into denial about this, Melva," Noelle said. "There's no explaining away the missing rope. If you try, you're calling Carissa a liar and endangering her further. Next time, she could be killed."

"Wait a minute," Jill said slowly. "You're saying that you honestly believe one of us tried to hurt our own flesh and blood?"

"I don't want to believe it," Noelle said.

"How *could* you?" Jill's voice trembled with betrayal. "That's why Cheyenne wouldn't let me accompany Carissa yesterday? Because she was being . . . protected from me?"

Noelle heard the accusation. "I'm sorry. The last thing I wanted was to hurt you, but we couldn't take any chances with Carissa's life. We didn't feel we had any choice. And now we're telling you about it because we need help."

"What kind of help?" Jill asked. "You want us to help you accuse family?"

Noelle caught her sister's gaze and held it. "Family or not, do you want to defend someone who abducted Carissa?"

"Just because the abductor called her name doesn't mean it was one of us," Melva said.

"Okay, hold it, let's stop arguing for a minute," Cecil intervened. Some of the high color had drained from his face. "You're right, we can't take a chance with Carissa."

"So Greg's actually been investigating *us* with all those questions he was asking yesterday?" Melva's voice shook, revealing more concern than her expression showed.

"Good," Cecil said. "He needs to investigate everyone. It isn't as if we have something to hide. Who's with Carissa now?"

"Taylor was with her," Jill said. "He told me Cheyenne and Blaze were due in shortly. Carissa's eating breakfast. She's in safe company."

"How can you be sure about that?" Melva asked. "Her abductor could've been a friend or acquaintance—"

"It was family," Noelle said softly, with a tremor in her voice she couldn't stifle. She became more certain of it all the time.

"You can't say that for sure," Melva said.

"I can." From the corner of her eye, Noelle once again caught her sister's sharp glance.

"How?" Cecil asked.

Noelle looked up and stared into her sister's eyes. "The same way I knew something bad had happened long before Nathan showed up on my doorstep and told me about Carissa."

Melva drew in a loud breath.

"When did you know?" Justin asked.

Noelle saw the alarm in Jill's face, the quick jerk of her head, as if begging Noelle to be silent. "Sometimes there are things I just know. This is one of those times. Nathan calls it a gift."

"If Noelle hadn't been drawn to the cave yesterday," Nathan said, "then Carissa might not be safe at the clinic now."

"What do you mean, Noelle was *drawn* to the cave?" Melva asked. "Noelle? Why would you be—"

"I believe Carissa could have stumbled onto some private information that could be damaging to someone," Noelle said.

Melva looked at her husband, then raised her hand to her mouth in a gesture of distress. "What kind of information would that be?"

"It must be pretty damaging if someone is willing to abduct a twelve-year-old child to protect himself," Jill said, then glanced at Melva. "Or herself. We sent her to the mill that night to get the ledgers. What did she see?"

"That can't have a bearing on this situation," Melva said. "Nothing at all. You've got to believe me." She turned to Noelle. "How *can* you accuse us of attempted murder?"

"I'm not accusing." Noelle held her hands up in entreaty. "I'm simply saying that Carissa needs to be protected."

"Fine, then I'll be there to protect her," Melva said, shoving her chair back with unaccustomed force. "I'm going to the clinic. Cecil, are you taking me or do I have to walk?"

"You can wait a minute or two," Cecil muttered.

Melva crossed her arms and glared at her husband.

Jill reached for her purse at the end of the breakfast bar. "I'll take you. We need to talk to Carissa." She looked tired this morning, every bit of her forty-four years. She slid the purse strap over her shoulder and turned to Noelle. "You want to come with us and play bodyguard?"

The sarcasm in her voice bit sharply. Noelle looked down at the table and shook her head.

"You do know about Justin, don't you, Noelle?" Melva asked. "About his little problem with—"

"Melva," Cecil said. "There's nothing wrong with Justin that a little discipline can't fix."

"Oh, stop it!" Melva snapped. "You can't be so worried about that codicil that you'd allow your own son to suffer without help. It's gone on long enough."

"Codicil?" Noelle asked. "What are you talking about?"

"Melva!" Cecil growled.

"The codicil to the Cooper trust," Melva said, ignoring her husband. "All this talk about the Cooper curse? It isn't OCD. If you ask me, it's that hateful codicil, which is just your grandfather's way of controlling everyone from beyond the grave. Jill, are we going?" She stalked from the room, and after a final look of exasperation at Noelle, Jill followed.

The kitchen descended into tense silence. Noelle glanced up to find Cecil watching her intently, the flush of anger gone from his face.

"What's Melva talking about?" Noelle asked. "What codicil?"

"Just another deep, dark secret," Justin said. "Nobody's ever told me about anything like that."

"Cecil?"

Her cousin closed his eyes and sighed.

Noelle didn't press for more. She'd ask later.

With automatic movements, Justin positioned his plate squarely in front of him, set the utensils in precise order from the plate, folded his napkin, then opened it and folded it again. Once more, he turned his plate, checked its distance from the edge of the table. Then repeated the whole ritual again.

Noelle couldn't stop watching him. His movements indicated a problem far deeper than a preference for order.

This was a torture. No wonder Nathan wanted so badly to help him.

Cecil sighed again and pushed himself from the table. He picked up his coffee mug and pressed it against his lips, sipped, swallowed. He met Noelle's gaze with a level, steady stare. "I hope you're wrong about this mess with Carissa."

"So do I."

"But you sound pretty positive about it."

Noelle nodded.

Cecil's gaze fell on his son. "Justin, you're coming with me to the clinic."

Justin stayed where he was, refolding his napkin, repositioning his utensils, as if he hadn't heard his father.

Cecil shoved the place setting out of his son's reach, grabbed his arm and pulled him from his chair. Still holding tightly, he walked Justin out the door.

Noelle watched them leave. "What was it you said about OCD?" she murmured to Nathan. "That the victim feels constant worry and guilt about a possible act of violence he might have committed?"

"That's right. It's heartbreaking."

"Justin's experiencing that worry and guilt."

"Looks that way to me," Nathan said.

"Cecil is, too."

"I can understand. He's just discovered his daughter was abducted, he didn't suspect it, it appears someone nearby did it and he wasn't able to control it. How would you feel?"

"Helpless. We need to keep looking, Nathan. We're missing something, and I've got a feeling we'll find it if we keep looking."

Chapter Twenty-Two

The cloud cover had lifted overnight, and the fresh smell of rain-washed earth wafted on the breeze in Hideaway. Nathan stepped from the curb in front of the general store, satisfied that the substitute he'd called at the last moment was working out well in the pharmacy. Everything was under control, so he strolled across the street toward his favorite bench, on the lawn five feet from the water's edge.

Dr. Cheyenne Gideon was making "rounds," which meant she would spend at least another thirty minutes talking to her two overnight patients, checking them out thoroughly and deciding whether to send them home, keep them or have them transferred to a hospital. Noelle was at the Lakeside Bed and Breakfast, renewing her old friendship with Bertie Meyer and eating a much-needed meal of strawberries and home-made goat's milk yogurt.

Nathan could use a little solitude and some time to pray. The morning sunlight gleamed across the surface of the lake as he neared the bench. Someone was paddling a canoe across the water, and tiny waves lapped against the wooden dock.

Nathan was just about to settle onto the bench when he heard footsteps in the grass behind him.

"Where is she this time?"

He recognized Jill's deep alto voice. So much for solitude. He turned to find her frowning at him, blue eyes reflecting the lake, hands on her hips.

Jill's attractive features were bolder than Noelle's, and there was a voluptuousness about her that men had always found appealing, which continually inspired some older Hideaway residents to attempt match-making between Jill and any available male at every opportunity. To Nathan, she'd always been Noelle's older sister, ever the disciplinarian. Today, however, there was an air about Jill that suggested vulnerability.

"She's finally agreed to have some breakfast," he answered quietly. "She's at Bertie's. Has Cheyenne released Carissa?"

"She wants to keep her around a few more hours. Did you convince her to do that?"

"Me?" He gestured for Jill to have a seat on the bench. "Cheyenne's the doctor."

Jill glanced at the bench but didn't sit. Instead, she paced to the water's edge, arms crossed over her chest. "I know you and Noelle didn't mean to hurt anyone with your announcement this morning, but I wish you could have handled this whole thing differently. Melva's still in tears, Cecil is morose, and Justin can't sit still. Cecil has decided to stay at the clinic with Carissa for a couple of hours, and would you believe Cheyenne's insisting he can't stay there by himself? It's like he needs a chaperone to keep his own daughter company. Believe me, it isn't going over well."

"What would you do differently?" Nathan asked, and was dismayed by the irritation in his voice. He blamed it on sleep deprivation. Though he'd slept a few hours in the recliner, it had been an uneasy rest, and combined with lack of sleep the night before, he knew he'd need to watch his temper.

"I don't know why you couldn't tell us yesterday about what happened, even if you didn't feel it was possible to tell us about your suspicions."

"I'm sorry." He injected a note of gentleness into his voice. She was obviously wounded. He would be, too, if one of his sisters suspected him of abducting a child.

"And would you please not encourage Noelle to exercise her intuitive ability? It's wrong, and it's dangerous."

"Wrong?"

"The Bible specifically warns against witchcraft or conjuring spirits."

"Jill, this isn't witchcraft, and it isn't something she's conjuring. Just as she said, I believe it's a gift from God. I wondered about it myself, until I checked her gift against Scripture. It's biblical, and she wouldn't have found Carissa without His direction."

"We can't know that."

"Carissa was drowning when we found her," he said softly. "A few minutes later and we would have been too late."

Jill closed her eyes and raised her face to the sun. "Okay," she whispered. "I'm sorry. You're right, it would have been horrible if you hadn't been there for Carissa when you were, but she's safe now, and Noelle needs to get away from here for a while. She also needs to stop blabbing to everyone about this 'gift.'"

"You try telling her to leave."

"She won't listen to me."

"And she will to me? You know better than that. You're doing it again, Jill. Stop trying to be her mommy and try just to be her sister. She isn't a needy child anymore. What she needs now is to know the truth about what's going on around here, particularly with the family business."

"For instance?"

"What were you and Cecil and Melva arguing about this morning when we arrived at your house? What's this codicil to the trust? And I still don't understand why Justin's crisis with OCD is being treated like some

248

big, horrible secret that must be kept at the cost of Justin's quality of life."

A tour bus pulled up at the curb in a wave of heat and diesel fumes. Jill watched as the doors opened to let off passengers. She sighed and strolled toward one of several gazebos that dotted the lawn between the street and the dock.

Nathan followed her, controlling his frustration at her reticence.

"Aren't we getting off the subject?" she asked. "I thought you and Noelle wanted to find out what happened to Carissa so it doesn't happen again."

"That's exactly what we're doing. That's why we need to know these things. Noelle's already called her partner to watch the store, so you're not getting her out of Hideaway until she has some answers."

Jill grunted and nodded. "She's impossible."

"She takes after you. And since she isn't leaving, won't you give us something to go on?"

"I don't have anything you need."

"You can't know that. For instance, Noelle needs to recall some of those things you tried to bully her into forgetting when she was a child."

Jill's steps faltered. She glanced over her shoulder at Nathan.

"She found an old journal upstairs in the house where you grew up," he explained. "In it you wrote about slapping her so hard you bruised her face."

Jill's features twisted. She raised a hand to her mouth. "Oh, Nathan, no. She read that?"

"She only wants to know why you did it. She loves you, Jill. She knows how much you gave up for her, but it's important for her to know why you did what you did."

"But why do you and Noelle have to stir everything up *now?*"

"Because Carissa's still in danger, and we don't know why. We're collecting data, and your past with Noelle is part of that data. Carissa and Noelle both believe someone close to Carissa is the culprit, and I trust Noelle's special insight."

"But Carissa's only twelve. How can she be connected to something that happened nearly thirty years ago?"

"She's been researching family history, remember? She's possibly discovered something damaging to one of the family."

"You can say that so casually because you're above suspicion," Jill said, slumping onto the steps of the gazebo. She buried her face in her hands. "Oh, Nathan, how could it have come to this?"

He sat down beside her. "Come to what? If you could just tell us—"

"Okay. Noelle and I need to have a talk. I'll tell her what I can, but I'm sure it was obvious to you at my house this morning that I'm not up to speed about everything that's going on around here, either. I hate fighting with my family, but getting information out of Cecil and Melva lately is like trying to suture gelatin."

"Noelle's at the Lakeside. Why don't you go have a talk with her?"

Jill nodded, rubbing her eyes. "Okay. I'll try. Maybe we can get some things settled."

Noelle sat on the deck of the Lakeside Bed and Breakfast and gazed across the surface of the water as she ate the last strawberry on her plate. She'd had a few minutes to talk to Bertie before a fresh crowd of diners had descended and Bertie was called into service to replenish the breakfast bar.

A group of teenagers sat at the table next to Noelle, arguing about the type of tackle they'd need to catch their limit of large-mouth bass. A chattering group of female senior citizens carried their trays to the big table at the far end of the deck. Noelle felt lonely, wishing Nathan was with her.

A stillness seemed to hover over the lake. The colors of autumn appeared to have deepened overnight, the beautiful hues of life at the end of its cycle. The sumac bushes flared red against the dull dying green of oak and sycamore, all the colors reflected in the lake.

The cliffs hovered just above the surface of water on the other shore. To Noelle, those cliffs looked comforting, like the welcoming arms of home.

But she didn't need to be thinking like that.

Her gaze traveled across the lawn and focused on a man and a woman strolling across the grass, deep in conversation. Jill and Nathan. As Noelle watched, they looked her way. She raised her hand in a halfhearted gesture of greeting, then rose to her feet. Time to talk.

She met them as they approached the main lodge of the bed-and-breakfast.

"You're pale," Jill said. "Are you okay?"

"I'm fine. You?"

"I guess you could say I didn't take your news well. And I'm worried about you."

"You're always worried about me," Noelle said dryly. "All that stress will send you to an early grave, and then I'll have more to feel guilty about."

"Nathan told me to back off a little," Jill said, glancing at Nathan, who stood beside her looking uncomfortable.

"I think I'll grab of cup of coffee," he said. "Why don't you two take a walk? And keep the shouting down to a bare minimum. Looks like we're getting a lot of shoppers in town today. Don't want to scare off business."

Noelle gave him a mock glare, then turned to her sister. "Let me guess, you want me to stop causing trouble and leave town."

"I know you don't understand, but I really would like you to leave, at least for a while." Jill turned to stroll toward the small church and cemetery down the road.

Noelle fell into step beside her; Jill taking her usual position between Noelle and the road, ever the protector. "You're right, I don't understand, and I'm sorry, but I can't leave."

"The nightmares you used to have? Do you want them to come back?" Jill asked.

"Good grief, Jill, I'm thirty-six. I'm not going to allow a few nightmares to disturb my life now."

"I spoke with Greg a while ago. He said Joel's alibi checked out for Thursday night."

"He really was in church?" Noelle exclaimed.

Jill dug into her pocket, pulled out a slip of paper and held it out. "Even more shocking, he asked for you to call him. He said he needs to apologize for some things."

Noelle took the paper and shoved it into her pocket. "I read your old diary."

There was a long pause. Then: "Actually, it's a journal."

"I found it in the same place I found your poem," Noelle continued. "I didn't know you had literary leanings. I also didn't know you were impulsive enough to write something down in a diary that might be damaging to you later."

By the sudden stillness in Jill's face, Noelle knew she was upset. "Been a while since you read your old journal, has it?" Noelle couldn't read her sister's expression, couldn't catch a trace of her emotions. Jill hid her reactions well.

"All this talk about being a mature woman, and you still go snooping through your big sister's private journal like a little girl." Jill's attempt at humor failed dismally.

"I told you I found it in the attic. I figured if you weren't interested enough to take it with you, you wouldn't mind my reading it." Noelle hesitated, shaking her head sadly at her sister. "You've wanted to keep my gift secret since I was just a little kid. I can't understand why."

"Because I always felt these intuitions of yours were wrong. Evil."

"No, Jill. Nathan has explained some of the differences between godly gifts and the power of evil. I lost my gift when I strayed from God. Now I'm back, and good has already come of it. Carissa's alive. What was the poem all about? And why did you hit me?"

Jill averted her eyes.

"I keep telling myself you must have had a good reason, and you were young," Noelle continued, "but there's never a good reason for slapping a child so hard you bruise her, and you were a teenager, old enough to know better."

"I was afraid, and I knew of no other way to keep you quiet."

Noelle spread her hands, unable to look at her sister's face. "Did Daddy know what—"

"No." Jill closed her eyes, taking a deep breath, then letting it out slowly. "He never knew. He didn't know anything about you, about the gift. I thought nobody knew. I had to keep it that way."

"Why?"

"Because not only did I think it was wrong, I was afraid it was dangerous," Jill said. "And I think I was right. You know that epitaph on Grandpa's tombstone? The family knew he had the same special abilities you had. Grandpa died young. I've always heard from Aunt

Pearl that the gifted die young. I didn't want you to die."

"You sound like Aunt Pearl. I talked to her last night and she warned me as well."

"Fine. Call me old-fashioned. I was worried about you." Jill folded her arms across her chest, face turned from Noelle.

Something about her behavior felt . . . odd. She was distracted. Or she wasn't telling the whole truth.

That was it. Honest, blunt Jill was trying to conceal something.

"What about this codicil to the trust that Melva mentioned this morning? What does it say?" Noelle asked.

Jill frowned. "Pearl hasn't even told you?"

"No. You tell me."

"First you need to understand why I didn't want to call you about Carissa . . . and why I deleted your message on Cecil and Melva's answering machine."

"What?"

"I'm sorry," Jill said quickly. "By the time I noticed the light blinking and played your message, Carissa was already missing. I knew then that you must have known it supernaturally. I didn't want anyone to know."

"But Carissa's life was in danger," Noelle protested. "I could have helped."

"I didn't know that, I thought she might be hiding somewhere. With all that's been going on lately, all the fighting and tension, I thought she might have gotten fed up and gone to spend the night somewhere, some

255

place we hadn't looked yet." Jill raised a hand of entreaty. "I honestly thought that, Noelle. And even while half of me felt guilty for not letting anyone call you, the other half of me remembered what that accident ten years ago did to you. And I remembered all those old stories I used to believe. I'm not sure I don't still believe them. I tell myself this curse that's been whispered about for years is a myth, but I know the gift isn't, because I know you have it, and so I'm afraid for you, even though—"

"Wait a minute. This 'curse' is only Obsessive-Compulsive Disorder, what Justin has. It's not dangerous."

"When I was growing up, the problem wasn't understood the way it is now. Grandpa saw it as a dangerous mental illness, a curse on the Cooper family, because one of our ancestors was so affected by it she became a recluse and never threw anything away—old newspapers, magazines, paper bags, boxes. Her house, packed with all the trash she'd been unable to toss over the years, caught fire and burned with her in it. The flames were so fierce they caught three other houses on fire, killing two other people."

The memory of Justin's actions this morning struck Noelle afresh. "Okay, I can understand why someone might leap to that conclusion in the past, but now we know that the disorder can be controlled by behavior modification and medical intervention. Why is it still such a big deal?"

"Because of the codicil."

Noelle stopped and turned to her sister. "What do you mean?"

"No one with the symptoms of the illness is allowed to control Cooper property. They can't own the land, they can't work it. Family members with OCD are left out in the cold if anyone finds out about it."

"That's crazy!"

"Exactly. There's a curse on our family, but it isn't OCD, it's that vile codicil."

Noelle caught her sister's arm. "Would you come to Pearl's with Nathan and me? She doesn't know what's going on, and I need to tell her. Maybe the four of us can talk this over. Pearl knows more about family history than anyone. Maybe she can shed some light on this for us."

Jill hesitated, glancing back toward the bed-and-breakfast. "Why do you need me? You and Pearl have always been closer."

"But you and Pearl both tended to shelter me. Maybe with you there she'll be more forthcoming. We need more information."

Chapter Twenty-Three

Pearl was working in her garden when Nathan and Noelle drove up to the front gate, with Jill behind them in her SUV. Aunt Pearl dusted the dirt from the knees of her jeans and removed her gardening gloves.

"Looks like I've got some company!" she called with

apparent delight as she strolled across the yard, gesturing toward the house. "How about some sassafras tea? Then you all can fill me in on what's up with Carissa."

Noelle recognized the reluctance on Jill's face as the three of them followed Pearl up the steps and onto her front porch. Ever since her mom's death, she had felt like a prize in a contest, pulled between her sister and her great-aunt, each believing she knew what had been best for Noelle.

Noelle glanced over her shoulder at Nathan, caught his wink and reassuring grin and knew he was remembering, too. It helped ease some of her tension.

Pearl's house hadn't changed in the past ten years, except for the fading paint on the exterior and the encroaching forest that had been allowed to creep to within two feet of the flagstone porch.

The large front room was packed with drying tables that held herbs, roots and blossoms. Pearl led the way into the kitchen, where the counters were completely covered with packaged herbs and bottles of homemade cough elixir.

"Health-food store in Branson buys just about all the herbs your store doesn't buy these days, Noelle," Pearl told her, "but I keep enough around here for the neighbors when the docs in town can't figure out the problem." She shot Jill a challenging glance. "Those who'll use it, who don't think it's just a bunch of superstition."

Jill's brows arched. "Aunt Pearl, I can't believe you

said that. Didn't I let you treat me for that cough last spring with those elm leaves?"

"Slippery elm," Pearl said dryly.

"Well, it worked, and you made a believer out of me."

"Oh, really? So you're not still telling all your patients about how conventional medicine's the only good medicine?"

"I've never said that . . . exactly."

"Good." Pearl turned on the burner beneath a kettle on the stove. "Maybe you're getting smarter, Jill. Remember the time you caught me doctoring Noelle's skinned knee outside the sawmill? You were just a little thing, but I thought I had a wildcat ahold of me." She glanced at Noelle and Nathan. "Knocked me down the mill steps."

"I was twelve," Jill said. "Mom scolded me about it, and I never lived it down, so will you lighten up? I told you I was sorry at least a dozen times."

Pearl chuckled and shook her head. "Sit down, kids." She pointed to the long, wooden table. "I'll make that hot tea instead of iced. It'll calm you, and it looks like you need calming. So how's our girl? Is Cis coming home today?"

"Not yet," Noelle said, glancing at her sister.

Jill raised an eyebrow, and Noelle read her meaning. No way was Jill going to tell Pearl about the bombshell that Noelle and Nathan had dropped on the family this morning.

"She can't be that bad." Pearl eased herself into a chair at the table with a groan. "She was chattering up a storm last night when I saw her."

"She's going to be fine," Nathan said. "But there's reason to believe she wasn't just lost. Someone chased her down the lane to the sawmill, then carried her to that cave."

Pearl's hand flew to her chest, her heavy frown deepening the lines of her face. She studied Nathan for a long moment, as if she might see something in his expression that he didn't want revealed. "Carissa wouldn't be letting that wild imagination of hers get a little out of hand?"

"No, Aunt Pearl," Noelle said. "Someone abducted her. Our climbing rope was taken while we were in the cave. It was someone close to her. Possibly someone in our family." She hesitated. "Most likely someone in our family."

"Do you know that—" Pearl leaned forward, fixing Noelle with a sharp look "—in *here?*" She tapped Noelle's forehead. "Or in *here?*" She tapped Noelle's chest.

Noelle placed her hand on her heart. Pearl leaned back and closed her eyes. The tea kettle whistled, but Pearl didn't seem to hear it. Jill got up and switched off the burner.

"Noelle, I warned you about this," Pearl said. "You shouldn't even be here. You've found Carissa, now you need to get away. And if Cecil and Melva will let you, take Carissa with you."

"You know that won't happen." Jill took cups down from the shelf and poured hot sassafras tea into them.

Nathan added a drop of honey to his tea and stirred it. "Pearl, you're here all the time. What do you see going on?"

"Not much," she said, giving Jill a long look. "Nobody listens to me much anymore. They've got all their new ideas, computerized programs, fancy equipment. Did you know we're all incorporated now?"

"It needed to be done," Jill said. "It's just too big an operation for one man to control."

"One man doesn't control it," Pearl said quietly. "Don't forget who has veto power."

There was an uncomfortable silence, then Nathan cleared his throat. "Pearl, has anyone in your family spoken much about the accident at the mill ten years ago?"

Another silence fell. Pearl stared at the table for a few long moments, then looked up at Nathan. "What about it?"

"Were you convinced it was an accident?"

She looked down again. "The sheriff checked it out himself."

"I know, but I've never been satisfied with the explanation. Have you?"

She shrugged, still staring at the table. "They said there was a malfunction with the locking mechanism on one of the chains holding the logs in place."

"I know what they said. Someone who worked there at the time said he checked that mechanism at least twenty times afterward, and there was no malfunction. It worked perfectly every time."

"Then maybe the loggers didn't fasten it right in the first place."

"It's possible," Nathan said. "But I don't believe that. I know Harry Mitchell, and he's one of the most careful loggers in the Ozarks. That was a valuable load of lumber—Harry personally locked those chains that day. I asked."

Pearl looked up at him, startled. "Sounds like you've done a lot of investigating already."

"I'm beginning to think I haven't done enough."

"Well, it's a pretty sure bet we're not going to dig up any more evidence this far along in the game," Pearl said.

Nathan leaned forward, elbows on the table. "Pearl, Noelle told me about the codicil to the trust on the way out here. Who added that?"

"My daddy, Joseph Senior, Noelle's great-grandpa. He never was a very compassionate man—if you'll excuse me for talkin' ill about the dead. I just hope Cecil doesn't develop the same tendencies, although it looks as if he's treating Justin the same way his own dad was treated."

Jill carefully placed her teacup in the saucer and stood. "I need to get back to town," she said, leaning over to give Noelle a hug and a quick kiss on the cheek. "Forgive me for being such a bully, Sis?"

"If you'll forgive me for being such a brat to you when I was growing up."

"You got it."

With a final pat on Noelle's shoulder, Jill walked out

the door. Noelle heard her pull it shut until it latched, then start down the steps. Through the window, Noelle watched Jill cross the porch, stop, turn and walk back to grasp the knob and push. When the door remained closed she nodded, satisfied, and left again.

It was a familiar gesture, and Noelle caught her breath. She suddenly remembered numerous other incidents through the years that she'd never before realized had significance.

"Noelle?" came Nathan's voice behind her. "You okay?"

She turned her head toward him, dazed by her racing thoughts.

"Noelle?" Pearl said.

"I'm sorry, I think the past two days have finally taken their toll on me." She returned her full attention to the conversation. "Aunt Pearl, what do you think about Harvey Sand's death?"

Pearl looked surprised, then confused. "What in the world does that have to do with Carissa?"

"I'm not sure. Maybe a lot. Something was mentioned recently that put his motives into question. Could he have known something about our business that someone didn't want him to know?"

Pearl's iron-gray brows lifted, her mouth dropped open. She leaned forward. "I guess I've been so busy lookin' at superstitions and curses, I never thought to look from any other angle."

"I know you and Harvey didn't always get along well. Do you think he was capable of blackmail?"

263

Pearl nodded. "I never did like that man, especially after I heard those rumors a few years ago about him doctoring records to hide income from the IRS. I never listen much to rumors, but Harvey sure did spend money like there wasn't any end to his supply. Maybe there wasn't. He could've been milking half the county, as many secrets as he was privy to. Want to tell me who you think he was blackmailing?"

For some reason, Noelle wasn't ready to reveal this to Pearl.

Pearl leaned back in her chair and sipped her tea. "There's nothing Harvey could have had on the Coopers, though he might've known something about a certain hot argument that took place ten years ago over shutting down the sawmill."

"Shutting it down?" Noelle exclaimed.

"Your grandpa and your father were thinking about it. Face it, with two thousand acres of Cooper land and plenty of beef cattle, they had their hands full. When Cecil's folks took off for Texas, they were more than a little overworked. Cecil was all for shuttin' down the mill, but Jill pitched a fit, and so did I. Melva—mind you, she and Cecil weren't even married at the time, she was just working for the company—made a big stink about it, and urged Cecil to stop them if he could. But Cecil didn't want to stay around. 'Course, in the end, he did, but it was a hot topic for a while."

"And now Cecil is responsible for the whole she-bang," Noelle said. She sipped her tea as the room fell silent. She pushed her chair back and stood up. "I want to look through some more old records. Nathan, do you want to come with me?"

In the attic of the old house, Nathan picked up the file box from Harvey Sand's office and placed it on the table by the dormer window for better light. "Something happened earlier, didn't it?" he asked Noelle. "You remembered something, or felt something."

She pulled the first file from the box, avoiding his gaze. "I have no idea what kind of records Harvey has here. I guess we should just search until we find something off-key, although I doubt we'll find anything. Cecil or Melva must have searched for anything that would incriminate them."

"Don't want to talk about it, huh?"

She definitely didn't. "Let's just get to work on this stuff."

"Your intuitions and memories may be more important right now."

Noelle frowned down at her hands. "I don't think my memories of my sister have anything to do with the danger Carissa is in."

"So, you did remember something back at Pearl's, and it was about Jill."

A sound penetrated the closed window, and Noelle frowned. Then she recognized the rattle of Pearl's old truck. The honking of the geese did not drown out the clamor of the ancient vehicle. Pearl was probably going out to deliver her herbs somewhere.

"Noelle?"

"Okay," she said, continuing to stare out the attic window at the cliffs. Beyond them, she saw the shapes of the gravestones in the cemetery. "Jill has OCD." She felt Nathan tense behind her. "When she left Pearl's a little while ago, she turned back to check the door, and I remembered how she always checks everything over and over again. When I was a little girl, I would watch her, and I made the mistake once of saying something to Dad about her habits. Later, Jill blew up at me. She slapped me. Hard. I bit her."

"You *bit* her?"

Sheepish, Noelle shrugged. "I was only seven or eight. She hit me again, harder, and told me never, ever to tell anyone else about her rituals."

"Did you?"

"No. But when I saw her struggling with the problem, I couldn't help being upset. I finally said something to her. Then she hit me, to make me leave her alone. That's the incident she wrote about in her journal. I never told Daddy, because, I guess, I couldn't help feeling loyalty to Jill. And she was so sorry after she'd hit me."

"What happened after you got older?"

Noelle shook her head. "By then I learned to keep my mouth shut and close my eyes to it. I think she believed that I used my gift to pick up on her compulsions, but I didn't. They were so obvious to me, yet she didn't seem to realize how noticeable they were, and we both denied the reality."

266

"So she must have known about the codicil even then?"

"Or she'd heard the stupid stories about OCD being a curse."

"I'm glad you told me," he said. "It's good to know these kinds of things about someone for whom you care deeply."

Noelle felt her face grow warm. "Maybe I needed to talk about it, too."

"I'm glad that you trust me enough to share it with me. Your memories are important."

"Yes, I know that," she said. "That's why I carried that old backpack out of the cave yesterday. Even after all these years, I miss my mother."

He stepped up behind her and put his hands on her shoulders. She could feel his warm breath on her hair. "I'm sorry you lost your mother so young, Noelle. I'm sorry you're going through so much trouble now."

She glanced over her shoulder at him. She was coming to know every inflection in his voice, every changing expression in his face. Though she'd loved him for years, she was now suddenly falling in love with Nathan Trask for the first time. Now, of all times, with so much at stake.

"I'll live through it, Nathan," she said lightly, not yet ready to reveal her heart. "Now let's get to work on these files."

Chapter Twenty-Four

Noelle has to die. I can't believe I'm even thinking this. Not Noelle.

I've been so blind. She can read me—probably always could. Maybe I've always known it, too, but just tried to hide from the truth. She's a threat to all of us. Not that the others would see it that way.

Why does it have to be this way? Why am I the only one who sees what has to be done? Everything could be destroyed.

This is all getting so . . . so hard. Why me? Why do I have to fight this alone?

After three hours of searching, nearly blinded by all the columns of tiny numbers and lines of small print, Nathan pushed aside the box from Harvey's office. He glanced at Noelle, who had waves of damp hair sticking to her forehead. In the last ten minutes, she'd become jumpy, starting at every birdcall outside, looking up every time a floorboard squeaked.

"What's bothering you?" he asked at last.

"I'm hot and very sweaty. We should've carried this box downstairs before we searched it. Too late now. There's nothing more here."

Except for one small notation on the back of one of Harvey's files that didn't match with the duplicate in the family files, neither Noelle or Nathan had found anything of significance. And that notation was definitely small. It said, Lower level, upper file. Home. That was it.

"Think that note could mean anything?" Nathan asked Noelle as she sank down onto a wooden box on the floor.

She glanced at the words again. "It might. But wouldn't all the Cooper accounts be at his office?"

"It says home."

"Fat lot of good that'll do us here." She brushed back her hair from her forehead. "Maybe we could contact the executor of Harvey's will. Do you think we might get into Harvey's house if we explained what we needed?"

"The executor is about as likely to allow that as he is to jump down the Bobcat Cave sinkhole. How would we explain—" He noticed Noelle's sudden inattention. "What is it?"

She focused on him, her troubled eyes darkening. "Smell that?" She stepped to the window. "Gasoline."

Before he could join her, she whirled around and rushed to the steps. "Someone's here." She crouched and peered into the lower lever of the house. She sniffed. Jerking back up, she turned to Nathan, white-faced. "It *is* gasoline!"

Even as she said it, a loud *whomp!* shook the house. Noelle screamed. Nathan ran forward and grabbed her arm.

"Get down the steps. Quick! We've got to get out!"

He followed Noelle down the stairs and nearly collided with her at the bottom. Gray-black smoke and bright flames were outside all the kitchen windows.

"We're surrounded!" Noelle cried as she pivoted and grabbed his arms. "Nathan, there are flames all around us! We're trapped."

Smoke seeped beneath the inner wall, blackening the wood around it—flames would burn with dangerous speed through the age-dried material.

A glance into Noelle's old bedroom off the kitchen showed the walls already blackening as tiny orange flames rippled along the crackling wallpaper. The sound of shattering glass echoed through the house.

"We've got to jump through the kitchen window." Noelle's voice was hoarse with urgency and terror. She grabbed Nathan's arm. "Hurry! We've got to do it before the flames get any higher." She spun toward the sink.

He stopped her. "No. Back to the attic."

"Are you crazy? The porch is below that window, too. The whole porch is burning."

"The cliff won't burn. We can reach it."

"We can't! We'll fall."

"I won't let you fall. No time to fight about this, just go!" He hustled her back up the attic steps as smoke clouded around them, thick and smothering.

Smoke was already wisping past the attic windows. A few more seconds and their last escape would be cut off.

Nathan unlatched the window and tried to slide it up, but it was swollen shut. He reached for a heavy wooden box, while Noelle pulled a bag of clothing from a corner and began digging through it.

"What are you doing?" he demanded.

"Protection. Here." She pulled out a pair of old wool slacks. "We can tear these in half and wrap the material around our faces."

Nathan heaved the box through the window, shattering the glass. Smoke rushed through the opening. He took the slacks and ripped the legs apart. Noelle took one leg and tied it around her face.

"Okay." Nathan urged her to the window. "Out. Now."

Noelle poked her head out. She gasped. "It's too far. We'll never get—"

"Climb onto the roof. I know we can do that." He grasped her around the waist, to boost her over the ledge.

"But I can't—"

"Climb! Swing your legs out. I'll hold you."

She stepped to the window ledge, allowing Nathan to guide her.

"Grab the edge of the eave," he instructed, pushing her farther out the window.

"I'm getting dizzy. The smoke's blinding me!"

"Close your eyes and grab the roof, Noelle. Just do it!"

He heard her breath catch with fear. The smoke was burning his eyes and searing his throat. Noelle grabbed the eave, kicked away from the window frame and rolled out of his grasp.

"Okay," she called down. "I made it. The fire's

spreading. Hurry, Nathan!"

Flames were eating the porch roof below, pushing thick, black billows of smoke into his face. Nathan tied the woolen material that Noelle had given him around his nose and mouth and reached for the window.

"Nathan, come on!" Noelle cried.

Choking, he pulled himself out of the window, swung around, reached for the roof and kicked off, in one smooth motion. Heat burned his legs through his jeans.

"Nathan, your leg's smoking. Hurry, swing yourself up!" Noelle grabbed his arm and pulled with surprising strength.

Closing his eyes against the smoke, he struggled onto the ledge of the eave, allowing Noelle's strength to help draw him up to safety. She beat at his leg with the wool in her hands until the flames were out. He took deep gulps of the clearer air, fighting against the stinging smoke in his lungs.

Noelle untied the fabric from around his face, her eyes huge with barely controlled panic.

"Nathan, we've got to get off this roof." She turned a desperate gaze toward the jagged side of the cliff in front of them. It was their last, precarious chance for escape.

With Noelle's urgent grasp on his arm, Nathan pulled himself to his feet and walked to the center of the peaked roof. He studied the cliffside.

"Look." He pointed to a ledge with room for both of them only about a foot above the roof. "We can jump to that ledge, then climb from there."

"Okay, let's do it." Noelle stepped to the peak of the roof. "Let's pray this fire doesn't follow us up."

"It shouldn't. The trees are far enough above us, and the breeze is strong and in the right direction to blow the smoke away from us. We've had plenty of rain. Everything's soaked." Eyes on the ledge, Nathan grasped a sturdy handhold of granite and pulled himself up. Then he reached back to guide Noelle.

Coughing and gasping for breath, Noelle, with scraped and bruised hands, pulled herself over the final ledge of cliff onto solid, horizontal earth. Nathan had been right—the breeze kept the smoke away from them; they'd made it to safety.

Nathan came over the final ledge behind her, and with the last of their energy they stumbled into the dense protection of the forest and collapsed side by side onto soft grass. The roaring, snapping torrent of fire was muted up here, less nightmarish. What caught Noelle's attention was a voice below, shouting, and the sound of a loud, insistent horn.

"Someone's found the fire," she mumbled into the grass.

Nathan rolled to his side and faced her. "The question is, who already knew it was burning? Who started it?"

Noelle closed her eyes.

"Anyone could have started it." Nathan's voice held compassion.

"We've got to go down there and let them know we're safe. Jill'll be worried."

"She'll just have to worry a while longer."

"What?" Noelle raised her head.

"We can't show ourselves yet."

"But we can't leave them to think we were in the house. It's cruel, and it's dangerous. What if someone tries to rescue us?"

"We'll watch them."

"Watch? Oh, Nathan . . ."

"It makes sense, and I also want to see how they react."

"How long do we hide?"

"Long enough to check Harvey Sand's house. Let's go down through the trees and see what's going on."

Chapter Twenty-Five

Panicked voices grew louder as Noelle followed Nathan down through the thicket that covered the sloped hillside. Melva's voice carried clearly, shouting to someone to call the rural fire department.

When they reached level ground, Nathan signaled for Noelle to keep quiet. He peered through the foliage at all the activity around the house. Noelle felt the pressing weight of guilt—she was spying on her family.

Looking between two cedar branches, she spotted Cecil and Melva several yards away, staring helplessly at the firestorm that now enveloped the entire house. Another cry echoed across the clearing, and Pearl came racing out of the woods from the direction of her house, her face a grimace of horror.

"Where are Noelle and Nathan?" she demanded, running toward Cecil and Melva. She grabbed Cecil's arm. "Where are they? Have you seen them?" She shook him. "They were in that house!"

Shock filled Cecil's face. *"What?"* He grabbed Pearl by the shoulders. "Are you sure?"

Pearl could only nod. Her expression went beyond horror, beyond shock. She grabbed at her heart, and her body sagged. Cecil caught her. With Melva's help, he guided Pearl to a soft patch of grass.

Melva glanced back toward the fire. "Cecil, she's wrong. She's got to be wrong!" She reached down, as if to grab Pearl's arm, when a shout from behind them halted her. Together, she and Cecil turned to find Jill running toward them from the track beyond the cemetery.

Still watching the scene from beside Nathan, behind their camouflage, Noelle felt tears trickle down her cheeks. "I can't do it," she whispered. "None of them started that fire, I just can't believe it. And look what we're doing to them, look at Pearl."

"It's only for a little while." Nathan's voice was unemotional, but Noelle could tell that his calmness required strong self-control. "It could have been forever."

"Why are you just standing here!" Jill shouted as she reached them. "The whole forest could go!"

Cecil answered in a voice too low for Noelle to hear.

But she caught Jill's gasp. "No!" Jill pivoted toward the burning house. "They can't be in there! Noelle!" She started toward the house, but Cecil grabbed her, holding her back.

"We don't know for sure," he said, his voice cracking. "It's just what Pearl told us."

Noelle reached to push back a branch to step through. "I can't do this," she choked. "I'm sorry. It's too—"

Nathan grasped her arm. He pointed at Pearl, who was turned toward Jill, her face regaining a little color. "Let's get out of here." Nathan pulled Noelle back through the thicket to the old livestock trail that led to the road to the west of them.

"This is wrong, Nathan! None of them did it, none of them could have done it. They were all shocked and horror-stricken. Didn't you see them?"

He didn't release her arm, didn't stop his headlong plunge along the narrow path. "A lot of killers are horrified by their own crimes after committing them—that doesn't mean they won't kill again. Especially if—" He slowed his steps, glanced at her, moved on.

"Especially if what, Nathan?" She hurried to keep up with him. "Especially if it's a compulsion they can't control? Is that what you're saying? You've changed your mind about OCD never involving psychosis?"

"I don't know for sure anymore what it is. I don't know what to think."

She jerked from his grasp and skidded to a stop. "You're ready to blame this on my sister, aren't you?"

You're thinking Jill's a compulsive killer!"

"No, I'm trying to be practical."

"Then don't forget about Justin. He's suffering from the compulsion, too." She couldn't control the tension that tightened her voice. "It can't be Jill. She's in agony back there, thinking we're in that fire. Why can't we just go back and let them know we're alive? I can't stand leaving them like this. How can you be so callous?"

"I'm not being callous, this is hard for me, too. It makes no sense. OCD is not a dangerous disorder, but this time—"

"Maybe it's not the disorder," Noelle said. "Maybe we're letting this throw us off. Could be I've been jumping to conclusions all this time, and it really isn't family. After all, I have no proof."

He placed his hands on her shoulders and forced her to look up at him. "You're wishing, Noelle. Would you risk our lives for that wish? Because our lives are at stake. How much are you willing to gamble?"

She felt her face contort with the effort to hold back her tears. She shook her head.

"You're the one who insisted it *was* family, and we've operated on that theory," he said. "It's become too real a theory to dismiss. Don't you see how dangerous it would be? Someone wants us out of the way. We're getting close to the source, or someone wouldn't be so desperate. Whoever it is will stop at nothing to keep us from getting to Harvey's house if they know we're going there."

"But to just leave all my family thinking we're dead . . ."

"We'll be back as soon as we can, and then we can announce we're okay. If we reveal ourselves too soon, before we have the evidence we need, we may not be alive long." He released her shoulders. "Can you understand that?"

"Why can't we let the sheriff take care of it?"

"Noelle, they've had all this time to find something in Harvey's house, and they haven't found it. Do you really want to leave that responsibility to someone else?"

She closed her eyes. No. "We have to do this, don't we?" she asked.

"I'm afraid we do."

She continued to tremble, but she nodded, swallowing tears, swallowing another protest. He was right, they were in terrible danger. But she could still feel her family's suffering. It took all her strength to follow Nathan, resisting a deep need to look back through the trees toward the others. She had to repeat to herself over and over that this was the only way.

Harvey Sand's house, a narrow three-story Victorian structure in the center of Hideaway, posed a problem. Nathan and Noelle stood in the alley, looking across the white picket fence into a tiny yard filled with trees, bushes and every kind of blooming rose, pansy and chrysanthemum. How were they going to get inside? In spite of the abundant plant life flourishing in the rich soil, there was no camouflage over the front or back doors—the only two entrances.

"Now what?" Noelle asked.

"We'll have to break a window behind the bushes on the west side of the house."

"Nathan, look at us. We're a mess. It's a miracle you're not seriously burned. We had enough trouble explaining our appearance to that man who picked us up. If we get caught—"

"So we'll have to make sure no one sees us. Any other objections?"

"No."

"Then let's go."

Glancing around to make sure they were unobserved, they darted across the tiny yard and ducked behind a stand of bushes taller than Nathan.

Noelle looked through the window, then sprang back. "Either Harvey was an atrocious housekeeper or somebody beat us here."

Inside, the room that appeared to be Harvey's home office was a scattered mess, with files and papers strewn over the oak desk, drawers pulled out and emptied onto the floor. Along the walls, bookshelves had been cleared. Harvey's collection of Zane Grey, Louis L'Amour and Jory Sherman lay in piles, carelessly dumped on the floor.

Noelle grabbed Nathan's arm. "Would any professional investor ever leave a place such a mess after a search?"

"Depends on what they're looking for."

"This doesn't feel right. It feels dangerous."

Nathan didn't respond. He tested the window and found the lock already jimmied. "Someone must've used the same logic we did, choosing this point of entry."

"Except he or she was way ahead of us. This is crazy."

"Life's crazy. Let's go." Without waiting for an argument, Nathan swung himself through the window, then reached out to help Noelle.

"Okay, okay, I'm coming." She shrugged off his hand and climbed through the window. "The intruder probably already found what we're looking for," she grumbled.

"Or helped us in our search." Nathan reached for one of the few books that remained on a lower shelf. "What were the words we found on that file in the attic?"

" 'Lower level, upper file. Home.' " Noelle shook her head. "Since there's no basement in this house, common sense says this floor is the lower level. So that would mean any upper drawer or shelf could be the hiding place. Except I don't see anything that hasn't been disturbed by the intruder."

Nathan stepped to the doorway to his left and glanced into the next room. "Kitchen looks worse. He must not have hidden anything in the freezer or the flour."

"What about the computer?" Noelle gestured toward Harvey's workstation. "Could he have put something in it?"

"Possibly, but more than likely he'd save any incriminating evidence somewhere besides his hard drive. Look for diskettes or tapes."

"For blackmail, he'd need hard evidence, wouldn't he?" Noelle asked. "Something like pictures or signed documents, letters."

"Makes sense."

"And if Harvey was blackmailing others, as Pearl believes, he'd probably need a fair-sized storage space for his evidence."

"Which is probably in this house somewhere." Nathan beckoned to Noelle as he stepped into the kitchen. "Let's see where else our intruder searched. Watch your step."

Hesitantly, Noelle followed him through the kitchen, stepping over piles of macaroni and corn flakes, skirting the edge of a thick dusting of white flour. When they reached the elegant dining room, she winced at the slashed blue satin padded chairs, stuffing pulled out and scattered over the carpet. Pieces of silver-flocked wallpaper had been ripped from the walls.

Every room on the first and second floors had received the same treatment.

When they stepped from the final bedroom on the second floor, Nathan paused at the polished banister of the stairway to the third story. He shook his head. "The man spent a fortune on this house."

"Sure, with his blackmail money. If one of his victims searched this place, they must have taken great pleasure in its destruction."

"Wouldn't blame them."

"But it's breaking the law."

"I didn't say I'd have done it myself. Besides, we're breaking the law, too," Nathan said. "Let's go, we have another floor to search."

"Hold it a minute." Noelle turned to glance back down the stairway. "Seems to me we're getting colder. I thought we decided lower level meant the first floor."

"It was just a guess."

"Okay, but we've already decided Harvey could have been blackmailing others besides Cecil and Melva, and I've heard Jill remark more than once that if anyone wanted a false set of books, Harvey was the man to see. So it stands to reason he could have had several victims. I just wonder why Coopers continued using Harvey's services for so long when Pearl didn't trust him."

"Pearl said he knew the business better than anybody."

"You don't think he had something on Pearl as well, do you?" Noelle asked.

"We could ask. Later."

Noelle studied the slashed carpet of the hallway where they stood, and saw the hardwood floor underneath. "What a shame to cover such a beautiful floor with carpeting." She reached down and grasped the ruined floor covering, then paused, head tilted. "Hmmm, I wonder which step he tripped over? You did say Harvey was supposed to have fallen down the stairs?"

"That was the story, but I think we're close to refuting

that, don't you?" Nathan turned and went back down the staircase.

Noelle followed. "We can't refute it without evidence, and so far we don't have a scrap—whoops!" Noelle's toe caught in a piece of slashed carpet. She stumbled and fell against the wall of the stairwell. "Ouch. This place is dangerous!" She rubbed her elbow, glancing at the unscathed wallpaper below the stairwell. "Here's one place that was missed." She studied the wall more closely, this time thumping it with the flat of her hand.

Nathan watched her. "What are you doing?"

Noelle frowned at the wall. "Strange, don't you think? All this wasted space below the stairs? Jill's staircase isn't enclosed like this."

Nathan met her gaze, a growing light of comprehension in his eyes. "Remember hiding under your grandpa's staircase when we were little?"

"I remember you always found me, but it sure was a good hiding place the first time I used it."

"Lower level, upper file." He climbed back up to the top of the staircase and sank to his knees. "Suppose Harvey made file cabinets out of these steps when he renovated this house last year?" He felt the riser of the top step. Nothing. He went down another step and did the same.

"Try pulling the carpet away," Noelle suggested.

Even as she spoke, he was peeling back a flap of the thick silver-gray pile, with the sound of ripping Velcro.

"How about this?" He reached forward and grasped a recessed handle. A drawer slid out. "We're geniuses!" He shot Noelle a quick glance. "Sorry, *you're* the genius. I'm just along for the ride."

Noelle knelt below him. "What's in it?" she asked.

He reached in and pulled out a thick accordion file. He flipped it open, and both he and Noelle peered inside.

A sudden, soft creak of wood from the direction of the hallway above them jerked their attention from the file.

Justin stepped into view from the alcove. He came forward with wary hesitation. "You guys could get in trouble for breaking and entering." He brought his right hand out from behind his back, and Noelle suppressed a gasp at the dull gleam of blue-black metal. Justin was carrying a gun.

Chapter Twenty-Six

"Justin Cooper, what are you doing with your dad's pistol?" Nathan stood up beside Noelle, the file still in his hands, and climbed to the top of the stairs.

"And what are you doing *here?*" Noelle added.

Justin looked down at the weapon in his hand. "I didn't want anyone to use it. You can't know who to trust anymore."

Nathan tried not to let his relief show on his face. "I know it's hard, son. Things are confusing for everyone right now."

Justin's troubled gaze met Nathan's for a brief moment, then returned to the gun. He switched it from safety to fire, then back again. With a metallic click he pulled back the chamber, peered inside as if he were checking for bullets, then released it. He unfastened the empty clip and peered at it as if he couldn't believe it was empty.

He pushed it back into place and looked up at Nathan. "These things are dangerous. Everybody knows where Dad keeps his gun. Now I don't even know what to do with it."

"Well, carrying it to town and pulling it on your cousin isn't the right thing," Noelle said dryly. "You didn't tell us what you're doing here."

"Probably the same thing you are. Looking for whatever Harvey may have had on Dad." He nodded toward the accordion file. "That it?"

"I think so," Nathan said. "How did you get here?" He doubted Cecil or Melva would let him use a car, especially not Cecil. Not now.

"Pearl let me use her truck. She trusts me—unlike some people." Justin frowned at their clothing, then sniffed and wrinkled his nose. "What happened to you?"

"We'll explain later," Noelle gestured to the gun. "What would you have done if someone besides us had come in here?"

"Hidden." Justin checked again for bullets. "I was going to leave this in the truck, but I was afraid somebody would find it. I thought about throwing it into the woods, but what if some little kid stumbled over it? I just didn't want to leave it where it was. We should be able to trust family, but now you're saying we can't. I just don't get it. Why would anyone want to hurt Carissa?" Again, he checked the gun, slowly and carefully following the exact procedure he had followed previously.

Nathan leaned forward. "You took the gun because you were afraid someone in the family might take it and use it?"

The teenager nodded. His hands never stopped their fidgety movements over the pistol, checking and rechecking.

"Justin," Nathan said. "I don't know what your father was thinking when he stopped us from working together on this problem of yours, but he didn't do you any favors. You need to get out of here now, before someone comes."

Justin didn't move. "Then so do you. And as for Dad, I think he's worried about that codicil, but I don't want to stay in Cedar Hollow anyway, so why does it matter?"

"The Cooper holdings are worth a few million," Noelle said, "what with the cattle, the farming land, the sawmill and equipment. I wouldn't dismiss it so lightly, but I think someone needs to seek legal advice about breaking that codicil from the trust."

"Pearl doesn't think it can be done," Justin said.

"Pearl doesn't know everything," Noelle retorted. "I hate the thought of a legal battle, but this has gone on long enough. We could get a good attorney and challenge the codicil as a family, requesting its removal from the trust. Then maybe we would all be out from under the true Cooper curse."

"Do you think we could discuss this later?" Nathan asked. "We need to get out of here."

"Wait, I want to follow up on a hunch." Noelle descended halfway down the staircase, then reached beneath the riser of another step. Again, there was the sound of separating Velcro, then she pulled out another drawer with another accordion file inside it. "Harvey had quite a racket going here. I wondered why he'd need to leave a note to himself about the whereabouts of his evidence if he only had one victim. No telling how many people he was blackmailing."

Nathan glanced at the file in his hand. Bingo. It was labeled Melva Cooper.

Noelle replaced the contents of the drawer she had raided, then descended another step and tried again.

"Would you stop it?" Nathan said. "Leave all those drawers for the sheriff to investigate. We have what we need."

"Looks like somebody really did kill Harvey, then," Justin said. "Sounds like there might be several suspects."

"That's up to Greg to decide." Nathan held up the file in his hand. "We need to find a telephone to call him, and we can all pray he doesn't haul us to jail for breaking and entering."

Justin's fingers traced the smooth wood-paneled sides

of the gun's handle. "Melva told me that Harvey had a copy of a cashier's check that Dad wrote more than ten years ago."

"The one to Frazier Logging?" Noelle asked.

Justin nodded. "Dad fixed the records to make it look like he was buying a bunch of equipment, but Harvey said he paid too much, and he started investigating."

"So Harvey was blackmailing Melva?"

Justin nodded. "Melva told me Harvey knew better than to try it with Dad, because Dad would've turned him in to the police flat-out."

"When did Melva tell you about this?" Nathan asked.

"A couple of weeks ago when Harvey came to the sawmill. She had to tell me, because I was there."

"You saw him?"

"Yeah, I was out working on one of the saw motors when he dropped by. Melva was working in the office, and he thought she was alone, I guess, because there weren't any other cars in the parking lot. He wanted more money, and said that he could make it look like Dad had caused that log slide that killed Uncle Frank and Great Grandpa and Great Grandma. Melva told me later, she was so mad she threw the first thing she picked up. It was a cant hook."

"But, Justin, Melva couldn't have believed your father would commit murder," Nathan said.

"She didn't, but she was afraid Harvey could make it look that way." Justin's lip suddenly curled in disgust at the gun he was holding, and he held it out to Nathan. "Would you take this? I don't know what to do with it."

Nathan accepted the weapon and slid it into the pocket of his jeans.

"Dad's paid all the money back now," Justin said. "But Harvey's had Melva scared for years that if Pearl found out about it, she'd fire Dad as the manager, because she has final say about everything. Melva was all freaked about it. She said Carissa and I had a right to our family land, that we'd inherit all of it someday, and it wasn't fair for us to lose out just because of some problems Dad had ten years ago. So she paid Harvey what he asked."

"And she got away with it because she was doing the bookkeeping, and Harvey was the accountant," Noelle said. "No other double check?"

"Not until they started entering data on the computer." Justin shook his head sadly. "If they'd kept up the manual ledger entries instead of buying the computers—"

"Are you going to look and see what's in that file?" Noelle asked Nathan.

He opened the manila accordion file and pulled out a copy of a cashier's check to Frazier Logging for a hundred thousand dollars, and bills of sale for a saw and a logging truck. There were copies of correspondence and a record sheet of all transactions. A small, folded bundle of green ledger sheets matched the pages Noelle had found on her first expedition to the attic—the same type of sheets that were in the ledger Carissa had been carrying when she was abducted.

"Nothing we didn't expect," Noelle said. "I wonder

why Cecil took the money in the first place."

"Dad and Mom got into debt gambling down at Hot Springs," Justin said. "Dad borrowed money from the company to try to win it back, then he kept losing and taking more, hoping he'd recoup their losses."

"That's it?" Nathan asked. "He wanted to pay off a gambling debt?"

"What was he supposed to do? I told you, he paid it all back."

"And all these years Harvey was blackmailing Melva, Cecil never knew about it?" Nathan asked.

"Not until Dad found out from Jill about the missing money. He's never done anything like that since. He doesn't gamble at all anymore. He learned his lesson the first time."

"Well, something else is going on, then, because someone set fire to the old house with us in it," Noelle said. "Someone tried to kill us."

Shock raced across Justin's face. "Fire!" He glanced down at their clothes. "That's what happened to you? You've been hurt!" He dropped to his knees to examine a burned spot on Nathan's jeans.

"We aren't hurt," Nathan assured him. "We got out in time."

Justin fingered the burned material.

"I'm fine," Nathan said. "Noelle smothered the flame before it reached my leg. I'm okay."

Justin's face was pale when he straightened. "When did it happen?"

"A couple of hours ago." Nathan held up the file.

"We've got what we came for, now we have to get back to Cedar Hollow and let everyone know we're alive. You want to give us a ride?"

Justin glanced at the file, and he frowned.

Noelle nudged his arm. "What's wrong?"

"Do you think the person who tried to kill you was also Carissa's abductor?" Justin asked. "Someone in the family, maybe, like you said."

"It seems reasonable that the person who set fire to the house this afternoon was doing it to destroy incriminating evidence about past history, and to stop us from searching."

"Yeah," Justin said. "Permanently."

"I think it's time for us to return to Cedar Hollow," Nathan said, fighting a heavy wave of foreboding that settled on him.

It was beginning to sound like a horror movie. *Return to Cedar Hollow.*

Chapter Twenty-Seven

That ugly fire! Why now? There's no sign of Nathan or Noelle, but that doesn't mean they aren't in there. The firemen are handicapped out here—there isn't a fire hydrant for miles.

I should be ecstatic, shouldn't I? All those records Carissa was so adamant about digging up—they're gone. Only a few more things to tidy up, and everything will be safe again.

So why do I wish I could die? Why did life turn out this way?

On the way out to Cedar Hollow from Hideaway, Noelle became aware of a spring poking up through the upholstery in the bench seat of Pearl's pickup. She was already frustrated with Nathan's silence—he'd had Justin stop at the general store, then made Justin and Noelle wait in the truck while he went in to use the phone, then he'd returned to the truck without a word. She was getting irritable.

By the time Justin pulled to a stop in front of Cecil and Melva's house, that spring in the seat was making itself known. Worse, there was a white car in the drive, with the sheriff's insignia on the side.

Justin turned off the headlights and glanced toward the glow in the night sky to the north. "I can't believe this is happening," he murmured. "Is Greg going to arrest us for breaking and entering?"

"No." Nathan cleared his throat, then said quietly, "Someone else is being arrested."

"Who?" Justin asked.

"He didn't tell me."

Justin shoved open the door and scrambled from the truck. Noelle slid out behind him and took him by the arm. "You may not want to go in there while—"

"This is my *family*." Justin pulled away and yanked open the gate. Noelle and Nathan followed more slowly.

Before they reached the porch, the front door opened and the sheriff's bulk filled the doorway. His cowboy hat sat low on his forehead—a sure sign he meant business. He always tugged it down when things got serious.

He held Melva Cooper's arm as he escorted her behind him. Her face was smudged, her nose red from crying. Dirt streaked her clothing.

Noelle stayed in the shadows beside Nathan and caught her breath at the sight of Melva.

"Melva?" Justin rushed up the steps.

She looked up in a daze. "I'm so sorry. I had no idea Nathan and Noelle were in the house." Her voice was unusually soft. "Greg told us they're okay. I wouldn't ever have done anything—"

"Melva," Greg said, his deep voice gentle. "We need to get you on into town now. We've got quite a few things we need to clear up tonight." He turned to lead her from the porch. Cecil and Pearl filed out behind them from the house.

Noelle stepped from the shadows. "Melva? *You* started the fire?"

Melva closed her eyes and bowed her head. "I didn't know." She looked back up at Noelle and reached for her. Greg gently drew her away.

Pearl clambered down the steps and grabbed Noelle in an exuberant hug. "Do you have any idea what you put us through? What happened? We all thought you two were in that house."

"We were," Noelle said. "We got out."

"If I'd only known you were in there," Melva said softly.

"*Why* did you do it?" Noelle asked. This was a nightmare after all, and it pierced her heart more deeply than she would have believed possible.

"Not to harm you," Melva whispered as Greg led her to the car. "Never to harm you. I didn't know, I honestly didn't know. I didn't feel I had a choice, what with all those papers stored up there . . . all those boxes with records. Records showing when I took money out to pay Harvey, records that might show more—"

Tears streamed down Pearl's cheeks as she hugged Noelle once more. "I thought we'd lost you for sure, and if you ever do anything like this to us again, you're not too old for me to smack your bottom good!"

"Aunt Pearl, we're all right. I'm sorry we had you so worried, but we had to do it this way." Over Pearl's shoulder, Noelle caught sight of Cecil, his arms crossed over his chest, tears shining on his face in the porch light.

"Where's Jill?" Noelle asked.

"Still down at the fire, waiting for the firemen to find you two," Pearl said. "Greg didn't tell us you were safe until he got up here. Better get down there, kiddo. She's never going to forgive you for letting her think you was dead. What happened to you two? Where'd you get off to?"

While Noelle and Nathan explained themselves and apologized, Greg gently helped Melva into the back seat of his cruiser. Cecil didn't seem to be functioning properly. Shoulders hunched, tears streaming down his cheeks, he stood watching as Greg backed out of the drive.

"I smelled gasoline on her clothes," Pearl said softly in Noelle's ear. "She finally admitted to setting the fire, though she never would admit to knowing you was in there. Now we know Carissa's safe, but poor Cecil's a mess. What're we going to do with him?"

As the taillights of the sheriff's cruiser disappeared into the darkness, Justin walked up to his father and put an arm around his shoulders. "I'm driving you into town, Dad. We need to be there."

Cecil shook his head.

"We've got to be there for Melva," Justin said. "She's always been there for us."

Again, Cecil shook his head. "Think of Carissa . . . how could Melva have done what she did to Carissa?"

"You're going to have to talk to Melva about that," Justin said. "I don't know how many times you've told me there's always more than meets the eye. You can't know what happened until you talk to her."

Cecil covered his face with his hands. "I should have picked up on it. I didn't know she was so upset about something that happened ten years ago. Why didn't she tell me sooner?"

"Because she didn't want anything to happen to you, and she figured you'd blow a gasket if you found out." There was no accusation in Justin's tone, only sorrow.

"Where's Carissa?" Noelle asked Pearl.

"She's at Karah Lee's," Pearl said. "After they discovered the fire, Cecil called the clinic and asked if Carissa could stay in town. I guess she's safe now."

Noelle closed her eyes. Would any of them ever be safe again?

Cecil caught Noelle in a bear hug, and she could feel him trembling. "I'm glad you're okay. I don't know what I'd have done if you two had actually been in that fire, set by my own wife."

"You need to go to her," Noelle said.

He grew still for a long moment, then slowly released her and straightened. "I know that's the right thing to do."

She nodded.

He rubbed his face wearily, then turned to his son. "Go get the keys. You're driving."

Noelle turned to Nathan. "We need to go find Jill. Aunt Pearl, you want to come with us?"

"Nope. I think I'll stay here and try to clear out some of the mess in the kitchen. This place has been a staging area for too many disasters lately."

Nathan and Noelle decided to walk the quarter mile to the old house, and they allowed the remaining light from the fire to guide their way.

Nathan took her hand. "How are you holding up?"

For a moment, she didn't reply.

"None of it makes sense, does it?" he asked.

"No." She sounded lost. "Melva has loved Justin and Carissa as her very own ever since she and Cecil were married. How could she suddenly turn on Carissa like that?"

Nathan didn't know what to say.

"But she admitted to starting the fire." Bewilderment threaded her voice.

Nathan released her hand and put his arm around her. "There's no sense of relief, is there?" he said. "No sense of accomplishment at finding a culprit."

"I don't understand it yet," Noelle said. She leaned closer to Nathan in the darkness.

He wanted to protect her from the fallout in this family tragedy, but there was nothing he could do. She was strong, he knew. He'd always felt protective of her, even when she didn't want that protection.

Now, it seemed, she welcomed it.

He remembered the times they'd walked together like this when they were growing up. He always wanted to be there for Noelle. He'd always cherished her and admired her inquisitive spirit, even though it had gotten them both in trouble several times over the years.

She sniffed and dashed her hand across her face.

He tightened his arm around her. "It's going to be okay, Noelle. Your family will get through this. *We'll* get through it."

"I know." Her voice was hoarse with tears. "I can't stop thinking about Melva. She must be so frightened, so hurt. She always tries to do the right thing. She always struggles to live her faith, even when people around her aren't living theirs. What went wrong? How did this happen?"

"Melva tried to cover for Cecil for so many years because she didn't want to lose everything he'd worked for. She got so caught up covering Cecil's past sins she didn't realize how far off the mark she was getting herself."

"But you heard what Justin said. If Pearl had found out about the embezzlement, she'd have forced him out of Cedar Hollow."

"Not necessarily," Nathan said. "Maybe they could have discussed it. Even if Pearl did force him to leave, would that have been such a bad thing? Cecil wanted to leave this place ten years ago. Maybe he'd have lost a multimillion-dollar inheritance, but that isn't the worst thing in the world."

"No, *this* is the worst thing," Noelle said. "His family is destroyed. What's going to happen to Carissa and Justin? Their mother abandoned them, and the step-mother they love might have abducted Carissa and left her—and us—to die?"

Nathan winced at the despair in her voice. *Oh, Lord, please touch this wounded family. Show us what we're missing in this mess. Give us wisdom and hope through all this, and work another of Your miracles.*

"Nathan?" Noelle's steps slowed.

"Yes?"

"Why does it take something like this to show us how desperately we need Christ in our lives?"

"I can't answer that, but aren't you glad it works?"

Pearl's geese suddenly honked, and Noelle stumbled to a stop.

Nathan tightened his arm around her. "It's okay. It's only the Cedar Hollow sentries."

"I know, but . . . something else . . ."

"What do you mean?"

"I don't know . . . a thought. Something . . . odd."

He waited. "Noelle?"

She hesitated, then walked on. "Must've been nothing."

He took her gently by the arm and turned her back. "What is it? Something's still bothering you, I can tell."

She looked up at him, and in the glow from the fire, he could see the confusion in her eyes. "Okay, you're right," she said. "I can't ignore it. It's not over." She glanced toward the fire. "I don't have any peace about Melva's guilt. I know she admitted to starting the fire, but she didn't acknowledge anything else. And this is *Melva*. We grew up with her. We *know* her."

"Did you ever think she would be capable of setting a fire?"

Noelle contemplated the embers in the darkness for a moment. "I think Melva would do almost anything for someone she loved. But she loves Carissa too. She would never hurt her. That's what doesn't make sense to me."

"Tell me who else might have done it, then," he said. "Remember that we decided this is family."

"I know, but still . . . Nathan, I want to check out that ledger book at the sawmill one more time."

"Why?"

"I'm not sure yet," Noelle said. "But I think there's

something there we've overlooked."

"But wouldn't Carissa's abductor have already taken it if it was incriminating?" Nathan asked.

"Not necessarily. I need to compare the pages to the ones we found in the attic."

"Then let's go," Nathan said grimly, taking her arm.

Chapter Twenty-Eight

Noelle switched on the light in the sawmill office. The file cabinets were bare. The four drawers in the cabinet by the desk held hanging folders containing invoices, accounts receivable, shipping information and financial records for the last three years. Nothing helpful. There was no dirt-encrusted ledger.

"I'll check out the workroom." Nathan took a flashlight from the desk drawer and aimed it into the cavernous area, then entered the darkness.

Noelle checked another cabinet and found bank records and personnel files. Still nothing significant.

"Nathan?" she called over her shoulder. "Did you find the light switch?"

"I'm getting there."

She knelt to check the desk drawer, then froze, suddenly concerned about Nathan in the darkness.

She turned toward the door and felt another familiar rush of awareness. Something was wrong. Tension and fear traveled through her as she rushed across the office. "Nathan! Get out of there!"

"Why? What's—"

There was a grunt and a muffled thud, then the sound of his flashlight clattering to the floor.

"Nathan!" She rushed into the cavernous sawmill. "Nathan, where are you? Please answer me!"

A muffled groan reached her from the center of the mill—the center of that darkness.

"Nathan!"

She stepped carefully down an aisle looming with machinery, her feet slipping on sawdust.

A human shape, barely discernable, lay across the sawdust drag.

"Nathan!" Noelle fell to her knees and reached for him. Her fingers felt his shoulders and touched the sticky warmth of blood near the back of his neck.

"Oh, no. Oh, God, please help!" She reached for the pulse at his throat, felt the throb of his heart's steady beat. Her hands explored further, gauging the depth of the wound at his neck. Her fingers brushed against a pointed metal tip. She felt the length of the curved blade and grasped the handle. The cant hook!

She had to get him out of here, get away from the danger quickly, before—

Somewhere in the darkness she heard the sound of a footfall, the brush of clothing—and a whisper. She held her breath, waiting.

The sudden snap of a switch warned her a second before the mill exploded into dark life. The saw engine groaned into screaming action, its power reaching the huge circle of knife-sharp teeth. The conveyor belt, only a few feet away, kicked into motion, drawing phantom logs toward the hungry blade.

Nathan's body jerked beneath Noelle's hands. She looked down, hope surging. "Nathan?"

Hope turned to horror.

In the dim light from the office, she glimpsed the movement of the sawdust drag, its shoveling cups pressing forward with the pull of the chain, catching at Nathan where he lay in the line of their forward motion, snagging at his clothing as they traveled toward the conveyor belt . . . toward the saw blade that screamed through the blackness.

"No!" Noelle gripped his shoulders. "Nathan, wake up! You've got to get up!"

One of the cups grabbed and held at the right leg of his jeans. The drag pulled tight, hesitated, pulled harder, hesitated, like a persistent animal hungry for food.

"Nathan!" she screamed, her voice lost in the deafening whine of the saw's engine. She grasped the denim material, tugged and pulled to dislodge it from the cup. She felt it rip, felt the chain jerk as she freed Nathan.

Then something tugged at her foot—a strong jerk that threw her off balance and pulled her inches before she could reach out to grab a conveyor support bar and brace herself against the pull of chain. Her left pant leg was caught, and she couldn't rip it free.

"Help me! Nathan!"

The engine drowned her cries. She could not kick away.

"Nathan!" She looked up and saw movement beyond his prone body.

A figure stood in the dimness, a woman staring at her, cupping her ears against the noise.

The dim glow from the office lights revealed her sister. *Jill!*

For agonizing moments, Noelle stared into her sister's face, the pain of fear and betrayal freezing her movements.

The sawdust drag gave another jerk, breaking her grip on the conveyor support. Again she cried out, grasping for another support beam, her feet less than a yard away from the screaming sawblade.

She looked up to see Jill turning away, running across the building. Running toward the power switch.

Relief strengthened Noelle's grasp. But only for a moment. Another shadow joined her sister's before she could reach the switch, thrusting Jill aside, then shoving her again. Jill fought back. The two tangled, becoming one in the shadows as Noelle's aching fingers weakened, her sweaty hands losing their grip.

It would do no good to scream, and she could not waste her strength. She had to hold on. The power of the drag might not be stronger than she was.

But how long could she hang on?

She could not see Jill now or see what was happening.

Nathan moved.

She saw his arms draw back to push himself up. He hesitated, raised his head, fell back. She couldn't reach him; he couldn't hear her.

He moved again, slowly pushed himself up, glanced back and saw her. His mouth moved. He shouted something, swinging around to reach for her.

"No!" she screamed. "Turn it off! Turn the switch off! Hurry!" She was too close to the saw for him to pull her to safety. She couldn't let go or the recoil of the drag would swing her into the hungry teeth of the monster.

Nathan understood. Staggering, holding the back of his neck, he rushed with unsteady legs toward the switch.

Noelle could feel air on her bare ankles, fanning from the motion of the saw. The fingers of her left hand began losing their grip; one by one, and fell away from the bar. At that moment, the drag chain flexed and heaved a strong tug. The force snapped the grip of Noelle's right hand. She felt herself being dragged backward.

Her scream was drowned out by the engine roar, which suddenly grew louder as the power circuit disengaged. The drag chain released its grip, just as the overhead lights threw a bright glare into Noelle's eyes. The steel edges of the saw slowed. Noelle reached down, ripped her pant leg from the drag, pulled herself free, and rolled out from beneath the conveyer.

The fading sounds of the mill revealed other sounds of struggle.

Two struggling forms were backed against a flatbed

trailer that was piled high with logs. Noelle saw gray strands of hair, a blue work shirt, a set of bony shoulders and recognized her great-aunt. With an amazing strength for her age, Pearl held Jill against the trailer edge.

Red-faced, breathing heavily, Jill grasped Pearl's arms. "I can't let you keep killing!"

"It's already too late, can't you see that?"

Noelle gasped. A memory, old and painful, suddenly surfaced. "Aunt Pearl!" She started forward.

"No!" Jill cried. "Stay back. These logs aren't secure."

Noelle took another step. "Aunt Pearl, please listen."

"Stay right where you are, Noelle, or this whole load of logs'll come down on us all. I've done it before, I can do it again."

Noelle felt as if she'd been kicked in the stomach. Aunt Pearl had done this before? Ten years ago? "We'll . . . we'll help you, Pearl!" How many people had she killed?

"Didn't you hear me! It's too late! Too many betrayals, too many deaths. My own father saw to it that I would never inherit if anyone found out. Harvey couldn't keep his foul mouth shut. I would have lost control of the land." Her voice caught. "That trust is destroying the whole family."

"That's not what's destroying the family, Pearl," Jill said softly. "It's your reaction to it."

Pearl shoved Jill harder against the trailer. "It doesn't matter anymore, though, does it? Everything's lost, can't you see that? I love this land more than I love my own life. I'd do anything for this land. No way can I leave it now."

"Aunt Pearl, please!" Noelle cried, stepping forward. She held her breath, knowing the logs could topple at any second.

"No!" Jill screamed, as Pearl shoved her harder against the trailer.

A log shifted on top. It rolled down to the next log, bumped against it.

"Look out!" Noelle cried. She stumbled forward over stacks of slab wood. The rest of the logs shifted, tumbling to the edge of the flatbed.

Noelle reached for her sister's shirt and jerked Jill toward her, out of the avalanche of logs. Together they fell hard on the concrete and rolled away. A second later, the logs covered Pearl.

Noelle and Jill found Nathan lying where he had fallen beside the power switches. Noelle dropped to her knees beside him, horrified by the sight of so much blood on his neck and shoulder, by his colorless face. She reached down and touched his cheek, still warm. Her fingers moved down to the pulse at his throat, the beat reassuringly strong and even.

His chest vibrated with a groan.

"Nathan?"

His eyes opened. He looked up at her with such intensity and love that Noelle caught her breath.

"I'm okay," he breathed. "Thank God you're safe."

He reached up to touch her face. "I didn't know if I'd reached the power switch in time."

She grasped his hand and kissed it, pressing it against her cheek.

Jill turned away. "I'll go call for help."

Nathan tried to sit up, and Noelle stopped him. "Try not to move. You've lost a lot of blood."

He lay back down. "What happened?"

"It was Pearl," she said. "I had the evidence staring me in the face today. I remembered the handwriting, and I checked those ledger sheets. They were more than ten years old. Pearl kept the books then. Her letters were always so precise, unlike the rest of us. I know that handwriting well, because she writes all the labels for the herbs we sell at the store. The ledgers had been copied multiple times by hand. Each page at least three times."

"So that's what you meant."

"And remember when you told me OCD didn't make a person dangerous, but some other disorder, or a head injury, might cause a behavior problem? Pearl herself told me about Jill pushing her years ago. She fell and it knocked her silly. That was even before Mom died."

The next moment, Jill was back with the news that Taylor Jackson was on his way. "It was Pearl," Jill said. "I did some snooping while you were all down here. I found the back rooms of her house filled with things she could never bring herself to throw away—empty cans, plastic wrappers, stacks of mail and newspapers. She had OCD, too, and she never told anyone about it because she was so desperate to retain control of the property. It meant everything to her."

"Where is she now?" Nathan asked.

Noelle looked at her sister. She thought that she had run dry of tears, but she was wrong. "She's dead. The logs fell on her." She swallowed. "I remembered something else. I heard Mom arguing with Pearl right here in the sawmill before we went to the cave the day Mom died. I remembered Pearl telling Mom they had to keep the secret. They were arguing about Jill. Later, I knew something was wrong with Jill, because I saw her checking the doors over and over again to make sure they were locked."

"But I got help," Jill said. "Sometimes I slip back into old ways of behavior, but most of the time, when the stress isn't overwhelming, with behavior modification, and sometimes medication, it's under control."

Jill reached down and touched Noelle's head. "It's all going to be okay. You stay here with Nathan. Taylor will be here any moment. I'll bring him in."

Chapter Twenty-Nine

For the second morning in a row, Noelle woke up from a night of restless sleep to the dim light of the clinic. This time, however, no nightmares had plagued her. The real events of the past two days had been nightmares enough.

Oh, Aunt Pearl . . .

She stretched her cramped legs and pulled herself up from the sofa. Voices floated into the waiting room from Cheyenne's office. Before she could talk herself out of it, Noelle pulled out the cell phone that Jill had recharged for her and punched in the number on the slip of paper that Jill had given her yesterday.

This was crazy. But holding grudges and being afraid wasn't exactly healthy either. If there was the smallest chance to put some more nightmares to rest, Noelle wanted to take it.

A sleep-filled voice answered on the fifth ring. It was Joel. She almost pressed the disconnect button, but instead she swallowed and took a breath.

"Hi, Joel. This is Noelle. I got a note to call you. Sorry it's so early." She glanced at her watch and braced herself for a hostile reply.

He cleared his throat. "Hi. Wow. You really called." He didn't sound angry.

"You asked me to." Yeah, but since when did she start considering requests from him again?

There was some shuffling, and Noelle heard a sleepy female voice in the background.

"I guess I scared you when I came into the store," Joel said at last, apparently waking up a little. "That wasn't what I meant to do."

"Okay. So I guess that means you really were just coming in for groceries?" Noelle couldn't believe she was having this conversation with a man who had plagued her sleep for so long—and they were actually being civil to each other.

"No, I was going to talk to you, but I couldn't make myself say what I needed to. I was afraid it would all come out wrong. I heard about your problems down in Hideaway," he said. "Carissa okay?"

"She'll be fine. Thanks for asking." So formal. So polite. Had they suddenly been transported to an alternate universe?

"I guess it amazed you when you found out that I really was in church," he said with a chuckle. "They have a recovery program, and I'm helping with it."

She managed not to laugh. "Helping?"

"That's right. My wife and I. One of the things we're supposed to do in the program is go back to the people we've hurt and try to make amends. I never did that with you because I figured you would be better off if you never had to see me or hear my voice again. Now I know I was wrong. I should have talked to you three years ago. It's what I've been trying to do the past couple of weeks."

Noelle didn't know what to say. She wasn't sure she knew how she felt about it. Could she believe him?

In any case, she knew he would have a struggle ahead of him. When someone was as deep into an addiction as he had been, the attachment was so powerful it never really let go. Even if Joel remained clean, he'd be struggling with depression and regression for the rest of his life.

"You've remarried?" she asked when the silence became ridiculous.

"Yes. First I made some changes in my life. I nearly

310

died before I did that, and if not for a preacher in California, I wouldn't've made it. I've been off the stuff for three years now. Rhonda's been clean for five. That's my wife."

To Noelle's amazement, tears stung her eyes. As she and Joel exchanged a few more pleasantries and agreed to meet—with his wife, and with Nathan—in Springfield in a few days to talk things over, she felt as if a heavy hand of oppression had released its hold on her.

"I forgive you, Joel," she whispered in the silent dimness of the waiting room after she'd hung up. "I wish you well."

Sure, they were easy words to say right now, and she knew there would be times ahead when she would struggle with that decision. But if she could forgive Joel, then she could forgive Pearl. And if she could forgive Pearl, she could forgive herself. Then, maybe she could release the past—and devote herself to the present . . . and the future.

"Thank you, Lord," she whispered. *"Thank you for showing me that living with bitterness and regret is not the way to live. Would You please show me what is the right way?"*

A few moments later, creeping past an open door on her way to the bathroom, she saw Karah Lee and Blaze, drinking their morning coffee and eating a typical clinic breakfast.

Karah Lee saw her and gestured for her to join them. "You look hungry." She shoved a small box of assorted doughnuts across the desk. "Help us out. The bakery always sends us too many, and I can't afford one more calorie or I'll pop my drawstring."

Noelle eyed the maple longjohn with interest. It was a far cry from goat's milk yogurt, but she felt as if a week had passed since she'd last eaten. Coffee beckoned from the corner pot, and she gave in to temptation.

Blaze pulled a chair out for her and handed her a napkin. "I just checked on Nathan. He's still asleep."

"How are his vitals?"

"Perfect. He's strong as a horse. He woke up about two this morning and asked if you were okay."

Noelle sank into the chair with a sigh. "Other than the crick in my neck, I'll be okay. Did Carissa go home with Cecil and Justin last night? I seem to have fallen asleep."

Karah Lee shook her head sadly. "She's still at my place. Don't worry, Fawn's keeping a close eye on her. She'll get to go home today. Melva probably will, too, if Greg has anything to do with it. Oh, and Carissa asked me to give you a message. She remembered what was so familiar about her abductor was the smell."

"What kind of smell?"

"Rosemary."

Noelle blinked against a new sting of tears. Aunt Pearl. "Did she say anything else?"

"She said Pearl kept saying, 'I can't do this. I've got to stay in control. I can't do this.'"

Noelle studied the shimmering black surface of her coffee. Obviously, her great-aunt had been fighting a fierce inner battle.

"Bertie's preparing one of her special breakfasts for Nathan this morning," Blaze said. "I'll go fetch it soon as he's awake. Maybe she'll let me have some, too."

"You've already eaten a bear claw and a jelly roll," Karah Lee complained.

"Hey, I'm a growing boy." He reached for another doughnut.

"Fawn's planning to walk Carissa to church this morning," Karah Lee said. "But Cecil and Melva had better watch that tomboy of theirs. She's got your looks, Noelle. She's going to be breaking hearts someday soon."

"She'd better wait a few years." Noelle sank her teeth into the maple bar and chased it with a sip of delicious coffee.

"So everybody's asking about you," Blaze said. "When do you start work?"

Noelle nearly choked.

Karah Lee shot Blaze a hard look.

"What did I say?" he protested. "I read that the best time to get somebody to do what you want is hit them up when they're eating. Their guard is down then."

"How about if I send you my résumé?" Noelle asked.

Blaze's dark eyes widened. "Well, what do you know? It worked."

"All right!" Karah Lee shoved a fist of victory into the air. "Did Jill finally talk you into it?"

"Jill doesn't know." But it was time to come home. "First, I'll need to break it to my business partner, and hire more help at the store." Yes, it was definitely time.

She talked with them for a few more moments, then brushed the crumbs from her wrinkled jeans and excused herself.

As she entered the room where Nathan lay sleeping, she saw his outline in the same bed that had been Carissa's. He breathed evenly and deeply.

His wound was not as serious as she had feared, and Karah Lee had indicated last night that Nathan would probably be released today.

Once again, tears of gratitude filmed Noelle's eyes, as she recalled hearing Karah Lee's words of reassurance last night. And now, as she stared at Nathan's tousled, dark-brown hair and his face, relaxed in sleep, she knew things would never be the same between them. Their old, easy friendship had changed beyond description, and she was eager for the change.

She stepped quietly to the window and gazed out at the lake, blanketed in fog. *Thank you, Lord, for so many things. Carissa's safe. Nathan's safe. Please deal gently with Melva, so she can remain at home with the husband and stepchildren she loves with such devotion. And please be patient with me as I learn to give it all to You on a regular basis. I'm a little out of practice.*

She heard the rustle of sheets and looked across to find Nathan watching her with a glint of sleepy humor in his eyes.

"I hope you'll be eternally grateful that I rescued you last night," he said.

She grinned at him. "Good morning. I'll take the matter under consideration, if you'll promise to try to eat something from your breakfast tray when it arrives."

He moved to sit up, then winced, reaching for his shoulder. "I may need help to eat it," he said, feigning a pitiful voice.

She chuckled. "Bertie Meyer's sending over her famous spread from her kitchen. You going to let a little sore arm keep you from her biscuits and gravy and omelet casserole? Or those black walnut waffles?"

"Nope. Karah Lee did say she was letting me out of here today, didn't she? I don't remember much else about last night, but I do remember that."

"She said *probably*." Noelle stepped to the end of the bed and reached for the control button. She pressed it until Nathan could sit up comfortably, then went to his side. "It seems to me you also remember saving my life."

"Only the relief I felt when I discovered you were still alive. As I said, I didn't know if I reached the switch box in time." He shifted to see Noelle better. "I'm so glad you filled in the details last night. I think I like being a hero." He winced again.

"Don't forget I rescued you first."

He laid his head back against his pillow and closed his eyes. "I'll never forget that, even if you'd let me."

She sank into the chair beside the bed and held his hand in silence for a moment. "Nathan, do you remember my telling you last night about the head injury Pearl received years ago?"

"Yes."

"It happened before Mom died. I haven't been able to get any of this out of my mind. Pearl caused those deaths ten years ago. She admitted last night that she'd killed Harvey. Do you think she was responsible for Mom's death?"

"Maybe we'll never know for sure."

"Maybe I don't want to find out."

He squeezed her hand, then raised it to his lips and kissed it. "Are you going to be okay?"

She nodded. "It'll take a while." Tears stung her eyes, and she swallowed, trying not to let them fall. "I loved Pearl."

"She loved you, too, Noelle."

The tears fell. "Jill found out what Pearl had been doing in the sawmill before you and I returned. She was going through those old log books that we searched."

"That's right," Nathan said. "Pearl kept those books years ago, before Melva took over. I remember hearing a lot of complaints about how slow she was. Now we know why.

"And she could never throw the extra pages away, for the same reason," Nathan said. "It all makes sense."

"Harvey must have found out about Pearl's problem," Noelle said. "He'd been the company accountant for years, so he must've known about the codicil to the trust. He could have tried to blackmail Pearl the way he did Melva. Pearl resorted to murder to protect what she had always tried to keep as a family secret."

"Again," Nathan reminded her.

"I fought hatred and anger all night long. It's so hard

316

to understand why Aunt Pearl would do something like that."

He adjusted his position once more. "Something occurred to me when I woke up in the middle of the night. Someone with OCD who has been brought up in a strict religious household would have a heightened sense of right and wrong. The compulsion would be to resist evil, not commit it."

"So that would mean what? That the 'family curse' might have even given her the impetus not to kill Carissa?"

"Or maybe it had nothing to do with that at all. Her response to the threat of losing Cooper Hollow was something completely unconnected to her compulsive tendencies."

"Perhaps her love for Carissa was what saved Carissa's life," Noelle said.

Nathan placed a hand over Noelle's and squeezed, then linked his fingers with hers. "That's what I'm saying." Again, he shifted, his discomfort apparent in his expression. "I could use a change of subject. How's business?"

She frowned. "Business?"

He leaned close, grinning. "Don't tell me you've already forgotten? Noelle's Naturals? You know, the store you prize so much?"

"It's doing great. Why?"

"Ever think of branching out?"

She suppressed a smile. He really did read her mind. Or maybe he'd been eavesdropping on her conversation with Karah Lee and Blaze. "Yes, as a matter of fact, Mariah and I had talked about opening a store in Branson."

At the sudden disappointment in Nathan's eyes, Noelle had trouble maintaining her serious expression. "I don't think Hideaway's ready for a health-food store."

"You might be surprised."

"Too expensive."

"There's a demand for the supplements, and I've thought for some time about expanding, buying my own building. I could see a merger taking place."

She considered this for a moment. "I suppose strong consumer interest could persuade me to move farther south, instead."

He took her hands. "Admit it, you're a country girl at heart."

"And maybe they'd accept my résumé at the clinic."

He grinned. "I don't suppose there'd be any other reason you might choose this area."

"Oh, yes. I plan to start a rock collection. I've heard rumors there are some beautiful crystals in this part of the state."

Nathan smiled wryly. "I suppose I could find a few for you down by the creek after the next rainstorm."

"I was thinking about the kind you find in a jewelry store, already set in gold."

Nathan's eyes held hers for a long moment. "Ever been to Thorncrown Chapel?"

"The glass church in the middle of the woods at Eureka Springs?"

He released her hands and reached up to touch her face. "That's the one. It's where they hold wedding ceremonies."

She smiled, then kissed him. "Is this a proposal?"

"Is it ever."

"I accept." Most definitely, it was time to come home.

Center Point Publishing
600 Brooks Road ● PO Box 1
Thorndike ME 04986-0001 USA

(207) 568-3717

US & Canada:
1 800 929-9108